2024 ©Kacy Granitsas
Edited by Kieran Ferrara
Published by Holy Grail Publishing
Cover Design by Miblart

I want to thank everyone who made this project possible, but especially a nice shout out to my editor, Kieran Ferrara, without whom this wouldn't have been possible to put together this year. I wish him luck with the best of his endeavors. I want to thank Miblart, and a number of writing and art individuals who took a look at the covers before submitting it for the final proof.

Dedicated to my mother. I love you.

No Happy Endings

Table of Contents

When I was a boy, one of the most defining thing my mother could have done, and in fact did do was to take me to the theater to watch Peter Jackson's LOTR. The film got me into reading the books because I simply couldn't wait to see how it ended, and with great joy, I found that evil and good was in a conniving battle of attrition with the forces of goodness at the forefront of victory. This moment in my life was defining because I feel in love with these stories, for good and evil, but when things came around and I got much older, my reading tastes had changed to permit morally ambiguous characters, and dare I say, the forces of evil won. While I presented this concept to my cousin at a camp we went to over the summer, he dismissed it as a very stupid idea.

Even growing much older, and my tastes in media began to change, and quite frankly, I started getting into horror where there is always an unfortunate ending. Sure, the protagonists might escape the Hell, but demons still followed them in their memories with wounds that would never fully heal. Trauma has a way to shape us, and keep us grounded in reality sometimes, even if that reality is always horrific. One of my favorite stories to date now is "Plague Tale" and I won't say much about the ending, but it moves you. Those are the stories that stay with you. Sure, every once in awhile we need to get back to finding some semblance of hope in an idea that Good will prevail, but the protagonist is oftentimes the antagonists enemy. We root for the protagonist as our minds put ourselves in their place and we can never truly associate ourselves to being evil, unless you're like me.

The stories I'm driven to now are the stories that don't always have a clear good and evil force, and where no matter what happens, hope always just seems to be an illusion: a postponed disappointment, if you will. These stories make you think, they make you cry, and yet, they make you feel an appreciation of life and your own circumstances. I know for many readers, we read to escape the present reality because the reality is horrifying for many of us, but if we consider the alternative, and focus on what that means, and we watch people, fictional or otherwise, explore that Hell, when we return to our reality we find it wasn't so bad.

As I undertook this anthology, I wanted the stories to have these qualities. A sad ending that will make you cry, think, or ultimately have an appreciation of your own circumstances. I'll admit, I undertook this project out of completely selfish reasons, but the result was a newfound appreciation of the grimdark of literature mirroring how bad the world at one point was, and ultimately, depending on what place we find ourselves waking up, is reflective of our own present circumstances.

MUD

Adam Conlon lives in Chicago, IL, where he works in pharmacy, writes stories, and plays with swords. Previous published works include the grimdark/war fantasy series "Wolves of War" novels The Threat, Storm and Siege, A Feast for Flies, and Crown and Conflagration, as well as the novellas Young Tiger, Mad King and Ghost Company.

1: AN ORPHAN'S OPINION

All Mada ever wanted was adventure. Sail the seas. Soar the skies. Find treasure. Live life. Lucky for her, adventure's all an orphan's got. Or unlucky, if you asked her.

The kind of adventures orphans have ain't the kind she had in mind. Still, adventure was all she ever wanted, so imagine her surprise when the wizard came to town.

The wizard was a shrouded man, with colourful robes of blue and green, and a cloak that covered his nose and mouth. Veils, masklins, and the brim of his hat pulled over his eyes. Made Mada wonder how he could see anything.

But that wasn't the only strange thing about the wizard. He breathed like a harmonica; smelled heavily of garlic; and silver bells of different sizes and tones tinkled from the floppy end of his frayed hat to the ankles of his boots. Mada—and anyone else—could see and hear the wizard coming from a long way off.

The town of Windmühlenhügel sat upon one of the region's many hills. The windmills at the edge of town slowly turned wheat into grist. Sometimes Mada could hear the stony gristmills churning. The town itself was colourful, houses of rich brown siding and roofs shingled blue and red. Springtime, almost, but they were so close to the mountain, chill winds and rains stunted the wildflowers' growths.

They were buying dried herbs for medicine-making when the wizard jingled into town. Everyone stopped and stared. People came to ask questions, get advice, and have their fortunes told. He performed tricks, levitated, guessed hidden objects. Sometimes people left frowning but mostly grinning and applauding.

Didact Gwenna stepped in front of Mada, shielding her view, scowling deep in her thin, taut face. Gwenna's eyes burned all the way down from her crooked nose. "Daydreaming again?"

"No, Didact Gwenna. Just . . ." she peered around the older woman, still staring at the colourful, jingling man.

If possible, Gwenna's scowl deepened further. She turned around and saw the object of Mada's attention. "So . . . *he's* back." She pretended not to care, but Mada could see a little worry behind her eyes.

"Come child," said Gwenna, tugging Mada's arm. "Gather your ingredients that I may pay for them. Need we not stay for *his* parlour tricks."

Mada needed ingredients for potions, salves, and everything else a budding herbalist might. War was upon them—well, not *them*, but west. Healers and surgeons of all experiences were expected to aid with the injured. Even though she was almost fourteen summers, Mada was no different. Soon, she would also travel west as a surgeon's apprentice, making sure the surgeons and healers had enough medicine and sutures to stitch up the brave heroes fighting against the rebels.

They'd *won*. Couldn't those westerly bastards *see* that? Why prolong their suffering and get more people killed? Why not just submit?

That wasn't for Mada to say. She was no diplomat. She was an orphan. Mada Dreck. Both her names meant, "mud." Goes to show how important *she* was.

When you're an orphan, you go where other fingers point. Despite what the other students might say, what they might call her, she knew that if it weren't for the teachers at Zauberschule, she'd be doing something much, *much* worse. So she could handle the hard work of the battlefield. Without another word—nor another glance toward the wizard—Mada gathered her dried herbs, and followed Didact Gwenna from the sundries stand.

———

Zauberschule was an old magic school. As much magic as it could be, anyway. Not much in the way of spellcasting. Usually *magic* just meant innate gifts, like seeing the future or having a certain knowledge of plants and animals or the way stars work. Until she came to Zauberschule, Mada never realised the "magic" commonfolk talk about just meant "academics." She still believed in magic, though. Maybe it was scarce now, but it was *somewhere* out there. Partly why she wanted adventure.

In the dusty tower of stone and wood and mortar, Mada looked for a table to sit at and do her writing. The girls' common room was well furnished, although not with the best furniture. There were pillows and cushions of crimson and green; chairs of dark wood plainly designed; shelves of books with yellowed pages and cracked binding; roughly sanded tables with ewers of water and plates of fruit. Best an orphan can get, outside the church. Better'n nothing.

"'Lo, *Mud*," said one of the girls, Stasia. A titter from the others behind her. Stasia was always with her duo of chittering chickens, Ida and Mia. Kind of impolite if you asked her—but what did anyone care about an orphan's opinion?

"Hey!" shouted Stasia, and she thumped Mada's head with a book.

"Gah!" she cried, rubbing the sore spot. "What's that for?"

"For ignoring me," said Stasia, and her gaggle giggled. "I was speaking to you. Best thing you can do is answer me. Is that understood, *Mud*?"

Mada glowered her most violent glower, still rubbing her scalp. "Fine," she grumbled. "What d'you want?"

"Yeah," said Ida. Or was it Mia? Mada was never sure, never bothered to learn either of their names. "Why are you talking to *her*? You don't want *lice*, do you?"

Stasia laughed haughtily, running her fingers through her silken tresses. Long, blonde, and falling perfectly down to her lower back like a sheet. Stasia was the kind of girl all the boys wanted and all the girls wanted to be, with milk-white skin and rose-petal lips and clear blue eyes.

And Mada was just ... *mud*. Brown hair, all limp and greasy. Brown eyes that didn't even get all gold like honey when the sun struck 'em. Reddish skin that looked about as delicious as raw clay.

Then, of course, there was that time she *did* get lice—or had them when she first came to Zauberschule. Didact Gwenna had all her hair shorn off and practically made her live in the bath to drown those bastards. Stasia and her friends never failed to bring it up.

"Rumours abound you saw the wizard on your walk today."

"What if I did? Ain't said nothing. Just jingled on his merry way."

"Well, I heard," started Ida or Mia, "that whenever the wizard comes through, he looks for a protégé."

"A protégé?"

"Mm-hmm. Someone he'll take away as an apprentice and teach special things to. Boy or girl, it doesn't matter."

Stasia tilted her chin and brushed her long, blonde hair. "But they say his instructions are far better than the school's. Those who go with him become so learned, they become fully fledged in their own skills."

"I heard," said Ida or Mia, but not the one that mentioned protégés, "that he specialises with incendiaries and makes firebombs."

"No, no, no," said the Ida or Mia that mentioned protégés, "he does things *much* more advanced."

"Such as?" asked Stasia.

"Alchemy. Turning lead to gold. Building homunculi or automatons. Forging unbreakable weapons. Things like that."

Stasia thumbed her milk-white chin. "Honestly, I remember hearing that he fights ghosts and devils. 'Tis why he obscures his face, wears all those bells, and smells so strongly of garlic."

"Think that's true?" asked Mada. "Which is it? Firebombs, alchemy, or ghost hunting?"

Stasia shook her perfect blonde head. "All that matters not. What matters is, we have the opportunity to leave this dusty old school. The wizard hand-picks an apprentice, takes them to a secret location, expedites their education, teaches them arts privileged and thought lost . . ."

"No bloody battlefields and surgeries," sighed Mada.

Stasia scoffed a laugh, and her two cohorts followed suit, giggling derisively.

"Oh?" asked Stasia. "And what makes you think he'll pick a muddy little orphan like you?"

Mada deflated. Too much to hope, it seemed.

"No doubt," said Stasia, leading her two companions away, but still talking loud enough for Mada to hear, "that in the next few days, the school will make an announcement regarding the wizard's visitation. And I heard this year, he's looking for a girl."

2: BILÉ THE WIZARD

Mada hated to admit it, but Stasia was right.

Two days after Mada saw the wizard in the market, the headmaster called an assembly in the great hall. Not that there were many to assemble. Magical abilities came scarcely, so there were only about thirty heads altogether.

Lots of students sat around her, but she still sat by herself. She could hear all the gossip about the wizard. Used to be a student, teacher, even headmaster. Was born in Zauberschule. Knew all the secrets of the school, the world, even the universe. Some of the same they were talking 'bout last night. Alchemy and ghost hunting and demon slaying and whatever else.

When Headmaster Grimsby stood up, the whispers quieted. Gaunt and wizened, tufts of cottony sideburns haloed his cheeks. He wore plain, brown robes under an ornate mantel with shining symbols and jewels around the hemline.

Standing next to him was the wizard she saw yesterday; all flowing robes, obscured features, and jingling bells. If Mada thought his garlic pungency was stifling in the open marketplace, in the confined great hall, it was *overwhelming* to the point her head swam. By all the gods and saints, it even seeped into their gruel, which made others like Stasia, Ida, and Mia complain. Not Mada, though. She'd already learned that any food is good food.

"Students of Zauberschule," boomed Headmaster Grimsby, "thank you for attending. We have an esteemed guest with us today. He's a longtime beneficiary of our school, a graduate, and renowned magician. I'm pleased to present, Bilé!"

There was no applause. Maybe everyone missed the point. Maybe Grimsby did. Everyone knew who the wizard was, but no one knew who he *was*. All anyone knew was that this wizard was a stranger come to take one of them away. So instead of applause or even words of welcome, there was hushed muttering and gossipy chatter. Except for Mada. She'd no one to chat with, so she just stared and smiled all friendly.

Bilé stepped forward with a jingle of all his bells. She, like everyone else, tried to glimpse something from under his veils and masklins. Couldn't. Had Grimsby and Gwenna not confirmed *he*, Mada would never have known if Bilé was man, woman, beast, or a stack of children under those heavy cloaks.

"Children of Zauberschule, know you why I'm here. Bilé is my name. My magic and workings remain secretive to all those except my apprentices. One of you lucky few will leave this school to aid in my continued work."

He paused for a moment to . . . do something. Mada wasn't sure. She couldn't see his face, nor his eyes. Did he watch them? Scrutinise them? Judge them? His voice was odd. It was like he had two—one of them high and airy like a piccolo; but also booming and present enough to cut through the din of mumbles.

"If you've seen me here before," continued Bilé, "you know what comes next. A contest. Should you choose to participate, you must complete three trials. If I deem you worthy, you will forsake your current path to join me on mine."

"How can we sign up?" asked one of the boys, Uwe. His hand shot up, but he did not wait to be called on.

"Speak with Headmaster Grimsby. He will tell you when and where the first trial will take place. Should you succeed, I shall provide you with the time and date of the second trial."

Stasia raised her hand but waited to be called on. Bilé shifted his direction to face her, complete with soft jingling. "Yes, Stasia?"

Her cheeks turned pink at her name. "Are there any requirements?"

"No restrictions. Anyone can participate. The trials will test multiple aspects of your education. Should you fail a trial, you shan't be allowed to continue. My judgement, and your assessment to continue, shall be decided then and not before."

Stasia kept her hand up almost defiantly. "But master, I heard that, well, seek you only *female* students this time around."

"Stasia. You already had mine answer."

Stasia knew when she was beaten. She lowered her hand and slumped in her seat. Ida and Mia rubbed her arm, offering encouraging words. Must be nice to have friends.

Friends or no, Mada felt resolute. Stasia was going to try. Ida and Mia, too, no doubt. They'd stick together. What if they were all in competition together? What would happen to Ida and Mia should they lose their Mother Goose? But most importantly, why did Mada give a damn?

She sighed, digging into her gruel, listening to the teachers and other students chattering. She was going to enter the contest. Would she win? Couldn't hold her breath, really . . . but at least, maybe if she passed the first round, they'd take her a little more seriously.

3: 1ST TRIAL

A week after the announcement, a small gathering of twelve students lined up outside. Mada may have considered it small, but it was half the whole school.

The air was delightfully fragrant. Springtime. Scents of wet earth, the sky after a thunderstorm, wildflowers reaching up to kiss sunshine. A chilly breeze rolled by, making Mada shiver. Despite the sunshine and flowers, it was still jacket weather. That was the problem being this close to the mountains.

Mada wondered when the trial would begin. Maybe this *was* the trial, and Bilé wanted to see who would stand in the cold the longest, waiting for a trial that would never come. She wasn't the only one that thought so.

"This is ridiculous," hissed Stasia. "We were all told the same time and day, weren't we?"

"Yeah, we were," said Ida or Mia. The one with a blue ribbon in her short brown hair. Which one was she again?

"Well," said Ida or Mia, who had reddish hair and a horsey face, "all three of us came together, so we got the time and date at the same time."

"Not us," said one of the boys, Uwe, "and we're here just the same as you."

"What about Mud?" asked Franz.

"What about her?" asked Stasia.

"Didn't she come with you?"

And the blonde girl made a disgusted face.

"Not at all," said Ida or Mia, the one with the blue ribbon.

"We *told* her she had no chance and recommended she not try," said Ida or Mia, the one with red hair.

"Why?" asked Franz. "You're friends, aren't you?"

"Absolutely not!" crowed the redhead. "She came of her own accord. No way we'd try this with lousy, mousy *Mud*."

The other girls laughed.

"Lousy, mousy Mud!" exclaimed Stasia. "That should be a song! It almost makes this whole adventure worth it."

Ida or Mia, the one with red hair, looked proud to make Stasia laugh so hard. Mada, however, shrunk back into her jacket, wrapping it tighter around herself. She dipped her head, avoiding eye contact. She wished she could blend into Zauberschule's brick walls and never have to hear or see them again.

So there she stood. Outside. Hands in her pockets. Shoulders scrunched up partly due to cold but also because of embarrassment; nearer the boys, Franz and Uwe, because they were nicer than Stasia, Ida, and Mia. Even though she was just a few strides away, Mada could hear the three girls laughing and making up a song about "lousy, mousy Mud."

The boys' company was indifferent, but at least they weren't rude.

"That's what he said, right?" asked Uwe. "Sign of the Bull, Day of Fire, during the Sparrow's Bell. That's . . ." He looked up to the sky, but had a hard time calculating because a large cloud had overtaken the sun ". . . I don't know, half a bell ago?"

Mada thought for a moment. "Sign of the Bull, Day of Fire, during the Sparrow's Bell." That's what she was told, also. Even wrote it down.

But she remembered something she'd read about dates counted by constellations. Wasn't there a different calendar? Not different, but . . . similar? Somehow? Used more west?

She remembered something about it. How the count didn't add up, how they were two weeks ahead? That would no longer be . . . but what if—?

Mada exhaled and stood a little straighter. She snorted vapour into the chill air and marched back inside, ignoring the boys' stares and the girls' giggles. Stasia crowed, "Giving up already, *Mud*?"

It was late before Stasia, Ida, and Mia came back in. Mada looked up from her book as they came in, her face neutral.

All three girls looked chilled to the bone. Hair all wind-tossed, cheeks all wind-burnt, wet from a rainstorm that Mada watched pattering on the windows. They ravenously descended upon the fruit bowl. Mada, of course, had her supper, and even now nibbled an apple as she read and worked.

After grabbing all the fruit they could, Stasia, Ida, and Mia stomped over to Mada. Before Stasia could open her mouth, Mada said, "Didn't come, did he?" Wasn't *really* a question.

That stopped the blonde momentarily. She regrouped and said, "You knew. I want to know *how* you knew."

"Nothing special," she lied, shrugging. "Just obvious he wasn't gonna. Now, if you'll excuse me . . ."

Mada turned back to her book and paper, started scribbling more notes. She tried her best to ignore Stasia, whose face turned redder with each passing second. At long last, Stasia had enough. She threw her half-eaten apple at Mada's head and wrung out her wet hair all over Mada's papers.

No chance to retort, Stasia, Ida and Mia laughed all the way to their rooms.

———

Two weeks later, Mada left the girls' common area, marched downstairs and was about to exit the courtyard when someone called to her.

"Where do you think you're going, *Mud*?"

Mada sighed, defeated. Stasia was right behind her. Mada turned around but didn't say anything. Didn't need to. Stasia, hands on her hips, demanded, "Don't you have a poisoner class today?"

"What's it matter?" asked Mada.

"Because you never miss a class."

"I . . . been working hard lately. Just thought I'd get some fresh air. Clear my head. Can't work all—"

"You're a terrible liar, you know that, *Mud*? Lousy, mousy *Mud* thinks she's sneaky." She crowed a laugh. "No friends. All you do is study. How could you possibly want *more* time alone?"

If her options were being alone or being with people like Stasia . . . but Mada said nothing. Dare she turn back? She'd be giving up her goal. But if she went ahead, Stasia would—

"You know what I think?" asked Stasia, interrupting her thoughts. "Bilé is out there. You knew it was going to be today."

"What? No. I was just—but now I'm going to class. Let's just—"

Stasia wasn't having it. She grabbed Mada's arm and dragged her into the courtyard. Sure enough, there stood Bilé in all his robes and shrouds and bells, still reeking of garlic. Others had figured it out too, like Franz and Uwe.

Mada tensed. Stasia didn't think of it herself. She just followed Mada because she was suspicious. For some reason, Ida and Mia were nowhere to be seen, and those three were inseparable.

"So, you've arrived," said Bilé. "A dozen students approached Master Grimsby for the trial. Here I see only five have made it. How astute of you. I said it would be the Day of Fire, during the Sign of the Bull, at the

Hour of the Sparrow. Calendars can change, and dates with them. Time can be measured based on cycles of the moon, cycles of the stars, or simply by counting sunrises. But not everyone counts the same. A good magician should know this because they'll never know where their learning might take them."

Mada'd been right. The calendars are under the current star signs according to the constellation maps. Out west, they hadn't been updated. Constellation maps shift over time due to the planet's movement. According to the most recent book on the matter, the westerly Sign of the Bull didn't start until two weeks *after* theirs.

Stasia whispered, "So *that's* why you—"

But she was cut off when Bilé shouted, "Mada Dreck!"

Stasia jumped back and so did Mada. She felt horrified. Never had anyone demanded her name so forcefully. "Y-yes?"

"Come forth, child."

For some reason, she shivered. Her legs felt leaden as she marched over, hands clutched to her chest. "Y-yes, m-master?"

Bilé dropped his voice so that only she could hear. This close, the garlic stench was overwhelming. "You were the first to figure the riddle out. You said naught. Tell me, your friend—"

"Stasia is *not* my friend." She didn't know why she said that. She wasn't in the habit of backtalking instructors, 'specially not one so scary. But she felt so frustrated about Stasia being called her friend. Immediately upon blurting it, her eyes went wide. She shrunk into her jacket and said, "Master Bilé, I'm *so sorry*—"

But he held up an arm so covered she couldn't even see a finger, and she shut up. "Your answer has given me all I need. You are the first to pass and will go on to the second trial."

Mada *did it*. She *succeeded*. She did what no one thought she could and was officially in Master Bilé's competition. What of everyone else, though? What of Stasia, who didn't solve the riddle but tagged along? Guess she'd find out.

As Mada stood behind Bilé, the wizard spoke up again.

"Mada Dreck was the first to successfully solve my riddle. She is exempt from the first trial. Erik Klein left some time later to do his own research.

Franz Browning and Uwe Veecher both went to Master Grimsby for hints. And Stasia Huber . . . cheated."

There was a small inflection in the wizard's voice, almost as if he was smiling under his veils and masks. But that was second only to Stasia's audible gasp. She fumed from her position but didn't dare say anything. Mada did her best not to look. Just stare ahead and smile, smile, smile.

The four students murmured to each other, looking confused. "First trial? I thought that *was* the first trial?" Everyone, that is, except for Stasia, who scowled, and mouthed, "You won't get away with this, *Mud*."

4: RHETORIC & HYPOTHESES

Mada knotted her hands around her jacket. What did that mean? What wouldn't Mada get away with? She'd solved the riddle fairly. The more she thought about it, the less it made sense, but the more it scared her.

So, she hoped that Stasia would lose. Somehow, someway. Stasia *should* lose. She had a fifty percent chance of making it. All Mada could do was hope. Hope and wait.

"The first trial is one of wits," said Bilé. "Just as the riddle was. A magician must be creative, imaginative, especially when in peril. Always will there be challenges—in homes, courts, on battlefields. We must narrow down three from five. I shall ask questions pertaining to your skills and knowledge. Those with the most points move on."

"Yes, Master Bilé," sang the other four.

"You find yourself on the battlefield," said Bilé. "An injured soldier is before you. His arm was struck, the bone cleaved through but hanging on by its meat. How do you help him?"

Mada gulped. The first question was already so grim. But it was a question for a healer. If it was her, she'd try to ask him what he wanted. The arm could be reattached with some magical herbs and a well-made salve. Even so, would she have those in her store? And there was no promise the arm would ever be the same. Better and more painless to just—

"Stasia."

Stasia had her pale hand in the air, looking eager. "Put the soldier to sleep, remove the arm and cauterise the wound. If the sleeping draught is strong enough, perhaps suture the loose skin." She smiled at Mada, if only for a moment. "Oftentimes we cannot afford such lengthy procedures on the battlefield. Even if we have the equipment and supplies, we may not have the time."

Bilé nodded. "Stasia is correct. Time is of the essence on the battlefield. We may want to help and give comfort to the injured, but spending too much time on one soldier—even to make a decision—means less time to aid other injured soldiers."

Stasia's haughty smirk returned. Mada deflated. She'd've been . . . *wrong.* Worry crushed her. Had Mada not already earned her victory, she might not have even gotten there. To make matters worse, 'twas *Stasia* who proved her wrong.

Bilé's second question was about a court seer, who discovers her lord, a count, will go mad in the future, similarly to how his grandsire did—a fact that was hidden from the history books. While the seer's evidence is largely circumstantial, she's able to see the past and doesn't want the court to suffer as it had under the lord's grandsire. What should the seer do?

'Twas Uwe who answered correctly, and expressed what Mada thought. Admittedly, she had to think a bit harder after failing the first question.

"Telling the court without evidence could cost the seer her life," said Bilé. "Indeed, if the seer brought it up before the other members of the court, it could get back to the count. With his grandsire's madness less than well recorded, the count and his court could take it as rumour meant to usurp or disrupt, which would endanger the seer. Instead, the seer should learn from the past, document her visions in her private journal, and monitor the count, consulting with the court physicians when the first signs of madness manifest."

After the next question, there were three. Erik had none, but Uwe, Franz, and Stasia all had one.

"Two more questions," said Bilé, "and those that answer them will enter the second trial. I'm afraid Erik is disqualified."

Erik huffed, clearly outdone. "Fine," he muttered, and skulked off inside.

Uwe and Franz looked at each other, determined. "Together," they said. Mada hoped for the same. Even if Bilé wasn't looking for a specific sex, it would be better than competing against Stasia. Was it so much to ask that Mada prove her superiority this early in the trial?

"A chimaera is ravaging the countryside. Indiscriminate in what it kills and eats, its victims range from livestock to travellers and even townsfolk. An illusionist is tasked with defeating it, alongside a knight. How would you go about aiding the knight?"

Mada blinked. This question was much more open-ended than the others. Chimaeras were legendary beasts thought demonic. As far as she knew, there hadn't been one sighted in centuries. As such, Mada was never really curious about what she'd do if she ever met one. Thankfully—luckily—she wouldn't have to answer.

Uwe raised his hand and answered. "Chimaeras have not roamed the land in centuries, and when they did, were quite rare. One must be aware of the three threats when approaching a chimaera. The lion's forebody has claws and teeth; the goat breathes fire and can kick; and the venomous viper makes the tail. If cornered or trapped, they become violent and may force their way from the illusion. Instead a skyward distraction was famously used in the past. Should one make the chimaera believe they're being attacked from above, the illusionist could also charm the knight with invisibility, allowing the knight to kill it with a lower assault."

Bilé faced him, silent.

"Uh . . ." Uwe looked confused. "Yes?"

"Your answer may result in failure," said Bilé.

Uwe swallowed hard. "I-I know," he said shakily. "But . . . that's the problem with chimaeras. With so many different ways to kill someone, there's no promise the attacking parties will be safe. At least this way, there's a better chance of success."

"I accept your answer," said Bilé. "Chimaeras are dangerous beasts. Due to their nature and physiology, they're difficult to kill. With careful planning and strategy, one *might* accomplish it. Alas, there exists no tried and true method. Please join Mada beside me."

Uwe exhaled, relieved. He clasped Franz's hand before jogging away, taking his place beside Mada.

"The last question determines who will proceed to the second trial." Bilé raised his heavily veiled arm. "A demon from the underworld has arisen. Its influence is palpable, holding sway over mortals, promising riches and power. It gains a foothold in court and holds power over lords and ladies."

Mada's eyes widened, terrified. Maybe Stasia was right. Maybe Bilé was a demon hunter, shrouding his face and feelings to hide from forces malevolent and invisible. Mada shuddered to think . . .

"You are whatever you want to be, even a master of all magical branches," continued Bilé. "You are learned, pure of heart, and thus unswayed by the demon's charms. You use everything in your power to break the curse held over the members of court but are ultimately confronted by the demon. What do you do?"

Mada blinked, thinking. "What do you do?" asked Bilé. Not, "How do you win?" or even, "How do you survive?" Would Franz pick up on that? Would Stasia?

Tentatively, Franz raised his hand. "We can be *anything*?"

"Within the realms of reality," answered Bilé. "No mythological weapons or powers. A demon emerges and you can only use the knowledge available to us *now* to stop it."

Franz furrowed his brow and lowered his hand. No sooner after did Stasia raise hers. "What powers does the demon have?"

A soft breeze rustled his fabric, jingling his bells. "Inhabitants of the underworld are formidable, but their powers may vary depending on many factors. I shan't trouble you with all the ways a demon's power can vary, but they are all destructive. Teleportation, duplication, hallucinations, demonic fire, invisibility, elemental manipulation, mind control, thought invasion. Need I go on?"

Mada thought and thought. Hopeless. Demons and devils had been defeated in the past, 'least according to some historical books. Only, those were under specific circumstances, and magic was much stronger back then.

Franz looked around nervously, hand twitching as though he wanted to answer. Poor boy even mumbled to himself. "What if you made duplicates—? No, no, it could see through. Or what if poison—? But isn't their *blood* poison? What to do? Heaven help me, what to do—?"

Stasia watched him in her snide, condescending way. Then her face changed, grinning like she had an idea. Again, her hand shot up. With a soft tinkling, Bilé gestured.

"'Tis impossible," said Stasia. "Mankind is not equipped to fight demons and devils anymore. Our magic is not as strong. People are not as innately gifted. Should any of us find ourselves in the presence of a demon, fleeing is best. Should it become hellbent on destroying us . . . pray, at least, that our soul isn't damned forever."

"Some say the only defence against true evil is prayer and faith. But you do not propose using faith to defeat the demon, merely to save your soul pending your inevitable demise."

Stasia looked at Bilé, who faced Stasia's direction. Hard to tell if he was looking at her or not. But after a few seconds of deliberating silence, Bilé finally said, "I accept your answer. You shall join Mada and Uwe in the second trial."

5: 2ND TRIAL

Mada moped in her bed, her clay-coloured hair frizzing in her vision.

After Bilé announced Stasia had won the first trial, Mada deflated. Hadn't heard the end of it. They both went back to the girls' dormitory, Stasia far more chipper. She bragged to Ida and Mia and any other girl who'd listen about how she overcame Mada's unfair advantage and secured her place in the second trial.

Ida and Mia, of course, were more than happy for her, issuing envious oohs and aahs, saying things like, "We wondered where you were" and "Oh, I wish I could've been there!" and even echoed Stasia's thoughts that Mada had somehow weaselled her way into the second trial, when Stasia unabashedly admitted to following her. Bilé himself said Stasia had cheated, but there was no way she'd admit *that*. No, she got there due to determination and ingenuity.

From her bed, in her room, two days later, Mada could still hear Stasia bragging. Mada might be able to shut her out of the competition, even if she couldn't shut her out of her mind. "I'll beat her," Mada whispered to herself. "And prove I'm not just *mud*."

The following morning, Mada met Uwe and Stasia. Instead of outside, they were deep in Zauberschule's undercrofts. Cesspools and sluiceways pounded their ears with rushing water. The stench was almost unbearable. Franz had joined to cheer Uwe on. Ida and Mia came to support Stasia. But no one was there for Mada . . . as usual. Just as well, because if Mada spent all her time with friends instead of books, she might not have made it this far in the first place. Still, there were less encouraging words and more nasally, shirt-over-the-nose complaints. "Gods, it *stinks* down here!"

Bilé approached with his typical furious jingle and jostle. If the stench of sewage and sludge affected him, he gave no indication. Even his odd voices didn't seem stifled.

"Miss Dreck," he said, "have you no one to cheer you on?"

"Don't need anyone," she said.

"What are you talking about?" asked Stasia. "All this slime and sludge. It's Mud's family reunion!"

Despite the overwhelming odours and dank, depressing environs, Stasia still found the ability to make fun of Mada—and her gaggle still found the ability to laugh. But all Bilé had to do was raise his hand, and the girls ceased their giggling.

"As scholars, we must be learned. As workers, we must be quick-witted. The first trial was to test your knowledge of history and how you may act in certain situations. The second trial is about teamwork. No matter the time or place, magicians must work well with others."

"Teamwork?" asked Uwe. "But . . . isn't this a competition?"

"It is. You won't be working together, though. You'll have partners." Pointing at each of them, the bells chimed. "Franz will aid Uwe. Mia will aid Stasia. Ida will aid Mada."

Mada's heart sank. Her and Ida? Uwe and Stasia got friends, but she . . . Mada *stomped*. Ida was her *enemy*. Certainly no friend.

The brown-haired girl with the blue ribbon sidled up beside her. So, that one's Ida. At least she wasn't the one who made up that contemptible song.

"I'm going to make *sure* Stasia beats you," she sneered.

If Bilé or anyone else heard, no one said a thing. Mada didn't, herself. For one, she couldn't believe this was happening. Would Bilé have done anything if she spoke up? Or would that be grounds for disqualification? How could she participate in a partnership without a partner?

"Sometimes our partners are ideal," said Bilé. "Other times, they are not. 'Tis the onus of the challenger to adapt. Sometimes friends can be as detrimental as enemies. Hidden around the dungeon are three trinkets—one per team. Each team must find a trinket and bring it to the designated point where the final assessment awaits. I will be watching, and judging. Two will enter the third and final trial. Off you go."

At the end of the first trial, Bilé had given Mada, Stasia, and Uwe each a map. He'd also instructed them not to let the others see—which proved difficult for Mada. She didn't care if Stasia's map was different, but Stasia cared about hers. In the end, Mada didn't get to look at it. She hid it in her clothing chest, in different books, anywhere she could to keep it away from Stasia and her friends.

Even as she led Ida through the sewers' tunnels, following the markings on a trail that was hopefully taking her northeast. Uwe and Franz went north. And before taking Mia west, Stasia gave Ida a knowing look that Mada didn't at all like. Didn't matter, 'cause soon the tunnels separated the three groups.

Mada furrowed her brow, occupying herself with the map. Not only were there directions, but clues leading to the trinkets. Best keep silent, she told herself. Best just lead and let Ida follow. Bad enough she had to find her way through these stinking sewers, she had to complete her task *and* keep an eye on Ida.

"Do you even know where we're going?" chided her companion.

Mada ignored her.

"You should let me see—"

As Ida reached for it, Mada yanked it away. "*I'll* hold it." Mada relaxed when Ida distanced herself. Combing stinking sewers for a trinket with one of her enemies. If anyone'd asked her yesterday, she'd've laughed.

After a few moments of silence, Ida asked, "Is there a reason you act like a rabid bitch all the time?"

Confused, Mada stopped. "What d'you mean?"

"You won't share the map with me. Your *teammate*."

"Can you blame me?"

"*Mud*, a lone wolf in her own little world. She doesn't *need* friends. You could've said something to Stasia, you know, instead of leaving us out there in the rain and cold, waiting for something that wouldn't happen for another *two weeks*."

"Wasn't it Mia who sang lousy, mousy Mud?" snapped Mada, and Ida winced. "Lousy, mousy Mud doesn't need friends. It's all Mud's fault she's all alone, ain't it? Don't got nothing to do with all your caterwauling 'bout how I'm filthy and stupid and mean? Lemme ask: I'd've said something, you'd've believed me?"

Ida looked at her, eyes wide, but didn't say anything. Dumb brain worked overtime for a retort she couldn't possibly find.

So Mada rounded on her. "I'd've said, 'Hey, won't be for another two weeks,' you'd've followed me? Wouldn't've accused me of lying for my own personal gain? That right?"

Ida stood stone still, avoiding her eyes, fingers rubbing thumbs and ankles rubbing knees, nervously trying to think of *something*. Mada felt like a cat watching a drowning fish. She relished in it.

"Well—" Ida sputtered. "Well—well—if you'd even *tried*—"

"You listening to yourself?" Mada started walking again, following the narrow brick pathway. All around, rancid water sloshed. The unbearable stench and the unbearable noise and the unbearable company. It all made Mada madder. "You *hate* me. Ain't no secret. You call me Mud and treat me like dirt. Want me to be nice? Sorry, but you don't get special treatment for being rude."

Mada stomped away. She wasn't even looking at Ida anymore. At first it was fun to see her so tongue-tied. Now she couldn't stand her pathetic wheedling.

Ida must've realised Mada had left her. She made a noise somewhere between a gasp and a squeak and dashed up, eyes all wide with fright.

"There a damn problem?" asked Mada. She didn't look at Ida; just kept her eyes forward or on the map. Just because she was mad didn't mean she needed to be *so* mad she stopped paying attention.

"Just . . . what do you want me to do?"

"'Bout what?"

"About . . ." She sighed defeatedly and gestured with her hands. "This place creeps me out. I don't want to be alone."

"Jus' a sewer," said Mada. "A river of shit and piss. Some of it's yours."

Ida shivered. Seemed she didn't like that thought much. "How can I help? I want to help."

Mada hated her wheedling, but . . . "Really wanna help?"

Ida nodded. "Yes."

"Really wanna help me *win*?"

"Yes."

"Why? Stasia also wants to win. Ain't you her friend?"

"Of course I want Stasia to win. But . . . I'm conflicted."

"How?"

"If she wins, she goes with Bilé and I lose my friend. But if *you* win, you leave and we never see *you* again. I think that's more appealing." She winced as she said it, shying away, eyes closing tighter. Brave words said cowardly.

Mada thought for a second, then closed the gap. She grabbed Ida by the neck of her robes and pulled her close. "Any tricks," she hissed, "and I'll push you into the shit river myself. Even if I lose, that's still a win for me."

Ida gulped. "Understood."

Of course Mada didn't trust her. But the whole point was having a partner. So, if she had to, she could work with her. And now, Ida acted like Mada was in charge. Damn good, and all it took was some hot words and rumpled robes.

"So what do we need to do?" asked Ida.

"Just follow the path until we find the trinket, then turn around and take it back to where we started."

"A race, like Bilé said."

Mada shook her head. "Never said it was a race. Said he's *watching* and *judging*. Speaks all cryptically. We don't have to be first. Just gotta get there *correctly*. Whatever that means."

"So . . . Bilé's watching us even now?"

"Said so. Don't ask me how. He's sneaky. Smart. Gotta be if you're a wizard like him. Ain't ours to worry over what or how he does. Just gotta do what he says."

"You're stronger than I give you credit for," said Ida.

"Yeah, well, mud lasts longer than any person." Mada stopped and lowered the map, eyes surveying her surroundings. "Can't be right."

"What can't?" asked Ida, but then she saw it too.

From the sludgy river arose a great, putrid bubble that continued to grow and refused to pop. The back of some great beast. With a great *surge*, it sloshed its massive, viscous, capsule-shaped body up onto the brick walkway.

6: MAP & MIRROR

Huge, paddle-like forepaws. Milky white eyes that seemed blind. A dark-coloured body somewhere between brown and purple that Mada couldn't see in the dismal light. It made a vacuous roar, its mouth stretching wider and wider. Thick strands of yellow saliva clung to three rows of perfectly flat, square teeth.

Mada couldn't believe her eyes.

"*What is that?*" screeched Ida. Apparently, neither could she.

Dammit. Magical creatures weren't Mada's strongest subject. Didn't have the mind for them like Uwe did, mostly 'cause she never thought she'd have to deal with something like whatever this was.

The sewer beast let loose another roar, wide mouth showing all three rows of flat teeth. Its forepaws gave a little hop toward them, but it didn't seem that interested in pursuing them . . . 'least for now.

Brow furrowed, Mada checked the map. "Bilé's trinket's just beyond."

"Just beyond?" Ida blinked stupidly. Terror as she suddenly realised, "You mean, beyond this thing?"

"Gotta get past it."

"What? How?"

"That's what we gotta figure out. Bilé knew I ain't good at magical creatures. Don't know how but it wouldn't surprise me if Uwe and Stasia were dealing with things they ain't too keen on."

For some reason, Mada got mad. She snapped, "Think, girl! D'you really think Bilé captured *three* of these things?"

Once more, Ida shrunk. "You really are mean, you know."

Mada's fists clenched and unclenched, and she breathed heavily through her nose. Didn't need Ida to like her; she needed to get past the sewer beast. So what if she's mean? Everyone else, even Stasia and her friends, acted like Zauberschule was optional. If Mada was going to survive as a healer and surgeon—even without winning Bilé's contest—she'd have to treat this as her only option. Because, as an orphan, what other option did she have?

"Need a plan," she finally said. "Gotta be a way past this thing. Ain't got time to go back and study."

Mada tried to think, and Ida wasn't helping. What did she know about this thing? It was a slimy half-fish monster that somehow scrambled onto dry land. Didn't know magical creatures, but don't magical creatures have some things in common with regular creatures?

"Got any food?"

"What? Food?"

"Look at this thing. Three rows of teeth and all flat. Don't that make you think of a dog or a cat?"

"What?"

"Or don't it remind you of a cow?"

"*What*?"

Mada scoffed and rolled her eyes. "Y'know, I'd be less mean if you were less stupid. Thing eats fruits and vegetables. Don't think it'll harm us; just looks scary. Great if we can sneak by. Better if we can distract it. So . . . got any fruits?"

"You're *sure* about that?"

"Pretty sure. Ain't chasing us. Just protecting what Bilé told it to. We get some fruit, lure it away, don't worry about it chasing us." Mada was tired of asking. She held out her hand expectantly. "So?"

"I got . . . um . . . an apple." She dug around her bag and pulled it out, dusty red and probably bruised inside.

"Better'n nothing," said Mada. "'Specially for a thing lives in shit."

Mada took the apple, shaking it like she might a ball for a dog. Didn't know why, though. The sewer beast seemed blind and its nostrils were clogged. How's something like that supposed to tell where its food is? That's why she hated magical creatures. Soon as she found one thing that made sense, she found six more that didn't.

Mada gave a halfhearted sigh and tossed the apple into the water.

Horrified, Ida gasped, "That's our *only apple*!" And Mada winced.

But the sewer monster scampered forward with its big forepaws and dove back into the water, following the ripples. For a moment, Mada saw all of it. It hadn't quite left the river. Its body was bulky and long, tapering down to a thin, sharp tail which it kept in the water. Probably how it sensed the ripples.

"Run, run, *run*!" pushed Mada.

She and Ida darted past the stinky wetness where the sewer monster once stood, turned the corner, and saw the thing lying on the ground.

"What is it?" asked Ida. "A weapon, I hope."

But it was just as Bilé said. A trinket. A hand mirror, wrought of silver with ornate etchings, filigreed with cerulean and aquamarine enamel.

"It's *beautiful*," said Ida.

"Yeah, maybe." Mada wasn't so sure. She picked it up, examining it, the mirror's gleam shining in her eyes. "Looks expensive. Why'd Bilé leave this in a disgusting sewer?"

"Seems like everything Bilé does has a reason, and a reason for that reason. Like he's telling a story. Maybe we'll find out when we take it back?"

Mada nodded. "Back the way we came, then."

Upon turning around, she saw a sight that damn near made her scream. Ida wasn't so stoic—she *shrieked*, and Mada winced and shushed her. The sewer beast was back in position, guarding the corner, milk-white eyes turned in their direction almost hopefully.

"It's already done eating?" squeaked Ida.

"Was a soft apple and its got three rows of teeth." She looked at her sideways. "Speaking of—"

"No. I don't have any more."

"Nothing?"

"No apples or oranges. Not even a citron. *Nothing.*"

Mada thought for a moment. "If we try to sneak by—"

"—we don't know what'll happen." Ida looked forlorn. Aside from bringing the apple, she hadn't been very helpful. 'Least she'd done *something*.

What Mada needed was to think. She wasn't being tested on her physical prowess or stamina, but her ability to resolve problems. What had she told Ida earlier?

"Can . . ." Ida cleared her throat. "Can I see the map?"

Mada breathed out. They'd come this far, hadn't they? She relented, handing her the map. Ida opened it, looking vexed. "What if . . . we try the mirror?"

"Mirror?" Mada considered it. Bilé was full of tricks. She held up the mirror toward the map. "See anything?"

"Y-yes."

Mada didn't like that she hesitated. "And?"

"I think . . . there's a hidden path?"

You think or you know? Mada wanted to say, but instead said, "Show me." A small dance exchanging the map and the mirror, and Mada saw what looked like a hidden path in the reflection. Not just a reversed image. The path they followed had been marked in black ink, and there was a trail of red ink that wasn't there before. "How d'you suppose he did that?"

Ida chuckled. "You really did need a partner for this. There'd be no way to see the path without someone holding the mirror."

"Would've been difficult, not impossible. Still, glad to've had you along."

Ida smiled. Mada couldn't have her panicking the whole way back. Despite what she said earlier, she didn't expect Ida to betray her anymore. They couldn't go back the way they came; they needed each other to find the exit.

As they walked, Mada heard a splash behind her. The bulbous, vacuous, viscous sewer beast dived back into water, and seemed to follow them. She could practically *feel* Ida's tension. Wasn't feeling so relaxed herself.

"Maybe we ought not to have fed it," said Ida.

"Maybe we should've brought more apples."

Mada kept her eye on it as they strolled down the sewers. Ever did the beast remain by their side, following. How did it know? Did Bilé control it? Damn thing unnerved her.

"Close now," said Ida. Mada took her turn and saw. Soon there'd be a tunnel or pipeway of some kind. That was their way back, away from the sewer beast.

"Maybe run for it?" asked Mada. "Get there just in case the monster gets there first."

"Think we should?" Ida looked at the sewer beast. Like always, it was right there. Waiting. Hadn't come back to shore. Why did it even follow them? The more Mada thought about it, the more she wanted to run.

But she didn't.

7: SEWER BEAST

They finally found it, a sluiceway behind a rusted grate. Mada and Ida investigated, wondering if they could just break through the bars. Behind them, the sewer beast watched them, waiting, a muddy bubble that pursued them wherever they went. Hopefully not for much longer.

Ida—either bravely or stupidly—rammed the grate, and fell backward. She gripped her shoulder, swears mingling with the impact's metallic squeal.

Dented, but not much else.

Mada looked at the mirror, curious. Everything came together. Everything came apart. She gripped the handle and gave a twist, hard as she could. It loosened. Her eyes widened and she continued twisting and turning and pulling until a tool was revealed. "Look, Ida."

"I see. I'm fine, by the way."

"Right. Right." Mada helped her up. Wasn't used to caring for anyone but herself. "Sorry."

Mada pressed the object into the grate and gave it a good pry. The rusty metal moaned, but damn if it didn't work. More and more, the grate creaked free. "Little more," said Mada.

Splashing behind them. Loud. Ida tugged roughly on Mada's sleeve. "What?" She turned around and saw the sewer beast had leapt again onto the walkway, directly across from them, staring with its sightless, milky eyes.

Mada gulped. Didn't like the look of that one bit. Returning her attention to the pipeline, she tugged all the more. "C'mon! Help me!" Ida slipped her fingers into the rusted crate and pulled, too.

Wet, sloshy stomps. Mada felt a shiver go up her spine. She looked back and damn if the sewer beast wasn't closer. *Damn, damn, damn.* She watched it, and it took a small step forward with each pull, each grunt, each creak. With one final effort, the rusted grate swung open. Both girls panted, exhausted. Looking behind them, they saw the sewer beast bound toward them. Ida squealed and Mada grabbed her arm, dragging her into the sluiceway.

Damn did it stink in there, the ground slippery with muck. Hard to take deep breaths when you're trying to avoid the shitty stench. Ida attempted to close the grate, but the sewer beast smashed through it, hot on their trail. Was fast in water; should've guessed 'twas fast on land.

"Run!" screamed Mada. "*Run!*"

They had to get away. Neither girl knew magical creatures. No telling what would happen if it caught them, but Mada didn't wanna find out. She wanted to look behind, see where it was. Bad idea. Focus on what's ahead. The floor was already so slippery, footing so unsure. No way to check without the risk of falling.

Just keep running. Just keep running. Don't look back and *just keep running*.

Behind them, the creature made the same yawning gasp. Mada tried to shake the sound from her mind—for the sound reminded her of the gaping maw with three rows of flat, square teeth.

And Ida screamed.

And the weight felt *heavy*.

So heavy, Mada slipped in the muck, shouting surprise while Ida shrieked agony.

But Ida didn't budge. Mada looked back in terror. The sewer beast had its wide mouth clamped around her arm. Her eyes stared helplessly, disbelievingly at her ensnared appendage.

"M-M-Mada . . ."

She knew. But she didn't know what to do. And then the beast dragged her backward. Ida screamed, "Mada! Mada, help me! Don't let it take me!"

What the hell could she do? The only thing she thought of. She grabbed Ida's arm and tugged back. Ida screamed, tears streaking through her slime-caked face. The beast pulled. Mada pulled back. Ida, caught in the middle, couldn't seem to decide anymore if she wanted Mada to let go or save her.

Then the sewer beast's jaw started working back and forth. Ida's eyes refilled with horror anew. A terrible sound—the sound of crunching muscles and grinding bones. Ida's screams flowed like putrid water, but Mada could barely hear them over her own heart pounding in her ears.

This wasn't working. There had to be something else. She reached down into the grimy mire, one hand holding Ida, one digging, feeling, searching. Ida begged not to let her go.

Mada pulled up the end of the mirror she'd dropped, slipped past, and drove it into its gauzy eye. The sewer beast let out another garbled roar, pulled back—and down Ida fell. The creature kept munching and crunching, backing away, the prying tool stuck in its oozing face.

8: FRIENDS

Ida looked pale. Deathly pale. Her arm was gone above the elbow, a chewed up, dripping mess of ruby meat.

Groaning and grunting, Mada grasped her up. "C'mon," she said, dragging her through the pipeline. She looked back, the sewer beast receding, leaving, not pursuing. Mada sighed with relief, but Ida didn't look so good.

"You awake?"

Ida didn't answer. Her head rolled to the side, eyelids fluttering, eyes unfocused.

"Hey, *hey*!" Mada hefted her to a good position to slap her face. Thankfully, some of Ida's awareness returned. "C'mon. We're close. Get you back. Get you healed."

"My arm's gone. Eaten," she croaked.

"Sure is." Mada concentrated, one foot in front of the other, careful not to slip and send them both into the shit around their ankles.

"Leave me."

"Can't do that. Stasia'd never forgive me."

"I don't . . . *want* to go back."

"Too bad, 'cause I'm your feet now."

"How will I be a healer—do any work—with just one arm?"

"Worry o' that when the bleeding stops."

"My arm's . . . *gone*. I'm trying . . . to wriggle my fingers. Can't feel anything. Except *pain*."

"Yeah. It's bad. Your arm's chewed and swallowed. Rest o' you's still with me, though, right?"

"Chewed and swallowed." Ida made a noise between a chuckle and a sniff. "You need to work on your compassion. Bedside manners, they're calling it. Do you . . . think a soldier . . . with the same wound . . . wants to hear what you just told me?"

"Gotta tell you something," said Mada. She needed to keep Ida awake. Aware. Couldn't let her drift off. Needed her talking. "Never thought I'd be here, helping you through the sewers. Maybe we're not friends, but a team."

"We're . . . not friends?"

"I got your arm all chewed off. Why d'you wanna be friends with me?"

"Wasn't . . . *your* fault. Besides . . . you're helping me. You risked your life for me."

This didn't feel right. Felt *wrong*. Didn't they hate each other? Wasn't she mousy, lousy Mud the orphan with no future and no past? Didn't Ida, Stasia, and Mia make her life a living hell every day?

"Yeah, well . . ." Mada swallowed hard, adjusted, and kept walking toward the steadily growing light. "'Fore this, I didn't know which o' you was Mia and which was Ida. Both just Stasia's bitches."

Ida chuckled again. "You *really* need to work on your bedside manners."

"Guess if we're gonna be friends, we gotta get to know each other a little better."

"I guess so."

"I like purple. Can't wear it 'cause my skin's too red. Y'know? What's your favourite colour?"

"Purple dye's expensive," moaned Ida. "I've got some dresses I don't wear anymore. Good colours. If you want to try them. Not fancy or expensive. Not like ladies' gowns. But I think we can find you *something*."

"Yeah," said Mada, not taking her eyes from the tunnel's end, "I'd like that."

They kept talking like that until they reached the big open space where Bilé waited. But . . . no one else?

Even though she was the first one back, Mada didn't care. No time to celebrate. She pulled Ida toward the wizard. So powerful. So knowledgeable. He *had* to help her. "Please. She's hurt. Please. We have to stop the bleeding. *Please*."

Bilé, all shrouded and impassive, said nothing but stepped aside. Behind him, a cookfire crackled, upon which a heavy iron skillet sat. Mada had questions. Was it safe to have a fire down here with all these fumes?

Whatever charms and enchantments Bilé had done made them safe. But Mada didn't feel safe. First, the dark questions of monsters and demons, then this terrible experience that left Ida in such a sorry state . . .

With billowing sleeves and jingling bells, Bilé gestured to the red hot skillet. Mada inhaled sharply. She knew what Bilé asked of her. Still being tested. She lay Ida on the stone floor, bricks stained greenish-brown. Damn she looked terrible. Skin so pale 'twas blue. Cold sweat across her brow. Hand so clammy. And that drippy, meaty, lump where her arm used to be.

"Don't go," groaned Ida. "Don't leave me."

"Shh, shh, shh . . . right here. Not going nowhere. Just need t' fix you up." Gotta cauterise the wound. Then gotta get her to healers who're worth a shit. "Here, here. For your mouth." Mada ripped a length of cloth from her tunic, folded it to something thick, and put the strip in Ida's mouth.

"Wha—?"

"Just for a little," Mada cooed. She took her jacket off, the stagnant air cold around her skin. She wrapped her hand in the thick wool and grabbed the skillet's handle. Gently—so gently—she raised Ida's arm at the tricep.

"Wha—?"

"Just keep that in your mouth. Be over quickly."

She wished she had help, someone stronger to hold her, another set of hands. She couldn't wait for anyone else. Mada pinned Ida down with her knee to her shoulder. Before Ida could even struggle, but just after her eyes widened, Mada pressed the skillet to the meaty stump.

Horrible. Everything was horrible.

The stench of the sizzling meat.

The searing sound of hot metal on flesh.

The awful screams Ida choked through her muzzle.

Mada felt hot tears streak her own cheeks. She wanted to gasp, scream, sob, retch. Later. For now, she applied pressure, moving the pan around to cook Ida's arm and staunch the flow.

Finally, it was done. She threw the cool pan aside, scampered away, and heaved a massive sob and vomited. Her whole body shook, eyes wide and blurry with tears. Ida, now free of Mada's weight, writhed in pain, fingers dancing above the blackened stump, indecisive of touching it.

"*Why?*" she howled. "*Why, why, why?!*"

"*Sorry,*" cried Mada. "Sorry, sorry, sorry . . ."

"What is going on?"

Mada looked up. As if things couldn't get any worse. Stasia stomped over, face quickly reddening, eyes livid. Red-haired Mia trailed not far behind. After everything else, now Mada had to deal with this.

"What did you do to her?!" Stasia examined Ida, mouth working furiously. She grabbed Mada by her tunic's neckline, pulled her close, screaming, spitting into her face. "What the *hell* did you *do to her*?!"

"Saved her life," said Bilé with his strange cacophony of voices.

Stasia softened—well, her grip slackened, but her face remained a screwed up mess of anger. Honestly, Mada never saw her more dishevelled. Anger aside, her eyes were bloodshot, and her hair was a matted mess. What was once silky blonde was now matted, streaked with green and brown slime. It even looked as though it had been shorn ragged from her head. Both she and Mia were coated with grime—though less than Mada and Ida.

"Looks like we all had trouble," croaked Mada.

Stasia blinked back tears. "Yeah."

"Really did try to help. 'Least your hair'll grow back."

"Yeah." Stasia faced Bilé. "I had to give up my hair. She came back and Ida's missing an arm. Take her out of the contest."

Mada's breath hitched. Almost wanted it, too. If Bilé agreed, she wouldn't've argued. But Bilé said, "Mada solved my tricks and returned first. She did as instructed. She did not lose."

"And me?"

"Follow me." Bilé faced Mia's direction. "Stay with Ida. Take her to the infirmary if necessary. But leave not her side."

Mia nodded, looking somewhere between frightened and determined. But she crouched beside Ida and did her best to comfort her.

Mada and Stasia followed Bilé through another tunnel, following a trail of slime. Mada had to ask, "What *was* that thing? The sewer beast?"

Stasia eyed her, confused. "S-sewer beast?"

"A Bøjg," said Bilé.

"A what?"

"A morphological creature, made when a slug is kept in total darkness with a golden ring."

"And you made one? And it attacked us?"

"We must be prepared for *anything*. I've read every contestant's paperwork, discovered their weakest subjects—amongst other weaknesses."

"Solving my riddle was far from easy," said Stasia. "A door that only opened with yellow hair." She shook her head. "I panicked. Mia just kept feeding it. I was crying because it took—" And she gestured to her head.

"Yeah, I get it," said Mada. "It's just . . . *we* could've—"

"*Died?*" Was it magic or coincidence that a cold breeze blew through, making her shiver? "Never did I promise safety."

"Never promised *harm*, either—"

"Incorrect, Mada. Students and teachers are well aware of my methods. My contests quicken skills and knowledge because they put the contestants' minds and bodies in danger. They require cunning, wit, and sacrifice."

At the end of the aqueduct, which opened to the sluiceways and shitty river, Bilé spread his arms wide, as if to say, "Behold!" to something miraculous. Mada guessed that miraculous something was that . . . he was right.

On the filthy brick floor, Franz sat on his knees, face buried in his hands, weeping. All that remained of Uwe was a greasy red smear on a far wall, apparently made by a construct of heavy spikes and tripwires all connected to a puzzle. Mada could've solved it easily. But her own, Bøjg, would've been easiest for Uwe and Franz.

"I don't know what happened," cried Franz, aware of their presence.

"Zauberschule has lost a good student," said Bilé. "Come. There's naught more for us down here."

But Franz didn't budge. Not right away. Lost his friend. Didn't wanna move. Mada couldn't blame him. Or maybe she could've. That's the risk you take when you have friends.

9: 3RD TRIAL

When Bilé gave his little speech about death and dismemberment, he thankfully did it away from Franz and Ida. 'Least he had *some* tact. Still didn't make Mada feel any better, though.

"A magician constantly faces death and dismemberment. One cannot get too attached to people or things—even themselves."

Blah, blah, blah.

All Mada knew was that Franz was so horrified, he left Zauberschule. Went to be a milkman or candlemaker's apprentice or something.

Ida . . . well, she was healing the ugly stump of her arm in the infirmary. Mada thought she should visit. Wanted to, but . . . would Ida wanna see her? After all, Mada blamed herself for her arm. Didn't Ida blame her too?

Mada couldn't even find joy in the sneers Stasia received from her hair. Shearing it off to feed some magic lock, bald in some places, horribly stained. The other kids laughed at her so much, she had it *all* clipped off.

But Mada didn't laugh. Firstly, her voice was scraped sore from all that screaming. Even if she wanted to be, she wasn't completely heartless. How could she laugh? Stasia constantly cried about it in her room. Sometimes she burst into tears during meals or class. Sure, wasn't an arm like Ida's, but down in those sewers, everyone'd been traumatised.

The night before the final trial, Stasia appeared by Mada's bedside. "Hey," she hissed, and shoved Mada awake.

Still dark. Couldn't she get some rest? "What?"

"Just us two. We're the last ones." She did that thing Mada hated, that noise between a scoff and a chuckle. Thought it'd lose its edge without Stasia flipping her perfect blonde hair, but nope. "I didn't expect you to get this far."

"Yeah, well . . . I didn't *want* you to get this far."

She made that scoff-chuckle again.

"Even Ida said she wanted me to win. Wanted me to leave Zauberschule and you'll never see me again. Can't say the thought don't appeal to me."

"You, er . . . bonded with her, did you?"

"I don't know shit about magical creatures." Mada hugged her knees. "Didn't know what to do. Never heard of Bøjg afore." Her head flooded with doubts and should'ves. Should've split the apple. Should've found a weapon.

Should've studied more. Should've realised there's always a trick. Should've never trusted Bilé. Maybe should've never entered the damn contest.

Problem with should'ves is they always come *after* you did the damn thing.

Stasia seemed to soften. Mada hadn't said it, but she knew what she meant. Strangely, Stasia touched her shoulder and said, "Her . . . *injury* wasn't your fault."

Mada sat up and looked at her, brows furrowed. Hard to see in the darkness. "Mean it?"

"As difficult as it is for me to admit, I don't believe you meant Ida any harm."

"Yeah. Thanks."

In a too-familiar way, Stasia sat on Mada's bed. Uncomfortable, but what could she do? Maybe this was Stasia's way of apologising? "This contest means a lot to both of us. For me, more opportunities. The same for you, but you had also mentioned you wish not to be here. We haven't been the kindest to you."

"Or, y'know, at all."

"No matter what happens, tomorrow is between you and I." She held out her hand. "Let the best girl win."

Mada looked at Stasia's hand, mind reeling. Didn't feel right. None of this did. Sorta wanted to clasp it but wasn't that what this was all about? Started this contest 'cause she wanted Stasia to take her more seriously, stop picking on her. Never wanted friends or companions. All Mada wanted was to be left alone, study, learn, then go to the faroff battlefield and stitch cut men back together. Just wanted to be away from Stasia and her friends.

She took a deep breath—thinking, thinking. Stasia raised her eyebrows. Expectant. Hopeful.

Maybe she oughtn't've, but Mada slapped her hand away. 'Course Stasia looked startled, but Mada couldn't give into her sympathetic feelings. Why should she forgive Stasia who never even apologised?

"What's all this?" Mada stood up, shaking her head. "This ain't like you. You jealous I'm getting so far? Or afraid I'm actually better'n you?"

"I . . . don't understand—"

"'Course you do! You'd *never* act like this. You'd always find some way to win, 'specially if I was the one beating you. Which I *am*. You think I'm gonna soften up just 'cause you wanna win? I'm only gonna try *harder*."

Stasia looked dejected. Mada didn't mean to snap. She *did* feel kinda bad. But then she thought of something. Stasia *wouldn't* ever act like this. So Mada asked, "Stasia . . . is that even you?"

When Stasia spoke, it wasn't her voice. Two pitches, high and deep, woman and man's—*Bilé's*. "Congratulations, Mada—" Eerily, when she turned back around, it was him in all his bells and shrouds. "This was your final trial. And you passed."

Mada blinked, confused. "W-What?"

"In the world of magic not everything is what it seems. As you learned with Ida, sometimes you must trust even those you once thought untrustworthy, set aside differences, and work together. Other times, you might be deceived by someone you think you can trust."

Mada's hands clenched and unclenched. She'd been deceived but she'd *won*. She looked at Bilé. "How did Stasia do?"

"I've not yet tested her. Please. Come with me and watch her trial."

Mada went with Bilé. So many questions . . . Bilé was male and thus wasn't allowed in the girls' dormitory. Why was he here? Did Headmaster Grimsby know about this?

There was something eerie about creeping about at night. Not a single candle burned. Mada was so concerned about stepping on a loose board and waking the whole place up. But it was so quiet. Bilé seemed to glide; not even his robes rustled against the ground.

Once in Stasia's room, Bilé waved his hands over Mada. Casting a spell, making her invisible. "Say not a word. Make not a sound," Bilé warned her. She nodded.

Then, he waved his hands over himself and—to her surprise—she was looking at her exact duplicate. The same clay-red skin, the mud-coloured curls, eyes dark and rich as soil. Her doppelgänger put a finger to its lips, reminding her to keep quiet.

Mada watched her uncanny twin slink beside Stasia's bed. Gently, it put its hand on her shoulder and nudged her awake. "Stasia? Stasia . . ."

The blonde girl roused, eyes opening. Sleepy confusion turned to angry awareness. Stasia bolted upright, almost ashamed at being touched by Mada, and hissed, "What do you want, *Mud*?"

Mada tried her damnedest to suppress a chuckle. *This* was the Stasia she knew.

"Just nervous 'bout the third trial." Mada watched her doppelgänger shuffle anxiously. So odd to hear it talk—did she really sound like *that*? "Couldn't sleep."

"Well, as you can plainly see, I *can*. So go back to your room, *Mud*."

"Ain't you concerned about the future? Can we really trust Bilé?"

"*Mud*. Go *back* to your *room*."

Stasia had never treated Mada with any respect. Why should she now? Bilé couldn't even begin to trick her because she didn't trust Mada in the first place; same as Mada didn't trust Stasia. She didn't think Bilé could trick either of them like this.

But then, something different.

Mada's doppelgänger leaned in close. "Not concerned, hm? Should be. Really think you can handle this? Any of this?"

"What did you say, *Mud*?"

"Lost some hair?" She scoffed. "So what? You don't know suffering. I lost *everything*. You really think you can do whatever Bilé asks when you *know* everything you've ever gotten was given to you. You don't know how to *work* for things."

"What—" but her fire was gone, replaced by confusion, sadness. "What are you saying, Mud?" Even that damnable nickname carried none of its usual harshness.

"Saying you're *soft*," croaked Mada's doppelgänger. "*Easy*. Don't got what it takes to do Bilé's work 'cause you ain't capable of doing *any* work."

Stasia's eyes welled up. Mada . . . didn't know how she felt. For the longest time, she wanted to say these exact words. Seeing Stasia's tears . . .

Mada's doppelgänger pointed its finger. "Truth is, you want *clout*. You ain't doing this 'cause you *care*. You wanna feel *special*. Better'n everyone else. Gonna sour real quick when you're out there with Bilé, 'cause Bilé wants someone who *is* special, not someone who wants to *feel* special."

Stasia's glittering tears spilled from her cheeks. "You're . . . *right*."

She was? It was?

"All I ever cared about is myself. I want to impress people. I never should've entered this stupid contest. Instead, I should've . . . made something up. Told a lie. Let everyone know that I thought the contest was beneath me."

She sniffled. "Now look at us. Franz left. I have no hair. Ida's got no arm. Uwe's *dead*." She squeaked the last word out. "It used to be I could decide your fate with the swing of my hair." She shook her head. "No longer."

Dammit, Mada *wanted* to be sympathetic, comfort her somehow. This didn't feel right. Stasia without her hair was like a toothless lion or a wingless eagle. But she couldn't give herself away.

Stasia sighed. "I don't think I can continue the contest."

"Thus, you forfeit," said Bilé's double-voice.

Stasia shook her head, pale eyes wide. "*What?*"

With a wave of his arms, Mada's visage fluttered away and he revealed himself. Stasia gasped and backed against her headboard, protecting herself with her threadbare blanket.

"This was your final trial. Allowed you yourself to be swayed by the shade of your adversary. Never did you question them, only yourself. Therefore, you fail. Mada Dreck is the winner."

10: MADA'S FAREWELL

Mada wrapped her jacket around her, shivering against the cold. One last look at this valley view. Green hillocks rising and falling. Sparse pine trees. Behind her, Zauberschule, tall and imposing. Very few other students came to bid her farewell, but it was nice the faculty did. Grimsby and Gwenna, Stasia and Ida, and at the end of the line, Bilé.

Headmaster Grimsby looked particularly pleased. Another success. He shook her hand and wished her well.

Didact Gwenna hugged her close, tears running down her beaky nose. "You would've made a fine surgeon," she squawked. "A *damn fine* surgeon."

Hadn't been too long ago Mada was thinking about that. Going west, healing some soldiers so they could fight more against those rebels. All in the past.

Gwenna wiped a tear from her eye. "No matter what happens, you'll always have a home here." She'd always been something of her caretaker. Mada was sad to leave her. Now Bilé was her master and guardian. She would go wherever he went.

But a home . . . yeah, that's what she wanted. In a way, Zauberschule was her home, even if it wasn't a proper family and she didn't get along with everyone. Odd to think she belonged somewhere else now. Fearing she'd also tear up, Mada said, "Thanks for everything" before moving on.

At the end of the line were Stasia and Ida. The dark stubble upon Stasia's head looked less coarse now; still short but soft. Ida was out of the infirmary, arm still bandaged but she looked good. After winning, Mada had visited her to let her know she won. Surprisingly, Ida seemed happy to see her.

"You'll do well," said Stasia. "We've had our differences. But I know, Mada, you'll do great things."

Mada grinned. Not *Mud*. Mada. Didn't seem to be any jealousy or animosity. "You too, Stasia. Hope we meet again soon."

Then she faced Ida. "Sorry 'bout your arm."

Ida chuckled. "It's fine. They'll find something for me to do. I can study, advise. Consult. I don't need two arms to be a scholar." She looked sadly at the stump, just above the elbow. "I can't explain it but my fingers *itch*. When I try to scratch them . . ."

"Yeah," gulped Mada. What else could she say?

"Don't worry too much." She smiled wearily but reassuringly. "I've got the best healers in the land taking care of me."

"I know. Wherever you end up, I'll come visit you." And they embraced, careful of Ida's still-healing wound. Awkward as it was, 'twas nice. A gesture of genuine friendship. Ask Mada a month ago and she'd've never guessed.

Bilé raised his colourful, shrouded arm. A quiet beckon. Time to go.

That was that. Nothing more to say, nothing more to do. She thought everyone hated her. Most didn't care to come out and bid farewell, but two of the three people she thought least likely were there. Maybe 'cause they all went through hell in those sewers.

With one last sniff and glance behind, Mada grabbed her rucksack—light 'cause she didn't have many belongings—and left with Bilé.

11: LESSONS LEARNED

Darkness everywhere. Light came in sporadic slivers.

Cold.

Lonely.

Hungry. Enough to pick the meagre meat from the bones in the corner.

Wasn't supposed to be like this.

Couldn't even tell where she was.

She pressed her bare back against the cold metal wall, sucking in breath.

Uncomfortable. Every time. Always so damn uncomfortable.

Had to crawl to get anywhere. Couldn't walk anymore. Had to pull herself by her bleeding fingers.

At the far end of the room, the creak of a rusted door. She closed her eyes. Didn't wanna look at him. Not again. Always so damn uncomfortable.

She heard the soft jingle of his bells as he approached. Best she could do was look away and wait. She tried to fight once. Learned quickly she couldn't. Finally, the jingling stopped. A rustle of fabrics—many-layered. Gauzy silk caressed her damp face.

"Mada, I knew it would be you as soon as I saw your smiling face."

Squeezed her eyes so tight a tear leaked out. Dammit. Wasn't supposed to be like this.

"You've learned my lessons well. Everything I have given you has led to this. I always wonder how pupils so astute always fail to see my true intentions. Believed I myself to be heavy-handed with mine hints this time 'round."

Mada's breathing hitched. Hyperventilating. Wasn't supposed to be like this. Dammit. She wanted to kick her legs but the damn things were all the way across the room, rotting in a pile with other bones of other students long dead. Same pile she forced herself to eat from.

Lessons learned. One cannot get attached to people or places or things . . . even themselves. One sometimes must trust the untrustworthy. Sometimes one shouldn't trust someone they thought they could. Never should've trusted Bilé. But that's the problem with should'ves.

Another rustle of fabrics. Mada turned her head away, not daring to look. First time she saw his face unshrouded, she recoiled—vomited. Forever would the image be burned into her mind.

Not human.

Insectoid.

Reptilian.

Hirsute.

Demon.

Devil.

Consumer of flesh and souls.

Her breathing hitched. More tears flowed. She recoiled at the memory, the barb that came from Bilé's mandibles. It stung her, numbed her, and her legs came off with such ease. A thousand clacking, slurping mouthparts picked away the flesh of her appendages. The remains—a mangled stretch of gristle, cartilage, and sinew—flung mockingly into the pile of bones. All because she tried to fight back, wanted to leave, wanted to be anywhere else. When the numbness subsided, pain and the overwhelming sense of loss. If only Ida could see her now . . .

Mada kept her teeth clenched so tight her jaw hurt. A thousand questions but none of them worth a damn. Bilé could answer them but what did it matter? She couldn't escape. Any information given would vanish in this cold, dark room. Same as her. Same as all the students in the bone pile.

"Grimsby knows." How could something without lips talk like it was grinning?

Mada's throat cracked with sobs. Didn't know why. She didn't particularly *like* the headmaster, but he never made himself out to be untrustworthy. Should've, should've, should've . . . that's all she had with lessons learned too late.

"Why?" she croaked.

"Devils are hungry. Many amongst us are equivalent to wild dogs. Like the aforementioned chimaera. But there are others, like me. Why lay waste to the populace when they can bring you a sacrifice willingly? A pact, you understand. A single life given willingly in exchange for countless lives taken."

A sacrifice. That's all she was. That's all they ever were. Even Gwenna said she would've made a fine surgeon. Did she know too? No one'd miss her. No one'd look for her. Stasia and Ida would never cross paths with her and they wouldn't think anything of it except a coincidence.

She'd lost even though she'd won. They'd won even though they'd lost. 'Least poor Uwe's death was fast. Horrible but she'd've preferred to be a greasy smear on a sewer wall.

Another rustle of fabrics. The sting of Bile's mouth-barb in her arm—then numbness. She shuddered. Whimpered. Felt something dully pulling at her arm like it was a hundred miles away. A twist. Sounds of tearing flesh, spattering blood, acid-cooked meat squelching on the floor. Hating the scent of her own cooking arm made her mouth water. That hundred-mile-away pull became a hundred-mile-away ache.

Emptiness where there was once something.

Her arm was gone. Didn't even have to open her eyes to know. Just knew something that was once there wasn't anymore. Thought of Ida. Tried wiggling her fingers. Thought she could still feel them a hundred miles away.

"Fear not death." Wasn't that the point of Bilé's lessons?

Mada had to pray. Didn't know if her prayers would be heard if she couldn't fold her hands or raise her voice. No use wasting time or breath on questions that didn't matter. She'd learned her lessons. She was doomed.

Humankind's powerless against demons. 'Specially if one's hell bent on destroying you.

Bilé's many mandibles click-scraped the meat from her arm bones. She could hear it. She'd die here, she knew. Couldn't run. Couldn't hide. Best pray, at least, like Stasia said, so her soul ain't damned forever. Best pray and wait for death.

The Hand that Feeds

By DB Rook

DB Rook is an author of fantasy with a promiscuous relationship with horror and all things dark. He has written for the tabletop gaming world and is not afraid to nail his nerd flag to the mast. After 15 years of working in the field of addiction he is now making efforts to focus his creativity into building new worlds.

His debut novel, (Callus & Crow) is the first in his Wayward World Chronicles series and was released in 2022. A weird West Odyssey of revenge and redemption with a sprinkling of steampunk, vampirism, and post-apocalyptic action/adventure.

Tempting as it is to deny, I was young in my career when the rebellious streak unfurled from a place deep within. A place neither me nor my mentors knew existed; a place that, until my internship began in the department of Watchers, was an undiscovered trove of seditious and fractious traits that would both help and hinder my climb through the ranks of collegiate leadership throughout the following years.

My initiation involved a silent and lonely year at the archaic controls of an Oraculum, followed by a dissertation on my findings, excerpts of which are presented here. Wondrous machines, they were, despite the necessity for the user to entirely interface with the subject's environment both mentally and physically, as well as the difficulties this created in separation once the period of watchfulness ended. Indeed, I fear I am not alone in my occasional cravings to revisit places I have never physically been. Such was the power of the Oraculum, that the minds and hearts of those surrounding our students lay open to the department of Watchers whether permission was granted or not, and it was those minds that eventually unified to lobby a change in our observation policies.

The Oraculums were decommissioned some years ago. In the end, it was the invasive nature of the machines that brought about their demise, particularly regarding those subjects not currently signed to programs of study at the Collegiate.

In an attempt to share both my journey and, I feel, the source of my aforementioned anarchistic leanings, an Otreyan named Ethna Vikreyus, I have compiled her story here in hope that those following in my ancient footsteps will understand the world beyond the Collegiate walls and will begin to adapt their learning to encompass all life, not just those that possess enough gold to weigh down the infamous Collegiate drawbridge.

***

The final deranged scream bypassed the eardrums, begging the brain for mercy. The warrior's ichor-splattered blade lifted to reveal it had severed the spine before crunching into bare earth. The last of their relentless pursuers fouled the forest air as it released its inner workings, steaming as it coiled black and foetid in the pale light of a waning moon.

Each of the beasts had died incensed and devoted to the cause of retribution for the company's blasphemous trespass.

Each of the group had been force-fed fear that night as they hacked and loosed, fled and fumbled their way through the dense black forest. Ever pursued and never stopping, never catching breath, never closing their eyes and never quite feeling the sweet rush of relief as the relentless threat finally ended. Until that moment.

"Fuck me, thank fuck for that!"

***

The common room was near empty. The remaining villagers slid their cradled pint mugs towards the bar as the hefty landlord gestured the bedraggled company to the fireplace with a stained rag in his fist. Keramin was the first to settle in and grab a poker, just as he would have on the road with a substantial twig.

Next sat Verrous, his hotch-potch chain and plate crashing onto the stone floor as he slumped and levered off one boot with the other. Daine and Greggim chose the creaking wooden benches over the floor, Daine removed his gloves to wiggle his grateful fingers at the fire while Greggim complained about the stink emanating from Verrous' liberated boots.

"Smells like a swamp troll with its guts cut." The broad warrior spat into the fire, adding an angry hiss to the hollow thuds of his blades as each drove into the scarred bench beside him, one after the other.

"You wouldn't understand. Stink comes from hard work, not tossing about with pointy kid knives." Verrous replied distractedly, looking over his shoulder as a young server arrived with a tray of beers. It was hard to tell if it was the young lass or the beers that caused his grey streaked eyebrow to reach towards his retreating hairline, crinkling the old burn scar as it went.

Keramin shook his younger head as he poked about in the fire, which grumbled in appreciation. The flames had built to a good size and the heat, in the corner of the old inn, stung the eyes, as did the vapour rising from the cold wet party as they made themselves at home and collectively shed armour, weapons and road weariness.

"Are we sure those two made it here before us?" Daine asked Keramin as he fussed with a buckle he'd had to mend with twine on the road or lose the pauldron. They were all in need of a smith and perhaps new gear.

"Yeah, she came ahead with Lialla. Said she had to meet this guy first so we didn't scare him off," the hunter replied as a haunted look locked his gaze on the flames.

"So where's Lialla?"

At that, Verrous laughed and took a glug of his ale before wiping his bearded face.

"She'll be introducing herself to the locals." He said as his eyebrows repeatedly rose and fell, his grin creasing his crow's feet.

Daine shook his head.

"Why does she...",

"It's the only way she can feel val... nevermind." Keramin interrupted as he tossed his twig into the fire despondently.

"Fuck me!" Greggim's eyes rolled as he slammed down his mug, ale sploshing over his massive hands. "Your jealousy is curdling my piss-warm beer, Kem." Keramin frowned at Greggim, momentarily unsure if he had the energy for conflict.

"Yes." He said in a quiet and controlled manner. "Maybe I am jealous of the strangers she chooses to fuck. Maybe I do think I could do a better job than some village fuck-wit."

It was Verrous' turn to laugh as he clapped a hand to Keramin's shoulder. "You can shoot a bowman's finger out at a hundred yards, Kem, but you can't..."

"Fuck you!" said the typically rational hunter. "And fuck you," he repeated to Greggim as he grabbed his bow and stormed from the corner of the inn towards the bar.

The remaining company looked at each other for a moment, and Greggim broke the yawning silence.

"Think we hit a vein."

***

Ethna arrived to find most of her company already snoring around the untended fire as it choked on its own soot. They had travelled for days and she hoped it had been worth it. After the botched temple raid - the raid she'd warned against, she felt they had hit rock bottom. She believed it was time to make a change. She had forged an opportunity to improve their fortunes, but hoped they were up to the task.

The inn was now empty, just the landlord barring windows and tending the barrels for the next day.

She looked at her sorry company. They had given her all they had and she had barely asked for any of it. In fact, she had never actually asserted herself as leader. She just started to share her thoughts one day and the burly warriors just grunted into line. She was sorely aware that each of them needed a mother and that, for now, she'd got the job, but it suited her as she rarely had to get her own hands dirty.

***

Upon reflection it may well have been Ethna's rough but motherly traits that endeared me to her so strongly. She was often oafish and confrontational, sometimes choosing to threaten or over-power her opponents to win an argument, but the raw and obvious love she felt for her friends was unquestionable.

My own mother was nurturing and proper, always considering of who was watching and how things appeared. She had a great deal of ambition for me and no doubt sacrificed a lot to give me my chance at the Collegiate. She was, however, often cold, and gave little thought to my ideas of a preferred future. I owed a lot to my mother, but as my period of watchfulness continued, my heart sang in the presence of Ethna.

***

Lately, their rewards had been meagre. People were paying less and needing more. Lords and landowners were sitting pretty and adding to their own crews. Crews of desperate folk that would do whatever was needed without questioning their unelected masters. The world was turning sour. The life was getting harder, and they needed a decent gig if they were to keep slogging it out.

She kicked Verrous on the floor, not too hard but enough for him to reach for his axe before he opened his eyes. It wouldn't be good practice to let them get too complacent.

Greggim slept in pain. She could see a deep red stain that had gathered under him. She could wake and then heal him, she mused, but she always valued the chance to practise.

She placed a tattooed hand lightly on his sweat-matted hair. Verrous frowned up at her reproachfully. Even in Ethna's circles it was considered ill treatment to overcome a person's defences when you could simply offer them healing, but Ethna liked to stay sharp, and she liked her crew to know how sharp she was.

She found his centre of power. Somewhat dwindled by poor diet, shame from poor morals and low self-esteem, but it was there. She spent a moment matching the rhythm of his spirit to her own essence and once the two flowed neatly together, she sent a piercing thrust of energy into and beyond his weakened protection, opening a small portal to slip in a fairly sizable healing notion. Her magic found its way to the source of damage and began to reverse the effects of the wound. She then slipped out unnoticed and tied off the flow from her hand with a triumphant smile.

She flicked Greggim's ear and laughed as he roared into life, swearing and flinging spittle everywhere, until, looking slightly abashed in her presence, he regained control of himself. The noise woke Keramin, who had eventually crept back to join the company like a sulking dog who missed the pack, and Daine, who scratched the deep scar beneath his shaggy black hair whilst forcing his eyes to open wide enough to wake up.

"There's a dorm for you lot upstairs." Ethna said as she rolled her eyes. "No need to curl by the fire like good hounds." They gathered their things in relative silence and filed past her. "Get a decent sleep. Tomorrow we change our fortunes." Greggim stopped and looked at Ethna.

"Working for them." He sneered, his frustration plain for everyone to see. "Like good hounds." Ethna let the insubordination go and held her tongue. They needed a rest and however they felt, she knew best. That was her job, was it not?

"Lialla's already abed." She called after them.

"No change there then." Greggim growled before vanishing through the doorway and upstairs to their creaky dorm.

***

Lialla was the first downstairs to join Ethna in the empty bar. Her red hair tangled and bunched atop her head, held in place along with her aching skull by a freckled hand. Her bare feet made no sound, but as she approached, Ethna put her book down and turned to greet her. Ethna had a knack for speaking volumes with a stare.

"You will feel like shit if you go guzzling wine and bedding strangers at every opportunity." She spoke with one eyebrow in total silence and pushed a bulging water skin towards the younger woman. Lialla perched on a high seat near the bar instead, instinctively close to her next drink and far enough away from her leader to dodge a wayward strike.

"You're going to have to be sharper than this when you meet him." Ethna said, folding her hands together with a smirk.

"I know Eth, I'll come around. It's still early." She let her hair fall to her shoulder as an idea forced its way through the fog of shame and booze. "How about a pick me up?" Indignation bulged Ethna's eyes and angled her brow, she placed her hands flat on the table to avoid using them in aggression.

"I did not study for *eight fucking years* in that monk infested *shit hole* so I could take the edge off your hangover."

***

I must admit to a break in connection upon Ethna's revelation. Fresh faced and passionate as I was, my appreciation of her relationships and her worldview was becoming emotionally aligned, perhaps to an inappropriate degree. To hear her speak of the Collegiate in such derogatory terms caused me some discomfort... but not enough to stop me from reconnecting with the Oraculum and diving straight back in to her world.

***

"I know, I know. Forget it. Was just a thought." Ethna briefly closed her eyes as she stood and stalked over, Lialla lowered her head and coiled slightly like prey. Ethna was around a foot taller even with the high bar stool. The sorceress grabbed a handful of red hair and lifted painfully. Lialla's eyes came alive with feral fury and she snarled before Ethna's magic-infused will held her in complete paralysis.

"We can't afford to fuck this up, Vialla! We need their gold and we need the stability." They stared into each other's eyes for a silent yet electric moment before Ethna forced her way through the thief's instinctive defences and forced the blood to speed up a fraction. She told Lialla's insides to send more moisture to the brain and released a quick flare of adrenaline to course through her ravaged body. The taller woman let go of the hair and tilted her head questioningly, a wicked and slightly triumphant smile creeping across her lips.

"Better?"

"And what if it's them that fucks things up, Eth?" Verrous' voice boomed from the stairway as he descended. Lialla, grateful for the distraction, crept her hand up the bar towards the next drink.

"Gods, Verrous, you couldn't be that quiet in the temple?"

"Don't change the subject."

"They won't fuck things up because they're the King's Guard, the Government, the Rulers of this land. Like it or not they're the ones with all the money and power!" Ethna's voice rose in volumes as she gesticulated her frustrations. There was a very slight shake in the earth and Lialla's abandoned water skin slipped from the table to splat on the stone floor. Verrous, not the most intelligent man but fearing nothing, pressed the argument.

"Is that what we need, Eth? Some goody-goody hero bullshit so we can all keep our armour shining and brush our teeth before supper?"

They approached each other, almost nose to nose. They were the same height but Verrous had twice the width.

"Verrous, what the fuck?" Keramin arrived, his palms both up. Verrous and Ethna stayed locked in scowling stasis as he circled them. "This is not helping us one bit."

Daine and Greggim both clomped to the bottom of the stairs and surveyed the scene. Greggim stomped to the bar despite the hour and before long was chuckling with Lialla. Daine scratched his scar then put a tentative hand on Ethna's shoulder.

"He's scared he'll be left behind, Eth." For a big man, Daine's voice was low and always calm. He had the ability to stay silent for hours, then cut straight to the throat when he needed to. Ethna broke the glare-off with Verrous and looked at Daine deadeyed as she worked through the flames inside her to find her way home, then smiled at him. An understanding and an appreciation passed between them.

"Let's get a drink and talk it through." She said finally, the tension draining. "Oh, and Daine." She said over her shoulder as she beckoned Verrous towards the bar. "Think you've got fleas."

***

"So, this is how it is now, is it?" Verrous lifted his hands in question. "Sitting 'round a fucking table making a plan without beer?" Keramin face palmed and Ethna visibly let out a calming breath.

"The bar's not open yet, Verrous. I thought you wanted to talk it through?"

"Nothing to say, is there? You've brought us here so we can be good guys. Go to church and kiss the fucking King's spotless arse."

The tension around the hastily conjoined tables strangled every voice. Each of them related to Verrous' barbaric objections, but common sense had forged a desperation in the company that required a change. They needed a stable source of gold and they needed to know that their way of life and the bonds they shared would not soon disappear like the muck and rust from an old blade struck on a smith's anvil.

"I know it's not ideal, but we're here to take their gold for doing what we do best. That's it. All we got to do is play the game and make out that we're good citizens that can follow orders," Ethna replied.

Greggim snorted loudly. The stunted laugh surprised him and he looked apologetically at Ethna, whose quick scowl could have melted steel.

"Ethna's right," Keramin declared as he braved his way into the conversation. "We can't carry on like this. There's no work! Every time we get a sniff of a job, some lordling has his crew all over it before we get our armour on."

The unison of nodding heads only seemed to annoy Verrous more. His fingers scratched at the table, picking at old scars and flicking away the spoils.

"But we're not like them!" he said. Some of his venom subsided. "Look at us. We're bloody outlaws, scum bags, none fit to kiss our mother's lips, never mind doing the King's work and lording over the peasantry. There's got to be another way."

Ethna's voice also softened slightly before she answered.

"You're right, Verrous. We're not like them, but we are good, and we can do a better job. Once we're back on our feet, I'll be the first to give them the finger and get us out of here. I promise you that."

There was a reflective silence. They'd had this conversation before, more than once, and agreed they would do what they could to get the job. Verrous was always the sticking point. He rubbed his stubbled head with a callused hand and puffed out a sigh. Then, with a slight shake of his head, he reached for his helmet, put it on his head and smacked it down with the flat of his hand as he always did before a fight.

"Come on then, let's get it done."

***

Ethna sat, nervously picking at a storage crystal. A booming voice had summoned her crew one by one into the room and, so far, none had emerged. She presumed there was another exit, and they were purposefully keeping them separate to avoid any collusion.

They were in a temple on the edge of town. She didn't recognise any of the iconography and she didn't really care. She was not a religious woman nor did she particularly respect those that were. This venue, she presumed, had been hired for a purpose, and the job on offer was unaffiliated with the white-robed acolytes that scurried past in pious silence every few minutes.

Why were they taking so long? She occasionally stood and paced the seating area, scratching away at a sharp corner of her crystal. She shook her head at her own anxieties and sat back down. Knowing they were extremely capable adults who had frequently performed feats of incredible prowess and had near legendary reputations amongst the mercenary community didn't seem to help. All they had to do was smile and pretend like they were good people who could do as they were told.

She stood up again for another circuit, this time clumsily bumping into a passing huddle of disgruntled acolytes.

"Next!" The booming voice filtered through the thick door. It was her time to shine.

***

Not for the first time, I found myself forced to detach and take a break from the Oraculum. Ethna's anxiety was running rampant in my own mind and body. My palms were sweaty and my heart thumped against my breast. I knew that should I discuss my increased connection to her, I would not only fail my initiation but also find myself grieving at the loss of Ethna Vikreyus and her friends. I took my leave for almost a full day of meditation and distraction before I felt ready to reconnect, assuring myself that this time, I would guard my emotions and carry out my duty to watch and report without undue empathy.

***

She pushed against the door, which was surprisingly heavy; it swung inwards in a great arc to reveal a long, flame lit corridor. She had expected to be immediately into the room; something about that extra distance gave her cause to feel a strange, uneasy sense of wrong. The sorceress gave her head a shake and started up the corridor, passing a small metallic opening in the wall at head height. As she passed it, a quiet voice caught her attention and she stopped. Silence. The phrase she barely heard was not meant for her, but the device had carried it through to the corridor nonetheless. Hesitantly, she continued up the corridor, pulling a small amount of extra power from her crystal before clipping it back onto her belt.

The white room was brightly lit and bare, save for the deep red curtains that served as walls and a heavy writing desk over to one side. It felt like a large room that had been cleaved down to size by the lush curtains. The sound of Ethna's boots suggested this was the case as she stepped inside, echoing from the high ceiling and out beyond the red boundary. For a moment she was unsure what to do. Presuming the smaller of the two chairs that accompanied the desk was meant for her, she approached.

"Just get it sorted and do not interrupt me again." The deep, familiar voice preceded a fairly short man with a bald head as he swept aside one curtain, closing it instantly behind him and smiling. His clothing was the height of some far away fashion; deep blue and edged with silver, hems riddled with runic patterns stitched by a team of tailors that would feint at the site of Ethna's ragged garments. Despite his small stature, the man emanated more power than anyone Ethna had ever known. His magical signature left a trail as he moved, gestured to the smaller chair and regally sat in his.

With a twitch of annoyance or a small smile, it was hard to tell, the man spoke.

"I must apologise. There has been a clerical error." He looked into Ethna's eyes. The apology was not there; just cold impatience and an eagerness to get the meeting over and done with. Ethna had not spoken. The room. The man. The wrongness of it all strangled her voice. She cleared her throat, but he spoke over her attempt to respond.

"We have what we came for." Ethna's pointed ears pricked up. Her senses tried to tell her something as she stared at the frustrated man in front of her. She experienced a strange paralysis as she opened her mouth. A thumping sound rhythmically pounded behind her, followed by a brief sucking of air.

Her instincts took the reins and she formed an expanse of solidified air behind her. There was a grunt of extreme effort, followed by a great sword smashing into her barrier. Ethna spun out of her chair and brought up her stave. Suddenly primed with the excess energy she had borrowed from her crystal, she formed a bolt of energy in her breast and with her free hand, aimed it at her assailant.

Verrous. Ethna swallowed a sharp breath.

Something in her heart twisted, her offensive energy cascading out of her hand to evaporate before it fell to the white floor. Verrous swung his sword again, hacking sideways but bouncing off the barrier. Again he swung and again his blade bounced. Ethna stood, mouth opening and closing, shocked and broken by the realisation that Verrous had turned on her Verrous' sword twisted as his stance changed and turning his shoulder, aimed to pierce the sorceress' shield with a thrust. He jabbed once... twice...

"Enough!!" Thundered the sorcerer from behind Ethna. From the corner of her eye, she saw his arm sweep, and she felt her barrier crumble like burning paper. Verrous' third thrust found its way, unhindered, into her chest, just below her left breast. The massive warrior's weight shoved the blade up to the hilt, forcing his face to touch hers in a perverse mimicry of a romantic embrace. His eyes met hers. He looked away and staggered back, releasing his sword as if it was suddenly white hot.

Ethna's knees gave up along with her heart and she dropped, hitting the cold white floor and sitting back; unable to fall as the great sword's length propped her vaguely upright. A cruel gesture of physics that prevented her paling body from embracing the floor.

Her red blood pooled, continuing to reach outwards as the sorceress twitched. Verrous, now a parody of a knight praising his sponsor on one knee, refused to look up..

The bald sorcerer calmly stood beside Ethna. Stretching out a hand, he leached what little vitality remained; a vague yellow vapour that twisted from her flesh and disappeared into his open palm.

Unable to move her head, Ethna's eyes turned to the sorcerer. With great effort, she forced whispered words from her bluing lips.

"I thought... this would be... by the book." Blood sprayed from her mouth on the last word, speckling her pale features.

The man sighed, more from annoyance than sympathy.

"You are right, you wretched thing, but unfortunately we wrote the book. Verrous!"

The command startled the warrior, but he looked at his new master, ready to obey.

"You have duties to perform, but for now, you have proved yourself worthy." Gesturing to the curtain, then abruptly turning, he vanished from the scene. Verrous gazed at Ethna's grotesque display and quickly looked away.

Angrily, he swung aside the red curtain, revealing the corpses of his former colleagues.

The King's man grabbed the closest pair of ankles and pulled Lialla's body from sight.

***

I felt that my heart would break.

Nothing had prepared me for the pain and grief should my subject be killed during my period of watchfulness. I disconnected for a number of days before offering my report. Ethna's betrayal had entirely permeated my thoughts. I ate little and barely found time to meditate, let alone study or take guidance on how to proceed. I mostly stayed in my small chamber, masquerading sickness whilst my stolen memories pecked and clawed at my thoughts, escalating the conflict between my emotional connection to Ethna and my previously resolute dedication to my duty.

Eventually, despite my ragged conscience, I reported Ethna's death. Knowing that my actions would initiate protocol which led to her recovery did not sit well, but I somehow found the strength to reconnect through the Oraculum. My mentor had coldly instructed me that my duty was now to observe the next phase in order to ensure the recovery was completed.

***

Dzawn had been riding hard for several days. The light from his device insisted on a relentless pace to force the exact moment and location of his arrival. As he dropped from his mount, he dulled the light with a gentle sweeping of his fingertips. A small relief flooded him; the device leached his spirit as it worked, showing him the where and when of his task meant a continual seepage of energy into the small box which powered its unquantifiable wisdom.

He stowed the device in his belt pouch, swapping it for wrappings to tie back his voluminous trousers. He was no longer an innocent foreign traveller, now his true work was to begin and his abilities would finally end his Collegiate debt.

Shadow was plentiful. The stone-cut corridors were dissected by quietly dancing flames on head-height sconces. Dzawn checked the oil reservoir of the first. The dish was shallow and would require frequent re-filling. Moving quickly and silently, he padded through the temple, his shadow strobing each light source as he traversed the maze-like passages until he found his way to a darkened stairway down.

Quiet but approaching voices came from below. He backed into the corner of the entrance of the steps and summoned energy into his air blade. Despite his dwindling reserves of spirit, Dzawn conjured a parchment-thin screen of solidified air by arcing his blade before him and, calmly, he invited the existing shadow to settle upon it, obscuring his position.

A huddle of robed acolytes appeared from below, talking quietly about some frustrating aspect of their nightly routine. Dzawn held his breath, and, as often was the case, his mind wandered back to his studies in the labyrinthine teaching chambers of the Collegiate.

***

Upon experiencing such memories, a strange sensation threatened to disconnect me from the Oraculum. The familiar rooms and even faces that I had seen in the physical world caused a loop of reality that was at once comforting and unsettling.

Though Dzawn studied a discipline far removed from my own, he held dear, as we all did, the tenets of the Collegiate:

"Those at one with the water need not wash their hands."

Behind his visual shield, Dzawn let out his stored breath with calm fluidity. His mind's eye projected an alternative situation with screaming and death; sticky red hands that resulted in clumsy strokes of his air blade amid the stalking whispers of guilt and shame.

He shook his head, clearing his vision as the acolytes moved on in ignorance and fled down the steps, his tight furred slippers a silent cushion. The air below was cold, and the chill left a clammy sheen on the surface of the walls. Greasy light bounced occasional flame reflections and the muttering of more disillusioned guardians echoed in the depths. Finding a shaded alcove, Dzawn checked his device. He was close, but his spirit was low. The plan was to find his target before summoning his artifact, but if his spirit was not up to creating a portal, it certainly wasn't strong enough to contain a sorceress.

Making a decision, he slashed his air blade, cutting a temporary gash in reality's fabric, and using a practiced hand, he reached through the portal into the Collegiate's requisitions chamber. Dzawn sweated. He was using spirit reserves and would soon tire. He held as long as he could until eventually the weight of the distant item settled into his open palm and he quickly withdrew his hand and closed the portal.

"Maybe a little trust and I wouldn't have to go throwing my reserves around when I have bigger concerns…just a thought!" Dzawn muttered under his breath, clearly frustrated with Collegiate protocol.

He continued his silent search through the bowels of the temple, occasionally descending further until the air began to stink and the light became sparse. He descended lower than the notice of whatever god they worshipped above.

The Collector produced light from a small hand-held lantern and, as the ceilings became lower, the stink became stronger. It seemed as though he headed towards the source of the smell, and when Dzawn reluctantly checked his device, his assumption was confirmed.

"Getting close." He whispered, the sound of his own voice taking the edge from the deep isolation as he moved gradually downwards.

Dzawn had very little spirit remaining, and he wanted to ensure he could still conjure a blade, if needed, once he reached his target but the stink was becoming unbearable. He thickened the air in his nostrils, partially blocking the horrendous stench. Flexing his nose for comfort, he continued into the gloom.

The passages at this level were more mined than carved. Low ceilings and poorly imagined angles and measurements gave the impression of caves over the upper isometric corridors of the temple. Smouldering braziers adorned occasional areas, but all comfort and light was forsaken at this depth. He saw no acolytes or any people at all. The stench he was moving towards obviously created a powerful deterrent.

Eventually Dzawn's light fell on a large opening into a seemingly cavernous room and as the footing became sticky, his stomach lurched and forced him to cover his mouth slightly with a tense hand. He stepped through the opening, his pale light fell across the space containing his target. He put one hand to his forehead as his mouth fell open.

"What the..." he said with a wet swallow. "You have to be shitting me!"

"Only a fool allows another's torch to set them on fire."

Dzawn's mouth remained open as he saw the mass of limbs and gore before him. Without taking his eyes from the pile, he lit a nearby sconce, and orange flickering light danced across the horror he had been smelling since his descent to the lower levels.

It felt disrespectful to vomit, so he maintained relative control of his stomach despite the rhythmic surge of bile that continued to threaten his gullet.

The large square pit before him was a charnel of human remains in various states of dismemberment. Buzzing insects skittered from one sticky limb to the next in frenzied ecstasy at the enormity of the feast. He knew not why the temple dwellers had need of such refuge, he only knew that amongst the broken and weeping bodies was his target.

"She... she will be amongst the fresh ones." Dzawn said, reassuring himself as he nodded unconvincingly.

Dzawn began to check between his device and the mound of death, ensuring he started in the closest place. "We owe a debt to the collegiate. They do not care what we must do to pay it off, only that it is paid." He muttered to himself.

He nodded one more time at the pile and began to roll up the sleeves of his robe, tying each in place whilst postponing what must be done.

***

Once again, I found the negative perception of the revered Collegiate difficult to hear. It seemed that from various perspectives, the methods in which these debts were accounted and remitted were seen as oppressive and unfair despite signed contracts that proved acceptance of the trade of knowledge for labour before the period of study commenced.

The multi-threaded experience that I was observing continually added to my list of questions and this, in no way, helped with the grief I still felt at the death of Ethna Vikreyus. Such was my state of mind that during one particular sleepless night, and against all better judgement, I chose to re-add Ethna's connection to my Oraculum's field of observation, despite firm orders from my superiors and the deep traumatic pain that her death had caused me to begin with.

***

To describe an inky blackness would suggest colour and tone. The void was lack of all things; no dreams of ascension, no lashings from vengeful demons, nothing. Time itself became nothing, and all memory, emotion, yearning, and momentum had ended.

A force crept into existence within the space between realities. Subtle at first, the sensation formed into an inertia that hunted, searching blindly in an unknowable realm. Like a desperate hand clawing for purchase, the idea of manipulation slowly, agonisingly, became a function. Shape materialised, colour in the abyss. Green was born and became woven into lines and form. Curling over perceived millennia into motive and momentum, threatening the emptiness of the void. The green evolved from colour to light, emanating light into the gloom with blasphemous clarity.

Wrongness appeared. Counterbalance. Opposing notions formed. Defence. Elimination. Punishment.

Suddenly, there was a pulse. A dangerous and approaching momentum pulled and forced open the senses, anchoring reality and reforming the ideas from before the void. Its rhythm pounded into the black, shocking with each wave and prying open a physical vessel.

"Fucking traitor!" Luminous green sprayed with Ethna's words, splattering her blood encrusted torso as she sat upright with eyes wide. She audibly gasped for breath, her mouth as wide as her bewildered eyes. Desperately sucking in air, the sorceress' head swivelled frantically, taking in the gore-covered stranger that stood over her. The Collector moved away from her face with an empty potion bottle. The remaining liquid dripped to the cold stone floor as he stood straight and looked down at her in satisfaction.

"What the fuck!"

Despite her reeling mind, Ethna's instincts quickly reached for what reserves of power she still had to protect herself.

Nothing.

She was dry as a bone. More so, she felt disconnected from her power source. A barrier held her magic away from her like an angry parent with a toy, waggling their finger in a smug learning moment.

She scrambled to stand, but he'd locked her hands behind her. She flexed and growled, but she was cuffed. As she screamed her frustration, her resurrector simply stared down as if waiting for her to tire herself out.

***

Despite the situation and the obviously traumatic and unnatural journey Ethna had been dragged through, I was comforted by feeling her draw breath and her choice of language. A completeness settled over me at her return to life, though in the back of my mind, I knew that my feelings for this sorceress were both unhealthy and seditious.

***

"It is quite typical to feel disorientated." Dzawn said. His accent was thick, but he rounded his words, making them easier to understand for the Otreyan.

"Who the fuck are you?"

"I may not have time to explain until we get on the road."

He lifted Ethna to a standing position. Each and every muscle protested. Her bones felt like dried and spindly twigs.

"Well, you better have a good fucking try! And what in ten hells is that smell?"

Footsteps approached. The man gave Ethna a slight smile before gently pushing her into the corner of the room. With bound arms and no balance she was unable to resist. Vulnerability swept through her and she allowed Dzawn to lead her until her back pressed against the stone wall.

The footsteps were quiet but fast. Dzawn pulled his air blade; a shimmering distortion the only indication that a blade protruded from the small cylindrical hilt. He readied himself in a combat stance that, to Ethna's eyes, seemed regimented and well-practiced. She had no idea where she was, or what was going on, until her eyes settled into the background. She saw the carnage of guts and gore behind the unfamiliar man, a horrendous charnel pile of bodies and armour. The revulsion in her nostrils finally matched her sight, which slowly and inevitably rested on a face she recognised. Pale and smeared in gore, Lialla's face stared back with lifeless grey eyes, striking Ethna hard and fast in the guts.

She screamed and railed against the bonds behind her back as robed acolytes with short swords thundered into the room.

"I am taking this woman from here. It is my duty and it must be done." Dzawn's voice rang clear and the building horde of dull white robes hesitated, bumping into each other and lowering their blades.

From beyond the great room came a deep baritone voice, a voice used to command and power.

"Stop them!"

Instant obedience sent the masses forward as Dzawn met them with certainty and finesse. He was first to make contact, spinning his body to allow his near invisible air blade to slice through multiple bodies, sending limbs twirling into the air. Screams and blood filled the scene as Dzawn twirled, cutting through sword arms and fumbling bodies in abundance. Figures fell into the charnel pit and crumpled to the floor, causing obstructions to their surviving colleagues.

A few came close to attacking the warrior, but his co-ordinated and athletic movements ran rings around the inexperienced acolytes. The occasional blade would come close only to be deflected by the whirling air blade as it shifted to defensive shapes, then instantly returning to the razor thin shard of solidified air that dismembered with minimal resistance.

Ethna's desperate fury abated slightly as she witnessed the martial prowess and the destructive capabilities of the air blade. Somewhere, hidden in her fuddled memory, was a familiarity in the way he moved and the awesome power he wielded, but her brain was struggling with imminent overwhelm since having to come to terms with the fact she was dead a few moments ago.

None survived.

Dzawn wiped his brow and turned to Ethna,

"I have come to escort you south. It would be easier if you..."

"Fuck!" Dzawn turned as the sweat and air in the room turned to ozone. Something wrong slipped in and danced up each of their spines. Dzawn grabbed Ethna's shoulder and pushed her towards the entrance he had used; she stumbled but kept her silence. They made their way to the doorway as the sea of limbs amongst them began to twitch. Across the vast room, heads lifted. Slowly and unnaturally, limbs joined the movement and previously dead carcasses disentangled from each other, climbing from their pile and preparing weapons or bloodless fingers to assault the living.

Ethna was unaccustomed to feeling helpless. She was only just acclimatising to being recently dead. Now she was surrounded by animated corpses intent on dragging her back to the void. She wailed. A mix of helpless fear and vulnerability combined with a dash of incensed hatred and aggression. Not her proudest moment.

She flexed her hands and pulled against her unseen metallic bonds with all the strength she could muster. Her ineffectual outburst did nothing to improve her situation and only highlighted the inevitable timeline of her second death in five minutes.

"Release me and I'll burn them all!" she growled as Dzawn continued to harry her away from the rotting horde.

Thankfully, the recently killed and now mostly red robed acolytes were slow to rise as they were in more pieces than those already putrefied in the charnel heap. Dzawn quickly stepped over separated limbs as he guided Ethna with a powerful hand on her shoulder. Enraged by her helplessness, she continually and violently pulled against her bonds until Dzawn cut down the first corpse. It was too late. She would have to focus her mind on escaping without sliding on the red human soup that covered the stone floor.

"If you decide within three breaths, never waste the fourth on hesitancy."

Dzawn sprung into the throng of approaching dead with inhuman speed, removing legs and heads with grotesque accuracy, then, recognising the need for defensive action, he retreated. He remained close to Ethna, aiding where necessary before breaking off and swinging his blade with devastating and pungent results. Thick clots of necrotic matter span through the air and splattered them both as they inched away from their undead assailants.

It was a crawler that first broke the defenses as they moved through the doorway into the outer corridor. The former warrior pulled its ruined legs through the morass and clutched at Ethna's. Its chest plate ground against the uneven rock floor and caught on a seam, stopping its advance. Ethna infused her stomp with all the ferocity and violent injustice that threatened to burst her brain, and her foot smashed through its neck, easily parting the blue and mouldering flesh, putting an end to her attacker's grasp.

With combat and savage death closing in, even Dzawn was losing space to manoeuvre in the face of overwhelm. Ethna kicked at those she could reach. Many broke apart at the slightest impact, but some advanced with feral tenacity that she could only avoid in her state of bondage.

They moved fully into the corridor with their snarling undead entourage. Dzawn's movement was becoming minimal, choosing to hold his stance and swing over practiced footwork. He was tiring. Ethna stole a moment to investigate a blueish light source that illuminated the roughly carved rock walls surrounding them.

Further down the tunnel was a robed man, his hands illuminated in front of him. He clasped a bright blue ball of light that sent silvery vapour trails into the air and beyond, into the room they'd escaped from.

***

It was during this moment, I believe, that my admiration for Ethna reached its peak, and her tenacity and strength of will affected my view of the world forever. It is this moment that led me on my path to steer my sheltered world towards one where everyone mattered. Simply because I observed that all beings had potential for victory despite a lack of assets or odds in their favour.

***

Without hesitation, Ethna ducked under Dzawn's back swing and ran, as fast as her weak legs would allow, away from the safety of the warrior and towards the presumed necromancer. She kept her head low, building up speed and momentum, while constantly at threat of losing balance and tipping onto her face. Without her hands to shield her from the rough floor, it would be messy.

The man ahead was oblivious to Ethna's approach. So intent on his necromantic weavings, his only movement came from the silent chant on his lips. Ethna resisted the urge to scream a ferocious battle cry as she neared, conscious that she may only have one shot at putting him down. At the last moment she set her feet, squatted slightly and launched herself headfirst at the man's face. Nasal cartilage and bone smashed as the single black stone in Ethna's circlet connected, sending bright blood splattering across both faces. The necromancer crumpled instantly, his vast white robe splaying as he dropped to the floor, unconscious. Ethna unceremoniously followed, smearing her face against the still body.

The silver-blue light went out, plunging the tunnel into darkness and severing the control over the animated corpses instantly. There was an almighty clatter as ragged bodies fell to the floor where they once stood.

A panting Dzawn ignited his small device and light filled the space once more. He was head to toe in dark ichor, bone, shrapnel and blood from multiple scratches and small wounds. Ethna struggled comically upon the necromancer's body, unable to put her feet on the ground as she writhed. Dzawn approached and lifted her upright without a word. Exhaustion drooped his eyes and slumped his shoulders. He gave her a push ahead, and they made their way to ground level and out of the temple in silence.

Outside the dark air was frosty but smelled of civilisation and life. Nearby sounds of revelry brought a sense of familiarity. Ethna smiled as they approached a horse hitched in a stable behind an inn. Dzawn silently grabbed handfuls of straw to wipe away the gore and stench that covered him. Ethna just sat, content to take stock of herself and her newly appointed existence.

Once satisfied, Dzawn untied his trousers and checked through his saddlebags, producing a wide brimmed circular hat of woven bamboo and placing it on his head, effecting the appearance of a common traveller. Ethna watched him curiously, still unsure who he was or why he'd brought her back.

"I don't know how the fuck you managed to rescue me without using my power. All you had to do was release my hands!" Dzawn looked at her in utter confusion for a long moment, then, suddenly burst out laughing. His mirth broke the tension of the night's trauma. He laughed so heartily that Ethna couldn't help but join in, though she didn't know why. Once the laughter had come to its end. Dzawn shook his head and looked at the sorceress, suddenly earnest.

"I have not come to rescue you." He said, wiping a tear from his eye. "I have come to take you back to the Collegiate. You have tuition debts that need to be paid!"

**

Five years passed. By this time, I had completed my initiation and was already gaining footholds in the political lair of the Collegiate leadership. I used Ethna's fire in my debates, her animalistic yet parental approach in any disciplinary proceedings and, such was my upward trajectory, I was able to gain permission to use the Oraculums to keep an eye on her. The practice, more often than not, left me feeling low and stirred a rebellious notion of assisting her towards freedom that, sadly, I never acted upon until it was too late.

**

The pious old ruin sat ancient and proud inside its cliff-side enclave surrounded by the spiralled steps that led down to its fortified viaduct. The waterway was the only entrance to the campus. To reach the ornate gate itself meant alighting a small ferry and enduring the silent indifference of the boatman. Beyond the gate was the sprawling Collegiate itself. Waterwheels, crude mining conveyor belts and guarded walkways surrounded the squat dome roofed buildings, which were illuminated by regular pulsing magic-infused lanterns.

Fat snowflakes dropped like winter tears and drifted in the gutters, painting the lead domes in white. Wand-like icicles reached for the earth like demonic teeth, ever dripping in runnels that eventually fed the tributary, leading gradually to the fierce Eastern Sea.

Ethna had aged. Five years in the Collegiate took the toll of a thousand. Her youthful appearance reaped as collateral, along with her freedom. She pulled her fur cloak around her permanently stooped shoulders and stepped gingerly from the warmth of the hall; the Dean had insisted she meet their guest. At least, she thought, she could break from the constant questions and demonstrations of teaching along with the tireless leaching of power that her students demanded.

She could see the approaching envoy as he climbed from the ferry, swaddled in furs and lacking luggage. Maybe he had left his effects at the cliff-top stable, she thought, a common mistake made by the rare visitors to the Collegiate. There was no short-cut, no fast-track to comfort or success within the walls of this place. The large man walked boldly towards her as she shivered. A familiarity in his gait stirred her adrenaline and squeezed her heart. His footsteps crunched the brown ice, turned partially to mush by the traffic on the bridge. She felt there was a hesitancy as he neared; he slowed his march and as he arrived, he lowered to one knee despite the frozen ground beneath him. Ethna could not see his face for the voluminous hood and the vast ice peppered beard that bulged out from within.

"Fuck me, Eth, I nearly broke my neck on them fucking steps."

Verrous.

Her heart betrayed her with his familiarity. She smiled despite the pain he had scarred her with, the life and death she had endured since his own betrayal. She was speechless as he pulled down his hood and shook out the beard. A moment stretched whilst each of them packed away their demons.

"You've got new scars." She said, nodding at the pale line that had almost taken his eye.

"Aye, inside and out, I can tell you." They both nodded, unsure where to go next in the conversation.

"I got a job to do now, Eth. You won't like it."

"It's true then? The bastard's bought the collegiate?"

Verrous nodded. "And it gets worse."

The big man removed a glove and fished inside his coat for a long dagger. He tossed it at Ethna's feet.

"He's banned Otreyans from practicing magic." He paused. "Them pointy ears of yours are a dead giveaway."

"So this blade is for me?" she whispered. Any fight she once had already leaked into the sacred earth of the Collegiate. She closed her eyes.

"No, Eth, it's for me." Verrous stood unbuckling his heavy coat, clods of snow slipping to the ground. "Fuck me, you know I'm not one for sentiment. What I did has followed me, Eth. It wasn't right, and it's time to cough up." He stripped to the waist, his tattooed skin turning instantly to gooseflesh. He held back his arms, offering his heart to his former leader and squeezing his eyes closed.

"I'm supposed to take you in. The new law means you should stand trial." Again, the moment stretched out. She had dreamed of vengeance for so long and it had ebbed the life from her. She stared down at the blade, envisioned plunging it into his black betrayer's heart.

"It's fucking freezing, Eth, if you could speed things up?"

She smiled at his way with words, then lifted her hands, filling them with power. Verrous' life did have to end, but she was unsure if that was cause to celebrate.

She felt for his familiar rhythm, finding it easily despite the years. Her unseen hands surged through his body, searching for the spark of human electricity that gave life to the heart. He did not resist. On the contrary, she felt an eagerness as if he guided those hands of ethereal judgement. As one, they found the spark. She felt it pulse through her: his life, his existence, his betrayal. Her eyes closed slowly as she engulfed the spark with her power. Verrous' body dropped instantly to the ice. She kept her eyes closed.

"How long have you been there?" she asked.

Dzawn stepped closer behind her.

***

As I observed, my heart began to struggle, its rhythm forcing a blood vessel in my eyelid to pulse. My chest tightened and my mind desperately rummaged through my knowledge whilst trying to maintain my connection. I knew that somewhere in the physical world I had seen the collector's orders. As powerful as I was becoming, I was unable to stop the creeping of time.

***

"Long enough to pay you the respect you deserve," he said into her ear. The warrior paced behind her, clearly using his three breaths to decide. Ethna was still, her eyes remained closed. They would send another. The King and his all-powerful Government had out played her and her kind. There was no life of freedom beyond the walls of the Collegiate, and she was unsure if she had the energy to fight for one.

There was a whoosh of cold air and Ethna's head left her body, floating momentarily before landing next to the corpse of her former ally.

"Before you take your eye from a scorpion, be sure to remove its tail."

The End

First Watch

By Marc Emerson

Born and raised on the Isle of Illusion, Marc has always been a fan of the imaginary and the irrational. After progressing in several different classes over the years, he recently took his first level of Bard. He resides in the Rabers with his animal companions. First Watch is his first professional sale.

Imatu used to be a paradise, where people lived a life of leisure in floating cities constructed of magical glass so they could better view all its natural wonders and be safe from the monsters roaming the surface. When magic suddenly diminished the glass reverted to sand and most everyone plunged to their deaths. The few hardened survivors banded together to form settlements and bring back civilization but were often overrun by monsters. To keep safe, they built a wall...

Daga hated the dark. Darkness hid dangers that you couldn't see, even if they were right in front of you. Soldiers needed to be able to see a threat in order to fight it, especially soldiers on watch. The very name of the duty, watch, implied being able to see.

This night was one of the rare times when all the moons were down, leaving the night dark enough that he could see the stars easily. But stars gave off far less light than moons, so it would be hard to spot any Zerks approaching the wall. The long walk from the barracks to the wall gave his eyes time to adjust to the lack of light.

Daga climbed the ladder to the top of the barrier wall with care, his scabbard thumping against each rung. Training and sentry duty were a soldier's main activities during peace. He didn't resent his military duties, even at his age, but he preferred his previous post in the Court of Karteran. The only sharp things he had to worry about there were the barbs tossed about by nobles.

He had not recognized the name paired with his on the duty roster, so his watchmate must be one of the new graduates. Breaking in new recruits was a burden, but there was plenty they didn't learn in their training, plenty that could be passed down. Some lessons were better learned from an experienced watchmate and not from a screaming drill master. The problem was that most recruits overcompensated. They either challenged his authority at every step trying overly hard to prove themselves, or they so meekly accepted everything he said that he might as well be standing watch solo.

As he stepped sideways off the ladder onto the top of the stone wall, he saw his watchmate was already there. Early was good. Even in the dim light, Daga could make out the shiny metallic copper hair of the new soldier. The lad, who looked barely old enough to shave, was a long way from home. This was the first copper-haired member of the wealthy Vendrani family he had seen since his last posting far across the sea. There must be a story there. Long night watches were good for stories.

"We have the watch," said Daga, touching the side of his head in a show of respect, even though he outranked the men they were relieving.

"You have the watch," confirmed one of the soldiers going off duty.

"Nothing much to see," said the other man with a chuckle. "May Kruuna watch over you."

The two relieved men climbed down off the wall and walked back to the barracks. On a normal night, Daga could have watched them open the door and go inside, but tonight he couldn't even see the barracks. At least the darkness couldn't stop the pleasant sea breeze from bringing the tangy smell of brine and seaweed to his nose.

"The name's Daga. Haven't seen you on duty before."

"I'm Jhyndra, just finished my training," said the other man.

Jhyndra extended both arms forward, palms up.

Daga responded to the offer by extending his arms, palms down but above the other man's, since he was the superior of the two. They completed the gesture by clasping each other's forearms. Daga felt the firmness of Jhyndra's grip and returned it in equal measure.

They began to walk at a slow and measured pace toward the far end of the wall. When more moons were out, one end of the wall could be seen all the way from the other, but tonight the darkness hid not only the terminus but the barracks, stables and other support buildings.

Daga sized up his watchmate the best he could in the dim light. Tall, but not as tall as he was; clad in a ring shirt for protection and with a scabbard sized for a broadsword slung at his hip.

"Jhyndra, it's good that you put on some armor. A ring shirt is a good choice for comfort during a long watch," said Daga as he stopped walking.

He paused and waited until Jhyndra made eye contact. Wisdom was meant to be passed from the old to the young. As a senior soldier, it was his duty to instruct the lower ranking men. Best to have Jhyndra come to the proper realization himself, and by asking the right questions, Daga could even lead Jhyndra through the lesson. Daga remembered a lesson he learned years ago. Tell a man something and he's likely to forget. Help a man to figure something out and he's likely to remember.

"What potential danger could we face tonight?" asked Daga after he figured out how best to get his point across.

"Zerks, of course," said Jhyndra with a quizzical look on his face, as if a senior soldier should know all about the dangers of Zerks.

"Correct," said Daga. "But we aren't in danger of a horde of Zerks swarming the wall. The scouts would have alerted us if that was even a remote possibility."

"No hordes," said Jhyndra. "But what about an archer? I heard sometimes they like to loose an arrow at men on the wall."

"There's only light enough to see movement at maybe a hundred paces, but sound travels far at night. We won't be taken by surprise," said Daga. "Plus, there's a brisk breeze to thwart the aim of any Zerks that have a mind to sneak up and take a shot with their war bows. Besides, Zerks aren't made for sneaking. Charging and screaming is more their style.

"Don't worry. They haven't hit anyone since I've been assigned here, but sometimes we find a war arrow on the wall or beyond it."

"Wicked metal heads with longer and thicker shafts?" asked Jhyndra.

"Yeah, the pull on their war bows is far more than what even our best archers can draw. Now, if the most likely danger on this watch is a Zerk arrow, why are you wearing a ring shirt?"

Jhyndra thought for a moment, then Daga could see the fear widening his eyes.

"Arrows go right through rings," said Jhyndra softly.

"Exactly," said Daga. He tapped the cured leather he was wearing. "This will stop an arrow fired from long range. The field beyond the wall has been kept clear of cover. A Zerk won't be able to get close enough to penetrate hardened leather. War arrows are devastating up close, but their extra weight means they sacrifice penetration at long distances, especially when shot uphill."

"Thanks," said Jhyndra. "I'll remember that. This is my first watch."

"First watch," said Daga, raising his hand in a salute. "May you have a long and distinguished career with the Gold League.

"It may be dark tonight, but it's always a quiet watch. I've paced this wall many times since I've been posted here. Never had cause to ring a bell. This is one of the easiest assignments I've ever had, and I've been serving the Gold League longer than you've been alive."

"I know. That's why I asked for this watch; figured you'd have better stories than the others."

"Asked for it?" said Daga with a smile. "Well, I hope I don't disappoint you. Even with stories it can be a long night up here."

"Up here? You say it like this wall is more than eighteen hands high."

"It's a work in progress. Northpoint has only been a Gold League protectorate for four years now. Give it time. Surely you had to haul blocks and fill up here while going through training."

"More than a few times," admitted Jhyndra. "Adding to the wall is used as a punishment. I'm sure they'll be forcing recruits to add to it when it's ten times this size."

"Know why the bells are low like that?" asked Daga, pointing to one of the many bells set at knee level every ten paces.

Jhyndra shook his head.

"They are low enough that you can ring one with a kick. That's important if you're in hand-to-hand combat," said Daga.

"And if you're wounded and fall, you can still crawl to a bell," suggested Jhyndra.

"You're a smart lad," said Daga. "But it won't come to that, I promise. It's going to be a quiet night. It always is when I stand watch."

At the end of the wall, they stopped for a moment, looked out across the cleared fields and saw nothing but the vibrant native grasses colored dull and washed out by the starlight. Daga watched to see how Jhyndra would handle the turn. Most recruits made a formal half turn. Formal maneuvers belonged on the parade field, not on duty. Daga was proud that Jhyndra made a casual turn, and not only looked out over the field, but back toward the barracks as well. The young man was both at ease and thorough. While watching the turn, Daga noticed Jhyndra was not bending his right knee much as he walked.

"Are you limping? What's wrong with your knee, can you not bend it?" asked Daga.

"Just a twinge when I pivot. I shouldn't have tried running across scree yesterday, but I'm not going to let a little pain keep me from my first watch. Don't worry, I can still run to a bell if there's an attack. And kick it," said Jhyndra with a smile.

"Kruuna forbid there's an attack, but your first watch is important. A lot of men believe that as goes your first watch, so goes your career in the Gold League."

"Do you believe that?" asked Jhyndra.

"I do," said Daga. "My very first watch was uneventful and my career has been—"

"Uneventful?" suggested Jhyndra.

"I would prefer to think of it as safe, and quite lucrative," said Daga. "I've seen action, but nothing too worrisome. Mostly, I've been paid to guard people and things. Come to think of it, that offering I made to Kruuna before my first watch was the best coin I've ever spent. You did make an offering to Kruuna, didn't you?"

"Uh no," said Jhyndra "I suppose I should have, with him being the god of soldiers and all, but I never quite understood that. Why do soldiers have their own God? There's already Bolaar, the God of war, and most soldiering is just killing, so why Kruuna and not Zhavos?"

Daga scowled at him. "Zhavos? God of murder? Soldiers may kill, but it's not murder."

"But isn't the only reason it's not murder is because someone in charge declares war?" asked Jhyndra. "If it's officially sanctioned, then it can't be murder?"

"I've been in some skirmishes that were part of a war, but like I said before, mostly I just guarded people and trade goods. I've killed other soldiers, and a few monsters, but it can hardly be called murder," said Daga.

Jhyndra noticed Daga's scowl and changed his tone.

"Don't worry, I made an offering, but not to Kruuna. I prayed for success and prosperity," said Jhyndra.

Daga was still taken aback that a soldier would forsake the god of soldiers, until he remembered Jhyndra's shiny copper hair marked him as a member of the wealthy Vendrani family. They had a special relationship with Dazmir, the God of wealth and commerce, and that relationship manifested in unique hair colors.

"To Dazmir, then?" asked Daga.

Jhyndra stopped walking and turned to Daga. Daga couldn't read the emotion on Jhyndra's face because he lowered his gaze as soon as Daga made eye contact.

"You may be a long way from your family," said Daga in a softer voice. "I doubt there are many in Northpoint that know the full story of Dazmir, your family and their special hair. I have served the Gold League for nearly thirty years, and have had fifteen different postings all around the world. I hear stories. I know what your copper hair means to your family. The Vendrani love their gold, and their golden-haired offspring—the copper-haired ones, not so much. I can relate. I may not have had my own family assume I was of little worth because my hair wasn't colored like precious gold or silver, but since they could do naught for me but let me farm on their already overburdened land, it didn't matter that they thought the world of me."

Daga looked at Jhyndra for his reaction. He might have pushed too far into the lad's personal life. Jhyndra's expression was somewhere between cross and confused. Daga put his hand gently on Jhyndra's shoulder. He felt the tension in the young man, and wanted to undo the pain he might have caused.

"The Gold League can be your new family," said Daga.

Daga felt Jhyndra's shoulder relax. Jhyndra walked slowly out from under his hand, and they both resumed the steady stroll of a sentry. Daga wanted to say more, but felt he may have said too much.

They reached the end of the wall, paused briefly for a look around, then turned back. Daga watched Jhyndra. The young man was lost in his thoughts, not paying close attention to the field below the wall, so Daga made sure to look it over with care. Jhyndra still favored his right leg, and his hand rubbed his thigh as they walked. Daga knew that Jhyndra wanted to say something, but had not worked up the courage yet. He would give the lad time.

The silence lasted half their route.

"My family loves their gold, that is true," said Jhyndra. "But they love their copper-haired children about as much as a single copper coin. There just aren't many opportunities in the trading houses for a copper like me. All the good jobs, the ones with the best prospects for profits, go to the ones with gold or silver hair. I joined the Gold League instead of keeping ledgers in a tiny room. My family was convinced that I would only ever be average. They may have been right. Damn them and damn their pledge to Dazmir."

"Nothing wrong with being average. Average gets you paid," said Daga.

"Well, I only scored at the proficient level in all my testing. Even my bonuses are copper coins."

Daga stifled a chuckle. The poor lad was average. Before graduation, and once a year thereafter, each soldier of the Gold League was tested in various contests: archery, spear throwing, running, etc. A passing, or proficient, score was necessary in all the required tests. Failure meant leaving the Gold League's army. Passing earned a bonus, one copper coin per test. For those that scored in the top ten percent, the bonus was a silver coin, and a gold coin went to those in the top one percent. There were many tests, so most people scored silver in at least one of them. Poor Jhyndra was quite average.

"I hate being average," said Jhyndra.

"It's good to have aspirations," said Daga. "Give it time. You're young. You have plenty of time to improve your skills. I'll wager you never had to run while carrying a sack of bricks on your back before coming here."

Jhyndra nodded and his teeth shone a bit of white as he smiled.

Daga smiled back at him.

"I have to admit though, your family does have a great motto," said Daga. "'Gold always shines.' I think if I ever start a noble family, I'll have to mention gold in my motto. Gold is important in this world. The Gold League even named themselves after it. Life is easier when you have plenty of gold."

Jhyndra scoffed, "Even a dull copper like me knows the value of gold. The problem is getting my hands on some."

"Want some advice?" asked Daga, answering before Jhyndra could respond. "Leverage your postings to make extra gold."

"Extra gold?" scoffed Jhyndra. "I'm only paid in silver and copper."

"Your pay will increase in time. Skills and seniority are valuable to the Gold League. What I meant was there are often opportunities for extra sources of coin. Not here though, Northpoint is a backwater, but's safe and a good place for my last posting. But if you have an assignment of guard duty on a merchant ship, you'll know where you're sailing to and what they're carrying. You're allowed one crate to travel with you. It's in the contract. Just buy some of whatever their cargo is, fill your crate with it, then sell it when you reach your destination. Merchants know what to buy and where to sell it. You can profit from their expertise."

"That's...inventive," said Jhyndra.

"The real money to be made is on the royal protection assignments," said Daga.

"You took bribes to—"

"Kruuna no, nothing like that. I'd never take a bribe to let an assassin into the royal keep. The royals you're protecting pay you extra to make sure you aren't amenable to bribes from assassins, and that's over and above what the Gold League pays you. The extra coins I received from the royals on my last posting exceeded my pay from the Gold League. I finally have enough to retire. I'll get a nice little place down in Northpoint—"

"Your last posting?" interrupted Jhyndra.

"Yes, my last posting was protecting the King of Karteran and the members of the royal family. I served them well, and they paid me well. You'll find that you can also receive bribes to look the other way if a royal wants you to keep quiet about what they're doing. They pay extra for your discretion. Coins aren't the only currency in court, you know. Gossip and information are often more valuable. Not to me, of course, but to members of the court and those trying to influence them."

Daga looked to Jhyndra to see if he was open to making extra money that way, but the young man was hard to read in the dark. A lad like Jhyndra needed help if he was going to ever rise above being merely average.

"Go on," said Jhyndra with a gleam in his eye.

Good. There was hope for the lad yet. He would get more than just copper coins if he followed the advice.

"So, if a crown prince of a certain persuasion wants to sneak out and bugger some handsome teen boy he fancies, I'm not against taking some extra coin to keep my mouth shut. You can't say no to a crown prince, not if you're a mere royal guard and certainly not if you're a handsome boy from a lesser family. I felt bad for the boy and reported it to my superior, but he said the boy was going to get buggered regardless, so we might as well get some coin out of it."

"Ah, so that explains it," said Jhyndra.

"Explains what?" asked Daga.

"Quiet. What's that?" asked Jhyndra as he looked out across the vacant field.

Daga had not heard a noise, but he followed Jhyndra's gaze out into the field to look for movement or anything that seemed out of place. From the corner of his eye, he saw Jhyndra slide his right hand up from his stiff knee to his hip. Odd, since Jhyndra's scabbard was slung on his left side, not his right.

Daga shifted his attention from the field to Jhyndra, just in time to see the young man pull something from his trousers and pivot with sudden speed. Jhyndra was so fast that Daga didn't realize what was in his hand until after it pierced his throat—a Zerk war arrow.

The arrow tore through his windpipe and an artery. Daga brought his hands up to his neck, trying to staunch the flow of blood as it spurted between his fingers and filled his lungs. Eyes wide in disbelief, he looked at Jhyndra trying to make sense of the attack. He tried to speak but only managed a bloody burp.

"I did make an offering tonight, just not to Dazmir. I serve Zhavos," said Jhyndra.

The god of murder.

"You might think I'm only an average soldier," said Jhyndra, "but I'm an excellent assassin. It was hard holding back, pretending to be average, so I'd never draw attention to myself or be selected for advanced training."

"She wouldn't tell me why she wanted you dead, and I was curious. Can't blame her, wanting to protect her buggered son's honor. You have a reputation for blabbing, so I thought I might get it out of you before the end of our watch.

"I hope you were right about my first watch being a sign of things to come. When I return home, maybe my sponsor will send me to kill the crown prince next.

"I'll just slip away next time my patrol is out scouting the badlands. They'll assume I was taken by Zerks. No one will miss me, not poor mediocre Jhyndra.

Daga's hands slipped from his neck. He couldn't feel them anymore.

"Don't worry though, I'm still a soldier. I won't neglect my duties. After you bleed to death, I'll make sure to ring a bell."

Path of Vengeance

by Ben Sherman

Other published works: The Book of Vashi, the Pool of Wailing Sorrows, 'The Crown of Laidun' in the Fable and Redemption Reclaimed Anthology.

The land of the God-Kings was dead, and men picked at the corpse. Dark men, not of skin or cloth, but of heart ruled the fell land. Cruel sorcerer kings and demon-summoners, slave masters and black acolytes. They called themselves the Exiled Ones, banished sovereigns from across the sea. But to those who knew them, they were the Dwemorlocks of the Anu'sar-Wastes

Traversing the dunes and cracked earth of the barrens was exhausting. Were Rhaak not tireless in his dogged approach, he would have fallen into oblivion long ago. With corded muscles and a strong back, the pit-fighter carried their rations without complaint. He kept his eyes forward and, his face grim, treating the desert itself as an opponent to brutally stamp out in a battle of wills. His city-dwelling companion was not so motivated.

Muk Al-matuk panted like a dog, trying not to groan from exertion. He all but stumbled across the unending sea of land, desperately trying to keep up with the young slave out of fear of being left behind. Rhaak had saved the weak merchant's life days ago from the dog-headed khamlyt raiders, moving in their sinuous gait and butchering everyone in the caravan who dared to breathe. Neither of them had ever heard a creature that sounded like the khamlyt, as if it were trying to breathe, snarl, and laugh all at once.

They had attacked with the surprise of a sandstorm, and only four of the caravan had broken free, fleeing into the desert sands with what little they could carry. Shazram was the slowest of them, the baker collapsing not a mile from what was left of the camels. The khamlyts that pursued butchered him and engorged themselves, leaving the rest to their fate in the sands. Ahmetab had moved quicker, but he became careless as the miles dragged on. Rhaak had liked the man, but he had died all the same. Stepping on a scython resting just beneath the sand had sealed his fate. The serpent's coils snapped his bones like twigs, but it was the dagger-sized fangs puncturing Amhetab's eyes that would stay in his memories.

Now there were only two of them, moving west with the west. The merchant had been given an ultimatum by the slave, follow him into the wastes or strike out on his own. Terrified of the dangers, he had stayed with Rhaak and clung to his heels. Only now was he starting to regret the decision, it seemed. He had gained a wild look in his crusted eyes, his thin limbs fidgeting when they had the energy to do so. Every day they passed what appeared to be the same mounds of sand and rock, baking in the sun. Only when they saw something truly horrible was it evident, they were still moving in a linear march. Jagged boulders with inhuman faces. Immense skeletons of black bone half buried in the sands. Monoliths that whispered as you walked by...

It was by the mercy of Hayashim that the two of them crested the next rise to find the shallow ravine Muk had spoken of, along with the water hole that glistened under the light of the dying sun. Rhaak felt a surge of relief, though it proved short lived when the growling of his thickly muscled stomach drew the slave's attention to just how hungry he was. The vegetation beside the water was sparse, but green. Stout desert grass and hardy weeds were splattered across the ground. A lonely fig tree drooped over the pond, stubbornly staying rooted and upright despite its depressed appearance.

Muk lifted his hands to the sky in thanks as he all but crawled towards the diminutive watering hole. He seemed thirstier than anything, slathering like a dog in his sudden run before shoving his face into the water, his big nose pierced the surface like a diving hawk. While he gulped down greedily, Rhaak approached more cautiously, eyes alight with suspicion. Such a place was the perfect area for an ambush, but as the seconds wore on, he could not deny that they were here regardless of the circumstances. Might as well drink his fill, and so he did in a similar manner to his companion. Muk's head surfaced a moment later, gasping for air. His eyes were glazed with exhaustion and sudden sluggishness.

"I thought you said there would be food here." Rhaak accused when they caught their breath.

"And you said the journey would take three days!" Muk snapped irritably, still harboring some energy in his paunch. He looked at the fig tree and gestured vaguely. "Help yourself."

Rhaak did so, making sure to remember his lack of interest when he demanded they stop for their next meal. The pit fighter picked what little figs there were. Rhaak was not short, but the tree was so bent, even Muk might be able to leap up and nab a few had he the mind. He popped one into his mouth, feeling the honeyed quality with a tinge of bitterness. Not in the best shape, but they would do. He began to put all the plucked fruit into the sack until he froze.

He did not know what it was. Perhaps he heard a voice or the trotting of hooves, it was possible he felt the smallest tremor in the ground. "Someone's coming." he said to Muk, who lay on the ground prostrated until he blearily raised his head.

"Hmmm?"

"Someone is coming," Rhaak remarked louder, as he put the last fig into his mouth and kneeled beside the water. He wanted another sip before he had to fight to the death. For his part, Muk scrambled to his feet, slipped behind Rhaak and looked back and forth, contemplating whether or not fleeing into the dunes yet again was the way he would survive just a day longer.

Camels loped around the corner. A dozen, maybe half a dozen... it was hard to tell in the narrow passage. Hooded men swathed in white cloth cantered their mounts forward, the shadows of the day neared indigo on their forms. The two saw a few were armed with swords of broad blades, but they did not look like mamluks or dwemorlock raiders. Muk cleared his throat and dragged forth his meager courage to stand before the lead man as the group slowed their camels beside the pool. The short and shaken Muk looked pitifully small before the mounted man, just the right size to be trampled.

The lead man gazed down at Muk, looking as if he would do just that. When he spoke, his sharp features cut the air. "Why is it that your slave drinks while you stand guard, good sayyed?" He did not look like one of the Dwemorlocks, or at least not full blooded. The men behind him were hard eyed and veiled, showing no hint of trust in this harsh realm. "Or have I mistaken a thief for a merchant?"

For all his cowardice, Muk rose to the occasion with pride. "I am Muk Al-matuk, purveyor of silk, satin, and suede. My slave here is all that stands between me and the dangers of the road, so I keep him well fed and supped to make the journey. I seek the city of Dak-Mirta. Do you come from there?"

"I am Thu'Natar," he said. The name was anu'sarian, but it could have been a given name used in dealings of the wastes. "And I would know your business in Dak-Mirta before you proceed further. I see you bring no goods, Muk Al-matuk."

"I have a contact there. I am here for business. A friend in Rhagba-Shahir told me of a man in Dak-Mirta who is interested in my services."

It was so flimsy a story, Rhaak would not have been surprised if Thu'Natar sneezed and he saw it evaporate into the desert sands. Perhaps Muk could swing it in that he traveled a thousand miles with no caravan and one slave to speak to a single man, but that was unlikely. The idle statement took Thu'Natar aback.

Muk did not grow daunted by the skeptical look. It was when Rhaak began killing that he blanched.

The pit-fighter, idly keeping to himself and eating, had snapped the branch of the lone tree in a swift, brutal motion and stabbed the end of it into the leg of the closest man. Blood seeped out of the wound immediately, and the fellow cried out as Rhaak pulled him out of his camel's saddle to hit the sandstone below, hard.

A man shouted in a foreign tongue and three of them drew their swords. Thu'Natar glanced back at the violence, and then smote Muk with an accusatory gaze.

"Filth!" he roared, unsheathing his longsword. Muk shrieked and dove under Thu'Natar's camel; scampering into his blind spots and keeping away from his swiping blade. He caught a glimpse of Rhaak, bleeding at the shoulder, parrying the blade of a man with a ferocious countenance. Two bodies lay at the slave's feet, and a riderless camel loped out of the ravine into the desert. Thu'Natar cursed and spurred his mount forward, nearly trampling the poor merchant who managed to squirm out of the beast's legs onto the sand.

Rhaak had not deigned to look and see if his companion was alive. He took another cut from a veiled man with long limbs who dismounted and assailed him with dual scimitars. He thrust one sword forward in a feint before cutting low at Rhaak's legs. The slave saw it for a feint, and instead of leaping back, he simply leaped upwards and shifted his body. His powerful legs shot out and connected with the fellow's face. The veiled man dropped his scimitars and hit the ground as the pit-fighter did. Rhaak had prepared for the landing, however, and recovered quicker. He rolled forward and wrapped his arms around the strong man's neck, snapping it with an audible crack. Drool oozed from under the veil, wetting the dead man's tunic.

A great cry rang out, drawing Rhaak's attention. He saw Thu'Natar barreling down upon him, longsword prepared for a sweeping strike that would cleave his head in twain. Rhaak put his thick arm above his head to vainly cover himself from the blow, but he needn't have bothered. A 'twang' echoed from the rocks by the cleft of the ravine, and a crossbow quarrel bloomed on Thu'Natar's neck. Blood bubbled out, and his nerveless fingers dropped the sword as he slowly fell off his camel, too busy grabbing at his neck to keep ahold of the reins.

Rhaak looked to his left and saw Muk-Al Matuk rising from behind the crags with sweat beading down his face.

"Good job," Rhaak said.

"I do not suppose that was enough excitement to make you rethink our course?" he asked, hopelessly.

"Get their cloaks and wash the blood off in the pool." Rhaak said, getting to his feet and grabbing what equipment they might need. In less than an hour, the two were riding deeper into the gorge. The rock was dry and devoid of life. Muk quailed twice. Once when he thought he saw a figure in the rocks, and another when he saw two horned statues framing the mouth of the path. Whoever had carved them had given them wings, and had shaped them so their chests were open, and their stone hearts laid bare as if in supplication. It even disturbed Rhaak.

On the shimmering horizon illuminated by the failing sun, a monstrous black wound festered in the sands. The walls were tall and grim, covering the base of the city's spires and minarets that erupted out of the sand. Rhaak saw a light from behind the curtain wall, sickly and grim, and yet somehow it illuminated nothing. It only bred further darkness. Despite the desert heat, looking upon it brought a chill to their hearts.

"You go ahead. I will, um, wait here and watch our backs," the merchant bade hesitantly, his eyes never leaving the sinister city.

"You would stay here?" Rhaak asked

For the first time Muk gazed away from Dak-Mirta, finding the two of them were in a wasteland pockmarked with sunken holes and rocks carved into the faces of demons. The handful of leafless trees that stood lonely in the vast space were cadaverous and drained of life. He stepped back, and his foot crunched on what he found was the skeletal forearm of what was once a man. The movement crumpled what small integrity that section of ground had, the sand evacuating into one of the many cavities in the ground. As the skeleton disappeared, he swore he saw eyes peering out from the one of the gaping holes.

"No, let us go into the city," Muk Al-matuk reasoned, stepping closer to Rhaak. "Let no man say I am not without courage."

Rhaak smirked. He found he liked the short merchant, as greedy as he was. They mounted their camel and set upon the road. As their steed cantered lazily, the sun was pierced by one of the towers.

"What do you know of the city?" the slave-fighter asked.

"Nothing. Nothing but what I hear," Muk said in hushed voice, shaken at their circumstances. "What I hear are things best left unspoken. We should pray to Hayashim they are but tales."

"What do you have the stomach to say?" Rhaak bade.

Muk Al-matuk hesitated, and then said: "The gates are watched by sleepless spirits who see all."

Rhaak grunted, taking him at his word. The city that grew closer and closer was inhabited by sorcerous, devil-worshiping dogs for men. There was nothing he would not believe after what he saw back in Zykrahir. The shadow that walked from man to man that had come for him and killed his master. He still could scarcely believe it, and he slew the demon.

Walls of obsidian loomed over them, and the sun was truly dimmed as if it had never been and never would be again. The gateway opened like a tiger's maw, two guards in ornate armor stood upon both sides. They were tall and muscular, gripping crescent moon poleaxes. Above them was an immense visage of iron, as if a diabolic mask had been forged for a titan. Its eye pockets were deep shadows of what one could only describe as hopelessness.

"Approach," the left sentry demanded. As Rhaak sent his camel into a slow canter and drew closer, he saw the Dwemorlock was covered in bronze rings, his tattooed skin pierced with silver and brass. Lazily they passed under the visage, its wide mandibles hanging over the two mounted men as if to devour them from above.

Rhaak felt a sudden presence; a pressure that probed him. It was unlike anything he had felt before, and his heart began to race. Briefly he considered charging forward and trying his hand at killing the guards, or even just turning tail and fleeing into the desert. However, whatever watched him left as suddenly as it had appeared. He looked up and saw one eye of the visage with a piercing red light at its center.

"Who is with you?" The right guard demanded, his voice strong even behind the cowl.

"Uh, I am a merchant from far off Izyria," Muk said, clutching Rhaak's cloak anxiously.

"This is Muk Al-matuk, a business partner. We come seeking Mephistok. Where is he?"

"Business partner?" The left one asked.

"Delay us no further, or kill us. But the lord awaits," Rhaak said acidly. Silence hung in the air for many moments as he stared at them, unblinking. His camel shifted uneasily, as if privy to their conversation. A moment passed, and the two pole-axes were removed from their path.

"Mephistok's chambers are to the south. Merely follow the bend upon the causeway."

There were men who could not believe the cities of the Al'ardbahja could have been made by human hands. They attributed their make to the giants of the elder days, before the men of iron broke their empire into a thousand warring tribes. Rhaak was unsure of great cities like Zykrahir, but Dak-Mirta was another matter. He could not believe its foundations or towers had been shaped by the Dwemorlocks or even the giants. They looked almost grown, summoned, as if the pits of hell had belched forth temples for which mortals could worship the lords of chaos at their pleasure.

The two passed one great spire that absorbed the light of the dying sun, seeing it was shaped of charred stone, smooth as steel save for the hieroglyphs engraved along the walls. Rhaak almost felt he were inside a living thing, and the smaller structures made by man of mud brick and sandstone seemed incongruous and lesser, wrought by mortals in a poor attempt to copy their masters. And yet the causeway led them past as many dwellings and meeting spots as any shrine or keep, where foreigners bartered, and the lower rungs of society fought for the scraps of the sorcerer kings. Slaves, both light and dark of skin, passed out of doorways with baskets of food and cloth. They averted their gaze and hurried to complete whatever tasks were set for them. Small cadres of Dwemorlock guards stood vigil or patrolled the paved streets, garbed similarly to those who met Rhaak and Muk at the gates.

The two meandered by what passed for a tavern in the city, but noticed that its outer wall of stone was used as a base for the ceiling of an even greater building. Rhaak and Muk crept by and gazed in awe. It was the entrance of a great temple. Powerful pillars framed a walkway deep into the base of a spire. Each pillar was made into the likeness of a great arm that reached out from the ground to hold up the ceiling, thicker than tree trunks and taller than six men standing atop one another. Braziers roared between each pillar, and the walkway fed into an archway shaped in likeness of a laughing demon. Rhaak had keen eyes, and by the demon he saw two people, likely slaves, impaled on iron spikes and writhing, somehow still alive.

"A temple of Amon-Hatsut." Muk Al-matuk shuddered. "The Devourer of Millions."

Rhaak did not ask how the merchant knew that. He did not say anything. He kicked the camel to continue, with the beast itself seeming eager to move on. However, once they passed the building, the camel began to dance in a panicked manner. Muk gave a cry as he clung to Rhaak, who called out to the beast and took its reins to calm the thing. He glanced behind them to see if some denizen had crawled out of the temple mouth, but the pit-fighter saw nothing. He sighed in relief and turned back around, only to glimpse something atop the stout awning of the next building. He squinted to focus on what looked very much like a massive pile of rolled up carpets, a huge block of stone resting at the edge. Realization dawned on him, and he gasped when he understood what it was.

Lounging atop the building was a massive snake, so large its coiled thews could strangle a full-grown bull. Its head was the size of Rhaak's muscled torso, and its body unfathomably long. Rhaak and Muk both recoiled at what they now perceived as a pale leg sticking out of its bulky coils. The pit-fighter spurned their mount on, passing by the slumbering beast as it rested after the hunt.

They passed by another patrol of men in spiked helms and spears, and less than a kilometer ahead the road ended before the throat of a great stygian palace. Its front archway opened like the underneath of a wave's swell, and behind it were pillars more massive than those leading to the temple, though they ironically seemed more traditional with columns that ended in faceted cylinders. And yet from what they could see, they led a traveler nowhere. It was a forest of stone structures that spread into darkness.

Immediately Rhaak realized going forward would lead him no closer to his target. Muk interrupted his thoughts by tugging at his arm and pointing southwards. Rhaak turned left and saw an entrance to one of the outer houses connected to the eldritch palace, a slave even now stepping in. The doorway was decorated with a colorful mosaic and framed by twin ferns of sharp, needle-like leaves.

The pair stepped within, closer to danger and yet glad to be out of the streets. The antechamber was small and packed with strange foliage, the room immediately feeding into a 'great hall' one might call it, if the intruders were not certain this was but one of many. Akin to a long gallery in one of the great basilean houses, it led to various different chambers and the slaves made good use of the space. Men and women in light shifts draped over one shoulder strode with purpose as they had in the streets. Rhaak spotted a guard with a fearsome sword striding out of the hall into a hidden room just as they entered.

Rhaak only had one moment of doubt before his senses were enthralled by the smell of freshly cooked food wafting out of the closest corridor. He felt his rock-hard stomach audibly complain, and the pit-fighter knew that even if he could withstand the temptation of the food, that if he did not eat soon, he would feel it in his limbs. Muk seemed similarly affected, but before he could speak there was a call.

Out of the lines of servants, a slave woman stepped out of line and approached them with a deliberate saunter. "Welcome, honored guests," she said with a honeyed tone, and she abased herself before the two men. On her supple arms were bangles of strange script, and her raven hair was fashioned by a cone of brass into a tall ponytail. Rhaak was too confused and hungry to speak, but Muk seemed elated. She drew up from the floor, though she was still on her knees. The woman looked at them from under long lashes. "How may I serve you, my masters?"

"Leave us alone," Rhaak started to say, but Muk spoke over him.

"You may serve by accompanying us to our destination, woman." he said, rolling his hand so she may get to her feet. "I am in need of a good servant, and perhaps if you serve faithfully, I shall allow you to drink wine at my table."

Rhaak shot the merchant a glare, but he was promptly ignored. Muk was just about to give her another command, but the pit-fighter pulled him to the side. "What are you doing? We don't have time for this."

"Do not tell me what we have time for! I am in the belly of a demon because of you!" Muk snapped, eyes wild with lust mixed with exhaustion. "Yes, you saved me at the caravan. But I saved you at the ravine. We are even, and I say I want a slave girl!"

Rhaak leveled his gaze at the short man. Muk Al-matuk had gotten a notch leaner in his belt, but even now he was not an imposing man. Rhaak was a barbarian to him, but the pit-fighter was trying to help the fool out of his old ideas of decadence. "No slave girls," he said evenly. "If we flee, we must flee fast. Take some gems, steal a golden cup, I don't care."

Muk sighed, closing his eyes. "Yes, yes, you are right." He held his soft hands up in defeat. "I am just tired. Lead the way!"

Rhaak nodded, almost smiling. He turned, not noticing the slave girl had gone. Instead, he crept toward the source of the sultry smell of food. He could also sense the faintest whiff of water, another welcome addition. The men of the northern river valleys would not know of this, but if a man went long enough without water, he could smell fresh water as clearly as spiced meat.

Rhaak left the central hall and entered the kitchens with the grace of a prowling tiger. Inside, the room was made almost entirely of well tiled stone save for the wooden chairs and various utensils made of wood or tin. At the center of the room was a large furnace on an island of sandstone, with a cookpot hanging over the coals by a chain that reached the ceiling. Smaller fires with lesser pots were arrayed at the left side of the room, a cook at all five stations. Shapely and succulent pork and beef were arrayed on porcelain trays, furnished with sauces Rhaak couldn't guess and vegetables he had only seen once before in his life when he fought for his life before the satrap.

One cooked turned to look at him, seeing a powerfully built man garbed in rags and stained in blood and dirt. He dropped his spoon, alerting the others to Rhaak's presence. Rhaak cared little; he just approached the food.

The cooks ran as he started grabbing freshly baked loafs and hot meat and everything else he could engorge himself on. Next, he found a jug of water, the liquid sloshing within. He was almost as thirsty as he was famished, but as he downed the pitcher of cool, clear water, he realized Muk was not with him.

Muk was hungry for bread and fruits, but he was ravenous for the woman. The travel over the desert had been incredibly dry, and he was a man unused to lack. He only felt the slightest pang of guilt at leaving Rhaak, but the merchant knew he would get over it. The brute was just an up-jumped slave that had given him an impossible choice, drove him across the wastes and led him into this hell. If he followed Rhaak further, Muk would just get killed.

There were merchants in this city. Muk could find a ship; he could barter his way out. In a month he could be back in his bed, with his money and his servants. Yes, he had lost revenue when the khamlyt had attacked, but it was not something he could not recover from, if he could just get out of Dak-Mirta.

Muk had disappeared between the servants, peeking into corridors and searching for the delectable slave. He stepped passed a brazier, shooing away a male servant who inquired to his needs. A fern brushed his nose, and he wiped his meaty hands on his sweaty face. He almost did not see the sentry, who's cable-like arms were crossed, and his back turned to the short man. Muk cowered and backpedaled again, thinking for a moment looking for the slave girl was too risky. As he scrambled on the other side of the pillar, he saw her again.

"You, girl!" he called imperiously. She spun, and for a moment he thought he saw hatred in her dark orbs, before they softened, and she looked at him with surprise in her keen eyes. Muk had seen many attractive women, but this one was sumptuous; her garb leaving just enough to the imagination to set a man's blood afire. "I was away on pressing business, but I have returned. Come, I demand you show me the way to the docks."

She placed a dainty hand atop her full bosom, nodding. She was too short to be from the Anu'sar Wastes, though she was taller than him. Her skin was a healthy bronze color, tanned but not as dark as his own people. Her full lips curved into a honeyed smile. "Yes, master. My desire is your desire," she professed.

Good, he thought. Despicable as the Dwemorlocks were, they trained their slaves well. She waved him over and danced into the next corridor, giggling girlishly. Muk followed like a dog, his eyes on the curve of her legs. He passed an archway framed with brass, and blinked in surprise when he found it led nowhere else. It looked to be a simple pantry, and the girl had disappeared, or so he thought. Muk Al-matuk heard a voice to his side.

"You're more foolish than my last master, and that is certainly saying something," the sultry voice said, and a white flash crossed his vision as he was struck by some crate. A roar filled his ears as his entire world went from white to black, and consciousness gave way to oblivion.

Rhaak felt sluggish after the feast he had participated in. He felt he should find Muk, and yet he knew he needed a scant minute to let the food and water drift down him lest, he be easy prey for any wandering swordsman. He allowed himself that, though he remained ever on guard, eschewing anymore food though he felt he could still tolerate more. In the meantime, the pit-fighter stepped lightly to the edge of the kitchens and peered out into the greater hall. To his astonishment, the army of slaves he had seen had at once, vanished. Instead, he saw two guards swathed in cloth and mail and bearing wicked swords, standing like statues on watch. The implication unnerved him, and immediately he felt they were discovered. He moved back into the kitchen, one of the pots now overflowing from the fire beneath it.

At once a guard appeared from a darkened corridor at the back, in a place Rhaak had assumed was a larder or closet. He was dressed as the two men in the hall. Both the pit-fighter and the guard paused when they saw one another, but the newcomer broke the silence first. He howled and launched himself at Rhaak, coming in for the kill with a smart thrust. Rhaak grabbed the closest implement he could, a large wooden pin for kneading dough. He batted the blade aside just barely, feeling the guiding strength behind the stab. The man was no slouch, however. He struck Rhaak across the face with a backhanded strike from his bronze bracer. As Rhaak's vision swam, he spun his blade and redirected it in a slash that would have separated Rhaak's head from his shoulder had he not lifted the pin on instinct, bracing it with both hands. The sword bit into the wood, and Rhaak spun the pin like one might twirl the wheel of a mighty ship. A testament to his skill, he kicked out at the same moment of the maneuver, knocking the wind out of the guard as he disarmed him. To the bastard's credit though, he recovered with lightning speed, tackling Rhaak and shoving his lower back against the stone table at the center of the room.

The two grunted and grappled there, but it was to Rhaak's advantage. The guard was strong, but Rhaak had thews like a tiger and was used to such combat. Gradually, he began to twist himself out of the man's grip, who changed tactics as quick as a mongoose. He shoved his hand into Rhaak's face and tore a serpent-like dagger out of his jerkin, stabbing down to skewer Rhaak in the eye. He would have succeeded, but Rhaak had expected the move. He ignored the hand that threatened to suffocate him and crossed his arms in a barrier that halted the descending arm. The blade now a mere inch from his eye.

"You are good intruder. I cannot afford to let you live to torture." The guard whispered viciously, pressing down with the knife to keep Rhaak's arms immobile. It edged closer to his face, and Rhaak was beginning to feel as if this was it, until he felt the heat from a cookfire to his left. The savvy fighter growled like a beast and used all his considerable strength to push the knife away a scant few inches with his left as he desperately reached to the right with his other hand. He felt something hot and metallic singe his hand, and without preamble he yanked it up. Water beyond the point of scalding smote the man in the face, easily burning through the cloth that hid his nose and mouth. Rhaak was not unused to cries of pain, but he had never heard such pitiful screams before in his life. The soldier grabbed at his face; flesh now mingled with cloth in a mockery of what a man's face should look like. He hit the ground and writhed violently, whimpering. Rhaak coughed and shoved himself off the table, regaining his posture and grimacing at the man wriggling at his feet. He took the now empty but still scalding pot, and beat the man's head in until skull fragments caked the floor.

"Be gone woman, or you'll be sport for my men." The half-breed spat, raising his hand as if to strike her.

The slave woman bowed demurely, and then spun on her heels and walked out into the antechamber, leaving the guardsmen their petty fantasies. There were far too few Dwemorlocks to be utilized as common foot soldiers, and so the footmen that guarded the archways and streets were of mixed blood. The bastard sons of their dark masters, most often borne of the coupling of a true blood and a slave. Ever resentful of being unable to attain hallowed status, they abused the slaves and whatever foreigners stepped out of line with vicious cruelty. The woman exited the antechamber and stepped into a larger hall, where Mephistok kept his collection of war trophies. Here every skull of every enemy the great sorcerer defeated was set upon raised daises of brass and gilded filigree... save for her own.

Calliope Kargasa was no mere slave, but the deposed queen of the Island of Calaverde. A sorceress and potent pythoness in her own right, she had once commanded a fleet of twenty caravels and carrocks, entertained princes and even once been a lucrative trading partner with Dak-Mirta, until the betrayal and her subsequent duel with Mephistok. The láthspell had drawn her in and utilized an ancient artifact she had not anticipated. The craven had not only left her alive, but had demarcated her powers with her accursed bangles and kept her as the lowest of slaves. She spat on the corner at the mere thought of that day three years before, and crossed into the next hallway. So deep in her thoughts was she that the woman took three steps before noticing she was not alone. Calliope gave a start at the sight.

At the center of the corridor stood the barbarian. He bore a new cut on his strong shoulder and one above his eyes, but he was very much alive. In his left hand he bore a sword dripping with blood, and in his right, he held the decapitated head of a guard by the hair, similarly staining the floor with crimson. She looked at him, dimly detached. For a moment she simply resigned herself to death, and calmly examined him. He was not unhandsome, in a similar vein to the dark masters of this citadel. He was built lithely, and yet he brimmed with muscle and powerful sinew. His mane of hair was unkempt unlike all in the city, even the slaves, and he watched her much like a tiger would its prey.

She only spoke when he began to move at her. She stepped back. "Master, what-"

He dropped the head of the sentry, and when she made to run, he leaped, shoving the sword between her and the exit. A callused hand grabbed her shoulder, and she was shoved against the mudbrick wall. Her head barely missed a brass wall hanging that would have cut into her skull. "Where is the merchant?" he asked her menacingly. "I warn you. Do not play coy with me."

"He was taken." she said, wincing from the pain.

"Where!?" he demanded, placing the blade's edge at her neck. This was not the first time she had been at the point of a sword, and she steadied herself.

"The black chamber. If he is not dead by now, he will be before you get there," she remarked, eyeing him to gauge his response. He cursed, and though death glinted in his dark eyes, he did not strike home.

"Will Mephistok be there?"

The question surprised her. She looked at him, and his appearance suddenly began to make more sense. She had thought they were lost at first, and then after seeing him here, she had figured him for a foolhardy raider. But now... "You're going to kill him."

It was a statement, not a question. At the moment she was not focused on how impossible that seemed. The man pressed the blade against her soft flesh. "Will he be there?"

"No, only his acolytes," she said quickly, causing his hand to go rigid. After a few moments, he withdrew the sword. Likely he would have killed her if he knew she had taken the fat little merchant, or maybe he had already figured it and was too focused on his vendetta to care. Either way, she saw an opportunity and took it. "If you are going to kill him, I will take you to him."

The two slaves hurried through the corridors of the dread palace, passing through chambers of torture, bedrooms of vulgar luxury, and rooms of an alien purpose. He did his best to simply keep his eyes open, for both traps and any tricks from the slave woman. He found himself ascending a spiral stairway just behind her, blindly following her through the immense citadel.

He could not guess why, but he felt the dimensions of where they moved was misshapen compared to the buildings he had seen from outside. Perhaps it was just his mind playing tricks. He had heard many rumors of the foul Dwemorlocks, even in the pits and cages of Izyria. Rhaak gazed up at his 'guide,' who moved with an undeniable purpose. He could see why Muk had been so distracted by her, now that his stomach was full and his path clearer. Her shoulders were slim, and her generous bottom moved alluringly every step she took. But he was not as gullible as Muk, civilized though Muk might be. He did not trust her. In fact he had nearly killed her, but he would not pass up help in locating the sorcerer. Even if it led into the very jaws of his machinations.

At the height of the stairway, they were in a dome of silver. At the center was a dais with a stone of black crystal. The slave woman ran a slim hand over the peerless craftsmanship, only giving the glass a glance before she stalked out of the chamber. Rhaak did not know the significance of the object, but it had an unsettling abnormality about it. He pulled his eyes from its black depths and followed her into a strange hall. There was a sheer, tall wall, almost cliff-like, to the left of them. On the right were a series of curtain laden archways that fed onto a number of balconies. Rhaak did not see guards, but he did see figures past the draperies, tall and majestic figures. Some of the silhouettes were dining as others were merely looking over the balustrade, and still more had decided whatever was transpiring outside was enticing enough to bring them into lustful embraces.

The slave woman apparently knew they would be distracted, only giving cursory glances to the right as she marched up the gently sloping corridor.

Rhaak was content to follow suit, until he heard a scream. A scream he had become intimately familiar with the last few weeks. He grabbed her arm, and she hissed like a viper at his rough handling.

"No, that's Muk," he said.

"We have no time for this," she warned him, but he ignored her. Rhaak let her go, pushing past the soft curtains to step onto the closest unoccupied balcony. He heard her curse as she followed him, even above the rhythmic chanting of strange words echoing in the deep. The balustrade was carved in the likeness of wyrms devouring one another from rock gathered from the bosom of the desert. He placed his hands on the stone and peered down to witness what was transpiring below.

They were in a vast chasm of dark architecture, decorated with alcoves where statues of leering, fanged monstrosities knelt like silent guardians beneath large torches. Guards stood vigil every fathom, but they were unlike the guardsmen Rhaak had previously fought. Taller by a head, they wore infernal plates of armor and held great spiked halberds of obsidian steel. Their faces were hidden behind helms in the likeness of laughing devils. At the center of the room was a dark pit of which no bottom could be seen. Rhaak's eyes swept over all of this in a moment, but they focused on the figures to the left of the abyss.

Acolytes wearing cloaks of crimson and black stood around what had to be dozens of headless corpses. Blood pooled on the stone floor, and they stood, some ankle deep, with bare feet. The last prisoner, still burdened with his mortal coil, was the short Muk Al-matuk. His cheeks were puffy from sobbing, and two muscled men shoved him down upon his knees, arms bound behind his back. An acolyte stood over his prone form with raised hands, calling to whatever foul spirits he worshipped. It was hard to hear, but Rhaak knew Muk was begging the man for his life. Even through the pathetic crying, the acolyte did not stop. As one of the guards raised their halberd in preparation for the beheading, he did not stop chanting. It only grew louder, and Muk had time for one last screech of fear before the halberd dropped. The heavy blade chopping through soft flesh and hard bone like it was paper. He watched Muk's head bounce across the ground.

Rhaak exhaled a breath, and started to turn away. To his surprise, however, the head wobbled. Peering closer, he watched in amazement as the chanting acolyte waved his hands, and the head was lifted off the ground by a force unseen by eyes. Muk's head floated steadily over the stone floor, even as his body slumped onto the ground. It now hung over the vast black hole, and to Rhaak's horror, he saw Muk's mouth opening and closing like a fish out of water. The merchant's eyes were wide and wild. He could not look around, but he screamed a soundless scream, suspended there in the air.

Something beneath his head moved. A whirl of the darkness, as if the blackness were some physical thing. He and the slave woman watched in rapt fascination as an immense shape reared out of the depths of Hell. Rhaak could not tell if it were real, as it was just a silhouette; a shadow. Something was there, but mortal eyes could not perceive. He saw branches of shadow beneath its bulk, limbs; perhaps four on each side like a scorpion. What might be considered a head reared up, gazing down at the terrified but still very alive Muk. Lines of small light coalesced and spread across the head in a parody of a face. Its eyes sad and its mouth in a silent, howling panic. Rhaak suddenly realized that whatever this thing was, it mocked Muk's fear. Despite her mistrust and anxiety to leave, the woman grabbed Rhaak's hand to steady herself as she watched with him.

The shadow demon began to shudder as if a flickering torch threatened to snuff it out. And yet, it was only the thing's form moving in this limited, three-dimensional space. Like a scroll, the gargantuan creature began to bend as its blackness shimmered, and the last Rhaak saw of Muk Al-matuk, famed merchant of the desert sands, he was screaming a lungless scream as he was engulfed by living shadow. The blackness coiled around him, tighter and tighter, until the shadow disappeared out of existence as if it never was.

"What was that?" Rhaak asked when he found his words. The slave did not appear shaken like him. She looked in awe, even captivated. Slowly her eyes left the area where the thing had been and returned Rhaak's gaze.

"One of the servants of Amon-Hatsut," she said. "They were here before the God-Kings. Before even the Xerubians. Perhaps they are older than the world." She shook her head, and pulled her hand away when she realized had begun to run her thumb over his skin, having forgotten she was still holding his arm. She drifted away from him, and curtly gestured with a flick of her head that they move. Rhaak only hesitated for a moment before he followed.

"Was one of the men down there Mephistok?" he asked her as they continued up the hall.

"No. They are but his underlings." she said, and Rhaak noticed she sounded far more familiar than a slave should. "He no longer bothers himself with the raising of dark servants and demons unless they are hallowed days during an eclipse."

"Hayashim burn this filth," Rhaak spat, making the sign of the sun upon his breast. They passed out of the corridor onto another stairway. Immediately Rhaak saw a difference in style from the floors beneath them. The walls were the color of blood, and the ceilings were stygian. Tapestries of great god-kings and their conquests framed every door, and soon they reached a large antechamber that seemed a dead end to the vengeful pit-fighter. On the wall to the right, a carapace of a scorpion the size of a wagon hung, its exoskeleton polished and shined like obsidian. To the left was a mosaic of a majestic figure, standing atop the tower of brass as multitudes of servants worshiped him and abased themselves in subjugation. But what the slave woman stood before was the far wall, which held a huge slab of bronze, framed by twin skulls of the saurian visk of the southern jungles. Rhaak might have called it a door had it any sign of a crease or latch. Rhaak locked the smaller door behind them.

"What now?" he asked, impatiently.

She approached the bronze barrier and ran her hands over the immaculate metal, pressing her fingers in seemingly irrelevant locations. Her bangles glimmered in the torchlight as her arms moved sinuously. He was going to speak again, but she let out a cry of alarm as the slab suddenly parted before her. Rhaak expected a grating, but it opened silently.

"How did you do that?" he asked her, suspicious. "How do you know this place so well?"

"I did not do that," she remarked, not deigning to answer the second question. She backed up to flank Rhaak, who stiffened when he turned from her to gaze where she looked. The room was a large chamber, the ceiling a dome of pure gold. Lavish day-beds with velvet cushions gathered at the back next to a grand bed of gilded curtains. Neither Rhaak nor the woman were interested in such luxuries. Nor were they intimidated by the weapons of bronze lining the walls, the paintings of elder gods hanging high above, or even the lantern of which she had spoken. Standing upon a dais of marble, it was adorned by three heads: That of a great serpent, that of the mighty roc, and one of a snarling panther. Yet even that was not of most importance at the moment.

At the center of the great room stood a man of great stature. Over a head taller than the woman and even standing above Rhaak, though of leaner build. His skin was coppery, upon his head he wore a tall Sekhemt crown. His long chin was adorned by a lengthy postiche beard cupped with brass and black iron. His fingers were laden with precious rings. All of this took a secondary note to his eyes. They were green, but not green of the northern barbarians from across the sea. They were a lucid green of arcane power. If all the light in the room was snuffed out and all were left in blackness, you could still see those eyes.

When he spoke, his voice carried as if sound itself served him. "Calliope, it still seems you have a spine. I perceived you before your arrival, but who is this that you have brought with you?"

Rhaak glanced at the woman, but steadied his gaze on the man who he knew beyond any doubt was the one he sought. "I am the one you would have killed."

"Do not speak to him," Calliope advised. "Kill him. He is here before you!"

Mephistok laughed; a laugh that knew no joy or mirth. Its timbre rattled the bones upon the walls. "I have sought many to die, and they all have, boy. That tells me nothing. But you shall die for your impudence." He spoke as if he were sentencing a prisoner, with surety beyond doubt. "However, I would know your name before I killed you. Not many would pique the once mighty Calliope's interest so readily."

Rhaak was beginning to think he had stepped into a greater game than he had originally thought. And yet, his objective was the same. "I am Rhaak of Izyria. You sent a shadow assassin to kill me. It murdered my master. It told me it served Mephistok of Dak-Mirta when I slew it. I have traveled a thousand miles to take your head, coward."

The sorcerer-king paused, and he turned to Calliope, putting his full attention on the woman. "I see your mind now, bitch. A bold play." The Dwemorlock sounded impressed. He briefly regarded Rhaak. "Why do you not tell him? Tell him I do not wish him dead, if he is whom I believe. Do your dog the favor of telling him the truth."

"The truth?" Rhaak asked, angry and confused at this turn of events. Calliope's glare was as sharp as daggers, but she remained silent, though her fingers clenched in anticipation of some foreseen conflict.

"Calliope here is no mere slave, boy. She was a ruler in her own right, feared across the sea. I humbled her and took her under my dominion. But I did not believe she knew my mind and purpose so well." Mephistok smiled at Calliope. "I do not know how you sent the assassins, but it seems you are the reason all of my heirs are dead."

The statement hit Rhaak like a slab of stone. Were he a lesser man, he would have swooned. "What?"

"One year ago, I began a quest to find all of my lost sons. I sent my greatest scouts and even the denizens of the lower realms in search. All had died." Mephistok explained. "It seems Calliope here, even without her sorcery, had orchestrated their deaths. Her cunning led her to act as if she were my own extension. Bravo!"

Rhaak hesitated, struck with indecision. He looked at Calliope. She scowled at him, distraught at three years of scraping at Mephistok's feet seemingly being for naught. "Fool! Do you think he wishes to keep you alive for some benevolent purpose? He wants your blood!"

"Yes," Mephistok admitted. "The Lantern of Forlorn Souls takes a heavy toll. If I wish it to remain loyal, only my blood may sate it. Or that of my pure born children. But that is better than being dead, yes?"

Rhaak did not trust him. Did not trust either of them. But that did not solve his conundrum of what to do. He had come all this way... Would he kill his father? Was there even a resemblance between them? Had there been a mistake?

"You would be his plaything-" Calliope started, but her words broke off in a strangled gurgle as she was lifted suddenly off the ground by an unseen hand. Mephistok raised his own hand, glowering at her as she began to shudder from torture Rhaak could not comprehend. Whatever was happening to her, it was excruciating. She bit her lip, not wishing to give Mephistok the satisfaction of a scream, but every few moments she gave a sudden squeal, as if he were probing her for her most vulnerable nerves. Mephistok laughed cruelly. "This time, I shall kill you, witch. But I will not place your head with the others, in honor. I will use your skull as a pot to piss in!"

Rhaak moved as if someone else controlled him. He was aware of what he did, but he did not feel some great need to help this woman who had tried to kill him, who had likely killed Muk. He only knew that Mephistok was distracted, and he would get no better chance to get close enough to kill him.

Mephistok saw his charge, bemused.

"Has she beguiled you, boy? You would attack your own father for her?"

Rhaak did not answer. He merely raised the wicked edge of his sword. Mephistok released Calliope, the woman hitting the stone floor heavily. The sorcerer drew in a breath, expanding his illustrious chest before he spewed forth a gout of white flame. It was almost liquid, spreading across the floor like a wall. The heat was so intense, stone began to run like blood. Mephistok watched in amazement as he saw Rhaak sail over the flame in a great tigerish leap, unperturbed and un-slowed. Mephistok sent his hand in a great wave before him, and Rhaak suddenly felt enfeebled, as if his limbs were wrought of lead. He stumbled forward, and the sorcerer was easily able to disarm him and shove him to the ground. Rhaak hit the floor, but a flame ignited in his heart and he kicked-up, his legs shooting above him and flinging him from a prone position to a crouch. He moved too quickly for Mephistok to recover, launching his body up with a shove of his legs, his fist hammering into Mephistok's chin like the point of a knight's lance. The sorcerer-king staggered back, blood running freely down his mouth.

The Dwemorlock seemed more fascinated than harmed, however. He ran a finger over his lip and gazed at the blood. "You have done something not many could do, boy. It seems you have inherited my will." Rhaak noticed Calliope stumble into the room, having regained her faculties. Mephistok continued: "I have wasted much of my strength trying to halt you, not kill you. It seems I spent myself in folly."

He moved like lightning, punching Rhaak across the face. The pit-fighter stumbled back, dazed from the blow. It was clear Mephistok took melee combat as a tertiary skill, and yet the strength behind that blow was as powerful as a hammer. However, Mephistok did not pursue him. Rather, he raised his arms and breathed in through his nostrils, deeply. Rhaak leaped back, thinking he was to shoot more flames. Rather, the very room began to shimmer. Torches flickered and gold glimmered, and as one, every shadow in the room was drawn to the sorcerer.

His body ensconced in it, Rhaak watched as the statuesque man grew and twisted in shape. Before him was no longer Mephistok, but some beast of the nether. It looked like a horrible mixture of a dog and a baboon, but even that did not give the beast justice. He could make out little in its features, as it seemed to radiate black, as if a shadow was bright with darkness. He only saw Mephistok's green eyes, now gleaming and trailing green light that burned the retina.

The transformed sorcerer-king leaped upon Rhaak, bowling him over as if he were a mouse. Rhaak cried out and sent his best punches, kicking what he thought might be its groin. The beast ignored the blows, rending Rhaak's shoulder with its jaws and shearing through his battered tunic with its long claws. With a flick of its head, there was a terrible sucking sound. Rhaak felt an alien pressure at his side, a feeling he had never experienced before. He was launched a dozen strides across the room, bouncing across the floor. Vaguely, he lifted his head as if to get up, but to his shock, he saw something in Mephistok's jaws.

A muscled arm.

Rhaak looked to his right. He saw torn skin and bare sinew, blood pouring out of the wound. The fighter could feel little by way of pain or sensation, but he felt weak. He fell to his knees, shuddering as his vision began to fade. Through the roaring in his head, he was dimly aware of a bronze point erupting through the chest of the demon-beast. Mephistok screeched in pain, shadows vibrating like a living thing.

Calliope let the runic spear go, backing away from the flailing beast. It turned on her, eyes alight with hatred. The spear had certainly wounded it, but it now prowled toward her like a stalking panther. She backed against the wall, bumping into an ancient sword. Quickly she grabbed it, but even ornate, it seemed a flimsy thing. Mephistok snarled as it reared back to rend her flesh, but the demon was struck again. This time, by a light that melted its flesh. It gave a cry so horrible that Calliope dropped the sword and clutched her ears. Both she and Mephistok turned to see Rhaak, on his feet. His remaining hand held up the Lantern of Forlorn Souls. Fires hotter than the sun burned in its depths, and they saw his wound was now cauterized.

Rhaak had ignited the artifact with his blood, and had halted his own bleeding with hellfire.

The roc head dimmed, and Mephistok turned to assail Rhaak even as the shadow of his form began to dissipate. It took only three strides before Mephistok was no more, leaving naught left but a legacy. Calliope pushed off the wall, and after pausing for a moment, she cackled.

"Yes! Together we have done it!" the woman cried, and her dark eyes glittered when she saw his dismembered arm. A new source of blood, no doubt.

"Together?" Rhaak asked, his voice hoarse. She regarded him, and it was clear for any who looked that he could do naught but stand. His eyes were glazed and his breath shallow. But he lifted the lantern once more, turning it so the panther head, the door of dimensions, was presented forward. Hellfire ignited behind its eyes and maw, and suddenly Calliope sensed as much as heard something behind her. She turned, and before the woman was a door in the fabric of reality. A door where something stirred. She only had one moment to gasp as something long and sinuous reached out and wrapped around her slim waist.

"No!" she cried, desperately struggling. She was pulled in just as Rhaak released the portal. "No!" she cried again, and it echoed through the chamber even after she was gone from this realm of existence.

All was silent, save for a distant pounding of guards at the door to the antechamber. Rhaak did not care. He looked around the chambers of his father, and felt it was as good a place as any to die. He dropped the lantern, and then his body tumbled to the ground even as the door shattered open to find a dying man, instead of a sorcerer-king.

Blackness took him.

Keneira

By Armanis Ar-feinial

Armanis Ar-feinial is a Native American from Maine, and lives and breathes in Mass. He resides in the city for the most part, and attends church weekly. He enjoys reading, games, and shiny things. As a voracious writer, many of his works can be found directly on his website. "The Holy Grail War", "The Dawn of Forest Black," and more recently, "The Land of Dreams".

Keneira stared out towards the darkened skies, her sister clasping tightly to her free hand while her spare hand weighed heavily on her opposite side, a chain she held, a ball of iron and glass, lights and smoldering embers inside, cackling, providing illumination. The cobblestones in front of her was the road onwards toward the hunting grounds, some barrows, and an old cemetery Jera liked to visit, where their mother was at rest. It had been three summers since her passing as they walked the bare road. The green orbs up in the sky shone, it was safe, for now at least, as she took her first steps forward. They'd be back, just in time for dinner for her father's servants were preparing several boars for the wedding festival.

It was not a wedding she approved of, her little sister, barely past eight summers herself. To wed to the disgusting Lorshmo, son of Crushma, Prince of the North. Rumor had it the King himself went a little impotent, and the poor son, the bastard, was found early this morning balls deep in a damned hog, as if her father's brothels, of which were offered last night, were subsequently refused for the sake of purity. Of course, copulating with animals was as clean as well water. Dreadfully so, she must admit, this was her own fault for marrying a low-born, but she loved him, and wouldn't divorce him to save her sister. Oh Gods. To even think to have the same prick that defiled some hog inside her was disgusting, she nearly vomited at the thought.

"I want to see Mummy," Jera said, her hand squeezing her own, gently, as she could. "Come, take me to Mummy."

"But of course," Keneira smiled, looking at her sister with the flame lighting her face. The hair was tied into a nice little bun, the clothes were mournful, to say the least, just barely covering her shoulders, and with a weakness about them, her hand tucked a few strands of hair behind her ears. "Just let me take care of the light."

She twisted the iron clasp at the top, opening a port with the glass, and embers danced inside the cage, emitting a little more flare. No telling really how much longer those orbs would stay lit, and when they did, the Abyss would encroach upon them, and this lantern would be the only thing either of them had to shield them from the dark, and the monsters that dwelt within it. Yes, yes, the cemetery too was part of the Abyss, but with this lantern, they could traverse it safely, as safe as one ever dared. Tightening her grip on her sister's hand, they stepped forward, the metal cage creaked with each step.

"Keneira," Jera spoke in her high-pitched voice, a shrill to it, unusual even for her. "What was it like?"

"What was what like?" she asked, observing the road, seeing the break in the path rising upward, soil there was, and dying plants. *She is far too young for this.* She didn't want to answer this question.

"Marriage," she said. "What's it like?"

"Did father never tell you?" she replied, leading her sister up the path ascending. She turned her head to look down at her sister, her brown braid brushed to the side of her shoulder covered in a green tunic. The eyes were innocent, gaping as if she herself was crying, not ready to face her future, not ready to continue on with tradition. No, her father already had one child who broke tradition, he needn't another.

"No," she answered, and Keneira knew, her father too was bastard enough to give her the responsibility for explaining these sensitive things. The bastard!

"It is a wonderful thing," she replied, drawing from her own experiences, which will not Jera's lot in life. "Not without its difficulties, certainly," her eyes gazed up to the sky. The air seemed lighter.

"But I don't want to leave and be far from mummy," Jera said. The silence in the air was deafening, all things considered with the tantamount of responsibility being thrust on her baby sister's shoulders.

"Listen, Jera," she squatted down, the chains scraping against the stones. What was she to tell her sister? That everything was going to be alright? No, that would be lying. Or—could she lie to her sister? Knowing the foul deeds Lorshmo was capable of? Her father was reasonable enough, but there was only so far his elbows could be bent. And her marriage of the stableboy was enough of that. One of his offspring had to marry a count, or higher, and this fit terms. The duty, to keep the house atop. "Jera, sweet Jera, I know you're scared. But I'm here. What you're doing," *forced upon.* "Is to ensure that our House will rise above the rest," *the house would already stand. I'll hold the status of a Count.* "He will hurt you," she spoke sternly. *The damned pig.* "He will like it, and you will accept it. Bear his children for the new generation." *Gods! She's just too young!* And all for the sake of tradition. "Come, let's go. I don' want to tarry anymore, and let's go find mother. Stay in the light!" *Others will benefit at her expense, even me.*

"What's in the dark?" Her sister asked. Too young, and too sheltered was she from the opaque that such tragedies went amiss. Sometimes it was so easy to forget she simply didn't know. How could she?

"Monsters," Keneira sighed, stepping upwards, taking her sister with her. "Careful, and quiet steps must we take."

They stepped forward, the path of the soil was soft, easier on their feet. The light from the green orbs faded as they drew further away from the path, the light from the lantern swayed, and the Abyss, like black smoke swirled around them, trying to penetrate the shield of light it created, but to no avail. Funny thing, really, darkness cannot survive in the light, but this world had so little of it. The path brought them to a plateau, and the light shone several stones, metal rods stuck into the ground, bones, and makeshift plants from a world forgotten and gifts from those whose dead were buried here. Save for one, and she walked Jera to it, the stone, a large one, a slate like a book. Upon it was inscribed the details of her mother, really, just her name: Mira, Countess of Morin, wife of Kira, mother of Keneira and Jera.

And underneath that was written: May the traditions guide you.

"Here she is, but be careful," she spoke solemnly, the lantern rested on the ground as she knelt, hands clasped over one another. She silently prayed a prayer, but to which God, she knew not anymore. How could any God have wanted to create such a dark, pitiful place? None. For better, for worse, good, or evil, this world benefited no one, save for perhaps some sadistic lunatic who presumed the rest of the world was filled with masochists. Keneira decidedly was not one of them.

"Flowers!" Jera shrieked. "Keneira, we—we forgot to bring flowers!"

"Oh my," Keneira turned to her. "You might be right. Go and grab some by the garden over there."

"Nothing e'er grows the'e!" she whined, voice wavering.

"Yes, but still, why don't you look. Or take a flower from one of the other graves. Those still work too, just *stay* in the light." Keneira heard the steps scurry off as she continued to look at her mother's tombstone. Squatting down, her hand reached out to touch it, remembering what her mother looked like before she passed. A tear rolled down her cheek, bowing her head. "I love you." She wept with the coming of the passing of time, lips trembled together. "I can't. I just can't. Baudet is here, but he is not you, and Jera, she looks so much like you, Mother. It hurts to look at her sometimes."

"Keneira!" her sister shrilled.

She turned her head. The braid whipped past her. Eyes darting her vision towards the garden, a pitiful display of a flowerbed, there was nothing save the black canvas behind it. *Damnit.* She stood grabbed the lantern, her blood pumped through her veins with each step, the light surrounding her in the cemetery, and she traversed the darkness of the Abyss, the light penetrating its hide, and the swirls of black smoke pushed back with the strength of the embers flaring from within their chamber.

Braving the dark, she felt the sludge creep into her boots, grimacing, heart pounded as the cold of the Abyss caressed her as she passed through the unknown. Mist, did she exhale from her lips as she pushed through the sludge, following her sister's voice. "Jera!" she cried; the weight of the sludge weighed down on her. Each step was heavy, like a ball and chain tied to her feet, shackling her oppressively. Peering past her vision swept, as the dark touched the orb of light around her, she feared the worst, and then, a squeak, heard she in the middle of it, a ruckus of tumbling rocks striking the ground.

"Keneira!" the voice shrieked again. "Keneira!"

"Jera!" She called, a rasp in her voice, and she sprinted towards it, the swiveling lantern squeaked with the sudden jerk in the force she swung, and found her sister, the brave poor fool, dash at her from the dark. "Jera!" she snapped, kneeling down, hands on her arms, nervously looking for markings of anything, bites, bleeding, nothing. The light of the lantern faded just a little as it rested on the sludge, the arms of the deep closing in on their spirits. "What did I say?"

"But I smell—"

"It doesn't matter, you don't cross into the Abyss!" she spoke harshly with a pointed finger.

"Why!" Jera exclaimed. "You do it all the time!"

To get away from—what am I running from? She gasped, and that was all she could think. "It's dangerous. You don't know what's out there, and the Abyss can eat you," she reached forth, embracing her sister. "I'm sorry, I was scared. I didn't mean to frighten you."

"But Keneira," her sister spoke gently into her ear. "Come with me,"

"We really should be getting back now, did you find the flower for Mother's grave?" she asked, standing, her eyes locked with her sisters innocent gaze.

"I found lots and lots and lots of things," she said, a sneer curled upon her lips. Had it come from anyone else's mouth, she'd think she was up to something. "Come and see, you'll like them. You really will."

"Very well, but we mustn't stay for much longer. Hold my hand, and remember, stay in the light!"

"Yeah, yeah," her sister brushed off the comment, taking her hand and she pulled her.

Keneira let her little sister lead her for a moment, the sludge still heavy, and the air grew thicker, and warmer for some reason she simply couldn't reconcile. The light illumined the dark until they got to the mouth of a cave, stalagmites, and stalactites formed into a large ravenous mouth, and there seemed to be something fuzzy growing on the stoney teeth. Her heart raced as her sister brought her closer to the cave. She couldn't have a nefarious mind. . .could she? Perish the thought, but onward she went, and the air grew warmer. Walking further into the mouth of the cave; there was a large open space in the center, where it was clear, streams of water. . . in abundance?

With reckless abandon, she darted forward to the water, and her sister followed. The giggles echoed off the walls as they came to the stream. The metal lantern creaked, the light still shining through its glass. At the stream, she knelt down, cupped her hand, and placed it in the cool water, brought it to her lips, and the refreshing liquid poured down her gullet. Exhaling a sigh of refreshment, she looked up, her sister walked through the stream into a clearing, and there was an artifact, of some sort. A brown pole, thicker than a house, and vein-like shapes of itself crawled to the streams where the tips rested, digging themselves into the earth. Large things like those on the ground scraped the roof of the cave, some thick, some thin, all with green oval shaped bracts. Rustling, as they lay above her, and some arms stretched down, hovering over another pedestal. She walked towards it with her sister, hating herself for trusting something like this so easily, but she was drawn to the artifact.

One of these arms stretched forward, branching out even, like little firm hands. The light from the lantern lit up an orb on which it lay, a red orb, with another brown stick at the top of it, and another bract. She took her hand, covered it, brought it to her face, flicking it's firmness. Raising it to her nose, she sniffed it, but nothing caught her attention, and she opened her mouth, took a bite from it. Crunchy, hard, and. . .sweet. Moisture it was inside, the white pale flesh. She took hers to her sister. "Here, try it, it's tasty!" She'd never tasted anything like this before.

Her sister took it in her hands, and immediately, Keneira wanted it back. She didn't know what it was, but it was delicious, more delicious than all the other dried fruit, meat, and various breads she ate every day. Even living underneath the safety net of being the heir of the Countess' seat, there were limitations to what was available. Her sister took her hand, bit into the fruit, a bright blush filled her cheeks, smiling, she chewed the fruit, whatever it was, and walked towards the other side of this cavernous opening, and little flower bed, only, these flowers were vibrant, healthy, not grey or black like those above.

Her sister was enthralled by one such flower and took it in her hands. The pedals were bright yellow, a large red center, a thick green stem. Her sister discarded the fruit, and it rolled towards the stream. She resented giving it to her, but her sister was precious, even if she didn't share the rest of it with her. She'd never taste it again. . .but perhaps, she knew where this was now, she could come back? Yes, it wasn't a complete total waste. A flower, the golden petals, were plucked from the garden, and she came to her sister, reaching up. "It's beautiful," she said, reaching up and tucked it behind her ear. "Like you."

"Well, aren't you the sweetest thing," she fastened the flower behind her ear. "Did you find one acceptable for mother?"

Jera looked at the garden again, plucked a purple flower, and presented it to her. "This one, it was the color of her eyes."

"Yes," Keneira smiled. "That will do just fine."

"For Mummy," her little sister said.

"Yes," Keneira repeated. "For Mummy."

Keneira considered Jera's innocence for a moment. A child. She resembled a child. It only made sense after all, for he was a child. And yet, with the upcoming wedding, a nasty affair, she was forced to take on the role that should be left to adults. Hell, Keneira even knew she wasn't completely considered an adult, but might as well be, with her father's subtle ailing condition. Such big things should be left to adults, or children at least capable of pulling a wagon.

They left the cave, but upon approaching the cemetery, Keneira looked back to where the cave was, the darkness swirled around it. Such a place, where the world was left with lacking, with water in short supply, plants were dying, or lived rather shortened lives, in that cave, it was abundant. She might come back here, to get some water. It wasn't terribly far from their land. She looked up in the sky, in the distance, the faint green hue was beginning to fade. There was something inside that cave, giving nourishment to plants that existed not outside the rest of the known, and bleak world.

"Jera," she knelt down. "We must be quick, it's late. This flame can protect us but only for so much longer."

"Very well," Jera spoke sharply, scurrying towards the grave site, tucked the flower by the stone atop which their mother lay, and she retreated back to her side, ready to go.

Mother, I love you.

Keneira returned Jera to the fief. The land was lit up by torches of burnable metal that doesn't melt no matter how hot it gets, and other miscellaneous materials. Dogs and cats roamed with their owners keeping steady watch. A bonfire, cackling, roasting the smell of a boar. As she walked with Jera, her sister turned to her, and said, "Can I go play?"

"Of course," she smiled. "Just stay within the guard's sight, will you? And stay in the light!" She couldn't risk her thinking she could go into the Abyss without any form of protection. The Abyss, she didn't know all that was in it, except uncharted territory.

"Ken!" A hard, thick voice called out. She swiveled, and beheld a man in his thirties, strong like an ox he was. "Whe'e ye off to?"

"I was going to get change 'fore the—"

"Stop it with that, plenty enough time later," Jorgan spoke harshly, arms crossed over his chest. "Can't let ye a'm rust up now can we?"

"Here? You want me to duel here? Now!" She broke eye contact with her mentor and retreated a hand into her pocket; she didn't want people knowin' her stance was still weak when wielding her sword. A little kick to the thigh would send her tumbling down.

"Just 'round the road," he spoke, and he led her away from all the people to a dueling circle. "You carried yer sword with ye, did ye not?"

"Did ye bothe' ta look?" she said, her hand on the pommel of her blade. She wished she'd the time to set her crossbow down somewhere, it was heavy with the iron stock attached to it. Sturdy thing, that."

"Yes, well, as heir to the Countess' seat, you must be prepared, and disciplined," he said to her as they were well away from everyone's sight. "Didn't want to publicly disgrace ye, now, we best start workin' on that stance."

He was right, even a countess was fated to fight should the occasion call for it, and there was no shortage of callings for occasions with the Eastern nation, the brutish Nezkamas threating discourse on their flank. The men to the south rarely came to their aid, that was to say, never would they come unless they could raid and pillage and rape their women for hazard reward. Griping, she stood, drew her sword, two hands on her hilt. Her back leg bent, ready to pivot, but her front leg, still twisted at the ankle, more than half her body weight leaned on the hind.

"Steady that stance!" he said pointed. "Hold that blade tightly. Tighter! I said!"

"This is my tightest grip, ye bastard!" she swore.

"Ha!" he swung his sword at her. Tilting her body, she parried the blade, but the force of the strike pushed her. "If that is the tightest grip ye can muster, I'd hate to see the sorry fate your house will have. After all, yer the only one who can wield a sword. Poor little Jera is far too young."

"Too young! Poor baby girl," she said, swiveling her feet and she threw her sword at him, attempting to nick his finger, he retracted his strike, and kicked the end of her sword. "Who will ever come for her aid."

"Well," he thrust his sword at her, completely exposed, it grazed her neck. She ducked down, twisted her body, and danced on her feet away from his reach. "Not that you'll have to worry about that much, tradition and all."

"She's too young, Jorgan," she spoke, knowing he referred to the comfortable life behind the protection of the King's men. "Far too young to be given in marriage."

"Yes," he scratched his head, sheathing his sword. She did so in kind. " I think that's enough for today, your stance is improving."

"Thank you," she said, bowing briefly to respect him.

"Not much we can do about tradition," he said. "I agree, but tradition is tradition, what all with the rumors of the King and prince being true. Since none of the other counts offered their own offspring for it, the lack of a king would render our land in chaos. It's almost like they wanted this."

"Why not?" she asked. "My father is the head count—"

"Head count or not, doesn't matter, whatever the king says, he does," he snapped. "Keneira, you must discard your own found morality, you might learn something. There is no right, no wrong, there is just what is. The better you learn this, the sooner you accept it. Accept it, else all will fall into chaos."

"And for you, what is, just is?" she asked. This was a rather short sparing match, did her swordplay partner decide it was time for a good lecturing?

"Just. Just is. Justice," he grunted. "Traditions were set in stone, and they ought not be uprooted like pointless weeds. Keneira, you know, you know too well that my fate is tied to the house. The house survives, so do I. Justice," he growled. "Is just a mere word. There is nothing just in this world in which we live. Get used to it."

"What!" she exclaimed. "But what are our traditions that we s—"

"Your mother believed in our traditions, our customs," he said. She remembered the engraving on her stone tomb. "Who are you to deny them? We don't get to decide what they are. Trust me when I say—"

"No, Jorgan!" she snapped. "What are traditions but man-made constructs!"

"And what are you going to do?" he growled. It was more a statement than a question. One of several in which he had asked in the future, to stop her passion, to force a moment of logic within her. It worked every time. What would she do? Nothing. That's what. She'd see her little sister off, married to that pig pookin' bastard! Removed from their house, inherited the Kingship, while she would be left with the countship of his fief, with her lowborn husband. There was nothing she could do, or else, risk the wrath of the King, face his justice by way of public hanging, and the spectators would dance seeing her body swinging with creaking rope, gasping for breath.

"I don't know," she finally stammered.

"Good," he said. "Then nothing is what you should do," he finally sighed, taking a seat upon a rock. "Young as she is, it would be most unwise to deny the will of the King. The Prince, less than reasonable."

"I understand," she said.

"Good, see to it you do," he replied, standing and proceeded to walk towards one path leading to the butchery. "

The Iron walls echoed with the various footsteps in her ears. Golden hue of flamelight from candles layered across the grand hall. Loud conversations to be had on all corners of the room. Food, there was, aplenty, for the King provided for the feast, and her father, Kira, provided the venue, the servants to which would cook and prepare the food. The music played with leather instruments, strings from horse hair.

Keneira ate from her plate, a turkey leg. A boar was roasted in front of her as she looked from across the hall. Her father and King Crushma spoke to one another, laughing like long friends, but she knew, the purpose of such niceties was always political. The only thing she could understand was the laughter, and to their side, the future betrothed, Lorshma and Jera sitting at the King's right-hand side. The dreadful prince was already intertwining his filthy little fingers in her hair, laughing as his future bride looked away, keeping herself busy, occupied and distracted with the plate of grey lettuce on her plate.

"Try not to think on it too much," Baudet said at her side, reaching in, pecking her on the cheek. He scraped the plate with his eating utensils.

"Dravel, dravel, dravel!" she growled. "Dare I say you don't understand," and why would he? He wasn't high born like her. Perhaps she did in fact marry poorly. No. Objectively speaking, she did, all in the sake of adoreation, for love's sake. Perhaps her decision to throw tradition in the dung heap led to her sister slowly being groomed to mate with whatever that *thing* was. Only a *thing* would dare fuck a pig. "You wouldn't understand. Leave it alone."

"I can't leave it alone," he said, turning to her, brushing a strand of hair behind her ear. "You'll take it out on me later, and for once since this sta'ted, I'd like a good night's sleep."

"When have I ever taken out my problems on you," she said, appreciating the warmth of his hand against her flesh. "I love you. You know that."

"As do I, and I know you love me," his hand touched her chin, tilting her gaze up. "But you do it every day. Perhaps you conveniently forget I'm lowborn, a stable boy, that's all I ever was, but when I caught such infatuation from you, I couldn't help but pursue you." He gulped down the rest of his ale. "Speaking of which, I've horses to feed now. Try not to do anything rash will you?"

She shook her head, kissing him firmly on the lips as he left. The chair moved, and he disappeared behind the plains of people, and in the center of the room, people started to dance. Perhaps when she was countess, she could enjoy a dance with the stable boy, her husband. Lorshmo took her sister's hand and out on the dance floor. Of course, with the promise of tomorrow, Jera couldn't very well deny such a gesture for more reasons than one. He stroke her hair, the one she braided, and who knew if the dirty little bastard at least brushed his hands through some water first before touching her. Gritting her teeth, she took a draught of ale.

"Poor dear, your husband seemed to abandon you before the dance," a voice called, and she turned. A strong red-headed woman looked at her with a lovely dress. "Dare I keep you company? Or will you push me away?"

"By all means, Count Mala," she motioned to the empty seat behind her. "Take your seat, it has since become available."

"I see," Mala elegantly took her seat next to her. "Dreadfully, I must say, a girl as young as yourself should be out dancing. Such a shame he left."

"Well, he is a stableboy," she said. "Father doesn't approve of him."

"No," Mala replied, taking a sip of her ale which, she brought with her. "No doubt. A little strong about the shoulders; you know how to choose the right stock."

"We're not livestock, Mala," she frowned. "Treat my husband with some dignity. He gets enough of that from my father; he doesn't need it from you."

"Sorry to suggest that," Mala apologized. "Milady."

"Nothing to forgive," she permitted herself to smile as she turned her gaze back to her sister, and emotions betrayed her of the disgust she had for the King. She felt her teeth gritting.

"Milady," Mala said, her hand stretching forward, clasping atop hers with an iron grip. "Might I have your ear a moment?"

"Yes, Count Mala," she turned over to her, putting her hand atop Mala's. She had to admit, the countess' grip was tighter than she expected. "What pray tell, reason do you have to infect mine ear with your words?"

"Oh, what's court life without a little friendly gossip," she sneered, bending forward. "You see, I have it quite on good authority, dear, that you do not approve of this marriage."

"No," she replied, turning her gaze from her. "But that's hardly a surprise, I am quite vocal on this matter."

"Except now," Mala replied. "Think not that I wasn't listening to your minute quarrel with your beloved."

"She's too young, Mala," she said. "Too young."

"She's too young, he's not that old, perhaps just a few years older than you," she said, finger to her lips. "Marrying young, especially for such political gain, your father is no fool, is not out of our customs."

"To hell with our customs!" she whispered sharply. "To hell with them all."

"To that," Mala drank. "You and I are in quite the agreement. Such drivel. What those of the lesser stock than you and I understand, is if you understand customs and traditions, you can make them say whatever it is you want them to say. Things change, so do our twists on the old lore goes, to fit our needs. I didn't rise to my station by merely following tradition. Now, look at me, a Count, not a mere countess. When you come into the seat when your father dies, you can make it that your stableboy is the countess, and you the Count."

"And what did you do to make yourself the Count?" Keneira took the ale to her lips, poised to take a sip, and slid her chair closer to the Count. "Surely there was a more complicated solution to your individual disposition."

"I killed him," she answered with a smile as ale slipped down her lips, this seemed to her, not an unusual thing Mala would suggest. Keneira coughed. "The count, that is. After a night of enthusiastic love making, I poisoned his morning ale. It was beautiful."

"The Four Gods," she wiped the ale and spit from her chin with a cloth. "You're bold to admit that before me. What's to say I don't—"

"Hush now," Mala replied, two fingers pressed to her lips. "We could all stand a little more violence."

"Are you suggesting I kill my father?" she whispered. "I'll not—"

"No," Mala cackled. "That would accomplish nothing. You'd become the Count, of course, but it would still be expected to join the two houses, and Jera would still be wedded to the beasty prince tomorrow evening, and then, pair it with a lovely funeral. And where would you be? Count, sure, but alas, the whole point of becoming Count would be nigh useless to you."

Keneira choked, taking a cloth to her face.

"Though," Mala took another drink. "If something were to happen to the King and Prince tomorrow, I might be inclined to ignore it. Let it be known," Mala winked as she stood from her seat. "I'm not suggesting you do anything. After all, accidents do happen."

Keneira yawned as she walked her sister up the iron stairs through their home. It was a large home, some candles, torches, paintings on the walls were lit up in the lateness of the hour. Looking to her sister, she noted the little girl was rubbing her eyes with her dress, a few stains through messy eating. Keneira's, as she walked her sister to her bedroom to tuck her in for the night of such an abomination, mind was infiltrated again by the words, harsh, though they were, and yet, a certain subtlety about Count Mala, who presented her with a solution, though, not explicitly suggested. Accidents happened, and of course, the killing of Mala's own husband was suggestive enough. Despite the abomination, she doubted she could do go through such a solution.

Arriving at the door, she opened it, creaking it did, the iron as it swung on its hinges, brushing over the dust on the floor before violently berating the wall behind it. She led her tuckered sister to her bed, yawning. "I'm not tired," she protested as the door slammed shut behind them.

"Come here," Keneira giggled, taking her hand and led her to the bed. "Come, let's get you changed. You've a big day tomorrow. You'll need to be rested well enough."

"I don't like him," Jera growled. "I don't. Why do I have to?"

"Tradition and politics," Keneira sighed, kneeling down. Brushing with a finger a tear from her sister's eye. Her heart felt heavy with sorrow, the dread plagued her spirit, as it felt like her heart was being ripped apart. One side tried to reconcile these barbaric customs which no one dared challenged for they came from the Four Gods; the other side, her will to see her sister alright, chained forever by the glaring decision, and unwavering will of her father and the King, and that disgusting prince to marry off a child for their own political gain, if even, it meant keeping the lands in relative peace. For better or for worse. What if there was wisdom in this? And the choices of the other counts led to this? Were they to blame?

"But I don't want to; I don't like him, there's just, they will take me from mummy!" she cried. Yes, that was a certainty, for with her, her mother couldn't go, not while her corpse lay in a hole in the ground. "Can you talk to daddy? Make him change his mind?"

"Hey, hey, hey," she stifled a tear, kept it in the lid so her sister couldn't see the turmoil in her own heart, the cruelty of this barbaric world where people, no matter how high a station they held, were subject to be traded like livestock. "Listen, let's get you to bed. We'll talk more tomorrow."

"But Keneira!" her sister protested, too much. "I don't want to do this!" She cried, kneeling down. Keneira embraced the hug, permitting her sister to cry in her arms. "I don't want to. I don't want to. Let's leave." *And where would we go?*

"I don't know what, or how, but I will do what's good for you," she replied. "Whatever that looks like. Now, Jera, off to bed now. You've a busy day tomorrow."

"What will you do?" her sister changed into a night gown and crawled in her bed.

"I don't know," she said. "Hush now, let me think on it." There just wasn't enough time. Tomorrow will be too busy to think.

"Will you hum for me then, to sleep?" Jera asked. "One last time."

"Of course, my dear little princess," *the last time.*

She smiled gravely, and tucked her sister in, stroking her braids. She hummed a tune to her. A made-up tune, for she wasn't musical, but that bothered her sister none. The little ears complained little when something was out of tune and had not yet completely appreciated the talent others had for music, or perhaps, because this tune came from her own voice, her own beat, that it was tolerable. No. That wasn't it at all. It was because it came from her, that despite its musical flaws, she loved it, and thus fell asleep swiftly.

"Sleep well," Keneira whispered, her hand touched her sister's shoulder. Watching her sleep, she didn't dare leave the bed, for she knew not without any level of certainty, if she or her sister would sleep peacefully after tomorrow. This may be the last time she could look at her like this, and so, she could permit herself to abandon her husband in bed tonight, he might not understand, but he'll have to accept his lot in life, whatever the future would look like. Keneira crawled into her sister's bed, and cuddled beside her, arms wrapped around. The warmth was comforting, if, nothing else was in this world. With little hesitation, her eyelids drew themselves closed, and alas, she knew nothing but the solace. As much as she could tell, there was little else she could manage, and knew not how long this peace would last.

Dreadfully, she'd not thought of a lasting solution to her predicament, but gazing at her sister, her beautiful, subtle gown she held, ringlets of gold set upon her hair, pulled back and braided like she too had a crown upon her head already. Worthy was her sister, of the grandest of crowns. But not like this, not like the drivel that would be placed on her this evening, not like the drivel of a man, dung heaped, again, balls deep into one of her father's horses! That disgusting little wretch! *My sister!*

Jera seemed none too happy either, for why would she be? Not only was the wedding going to take place now, as she was walked into a room with which she would come out and walk down the aisle of the Temple of the Four Gods, but also, her sister had simply failed, or, Keneira guessed, thought her sister just simply did nothing for the sake of tradition. When she became Count, she would do away with all of it, consequences be damned, and whoever has to suffer will, as she had despaired.

"But—"

"You will go through with it," Keneira snapped and relented. "I'm sorry. I'm so sorry. There isn't anything I could do!"

"Fine," her sister sighed, looking down, and then, her eyelids fluttered. Onward then, a pathway to misery, resigned to her fate.

The door opened, and Keneira took her sister's hand, walking down out, crossing the threshold into the temple. The chairs were seated, a fire over yonder towards the altar of the Four Gods, humanoids, they all were, save for two, of which were fashioned from the dreaded Nezka race, the purple bastards. Everyone stood as the music played, and her sister took her first steps, walking rhythmically as she could, towards the dreadfully dressed king-to-be. The sniveling bastard wiped his nose with his sleeve, sick, no doubt, probably going to die by way of venereal disease. *You best not touch my sister with your nasty little prick!*

Mala was dressed in a beautiful gown, her ceremonial sword at her hip. A smile on her face as she traded words silently with one of her body guards. Not too far from her, closer towards the altar of the Four Gods, was Jorgan, dressed in a leather cuirass, but designed for ceremony, he was after all, expecting trouble, and so was the case with such royal weddings, one could never be too careful. The king, and her father were towards the center, looking onward. Keneira refused to scowl as other lesser men ogled their eyes at her sister, walking.

At last, the moment which she thought would never come, and she let her sister go, and joined the prince, the two held hands. Keneira no longer could tell the expression her sister had, but she imagined it was none too pleasant, least of all, the prince, eyes gleamed with excitement, orbs watered as they did. The man behind him, she knew not his name, but such a man was merely to be the best friend of the groom, no doubt, would try to turn her husband into a cuckhold, but she'd not have it. No, should the bastard try, he'll have two less fruits.

She stared angrily at the Prince, smiling as he was for a conquest he didn't deserve, was far too distracted to see her glaring at him. The friend however, seemed to finally avert his gaze from hers, and she looked at him like this throughout the entire ceremony, this angry, foul tradition. She would burn this temple to the ground. For the sake of tradition, and soon, ah! The sacrifice to cement the marriage. A boar was walked over here by the farmer which raised it and brought it to the priest who was about the say the sacrificial rites and raised his hand with a knife to slay the boar.

"Father, if I may," Keneira said. Was she really considering this? Her gaze shifted to behind the sanctuary, there was a door here, and it led outside. Did she really have it in her? "I'd like to slay it."

"It is strictly forbidden for those of the flock to offer sacrifices to the Four Gods," the priest turned to her, mouth gaped open like she'd gone mad. But she had in fact gone quite insane.

"Yes," she admitted, a sneer crept upon her lips as the Prince turned to the King. "It isn't exactly illegal now is it? Give me the knife," seeing the priest didn't comply, she turned to her father. "Father, may I slay the boar?"

"Doesn't matter who slays it," the king smiled, superseding the request for aid from her father. "Go on, give her the knife. We're to be one house after all."

"King Crushma," she smiled as she walked towards the priest. "I thank you."

The priest reluctantly handed her the handle of the knife. Gripping it firmly, she bowed to the priest, a smile creeping on her lips. She was going to do it. Her hand pet the boar, which groaned in reply to her touch, and the knife, ceremonial, handle firm within her grasp, caressed the cheek, the cold iron forced it to jerk away, but her hand reached forth, pulling upon its collar. "There, there, it's going to be alright." With uncertainty, she wasn't sure exactly whose nerves she intended to be calming. She took a large breath, the smokey air filled her lungs.

"You bastard!" she turned immediately, stabbing Lorshmo in the face. Retracting her knife, the corpse fell to the floor, not a sound as blood smeared across his face. Before his friend could do anything, she sliced his neck, and with a bloody hand, ignoring all the screams, she took her sister's hand in her own. "We're getting out of here!" But where were they to go?

Her sister squealed at the blood, some sprayed upon her face as she stumbled, jerked away. The priest didn't have enough time to respond, no one did, save for the screaming, confusion of creaking chairs scratching across the floor, and the boar, still growled, for it lived to see another day, or perhaps after tonight, someone would enjoy a bountiful meal. Disappearing behind the altar, Keneira knew she'd be hunted. She needed her sword! A sword. Didn't have to be hers. And so first, despite her husband being caught in the middle of the madness, there, he would remain a stableboy, and it would be like her marriage never happened.

"Lorshmo! My Son!" Crushma cried, running over to his son's fallen corpse. "Get her! Get her immediately. Kill her!"

He pulled up his son from the ground, nearly unrecognizable, wiping the blood from his son's face, his beloved child, his only one, lay dead with a slit into his face, bones cracked underneath that dreadful bitch's knife. Kira, he would pay for this. He will hang! Gritting his teeth, he looked at the count, of which, undoubtedly, wanted this. He put Keneira up to the murder of his son who had done nothing wrong. "Bring me his head!"

"Sire," Kira spoke gently. "It grieves me, truly, it does. I did not tell her to do this."

"And yet you respond as if knowing my thoughts," Crushma spoke.

"It's impossible not to know, my Lord," Kira replied. "Jorgan, go fetch them. Bring Jera back to us alive. If it is impossible, then kill Keneira. She is no daughter of mine."

"Don't you dare, he'll help her escape!" Crushma protested. "Mala!"

He looked at the other Count who could be bothered to show up to this wedding. "Seize him!"

"That won't be necessary," Jorgan replied, hand on his pommel.

"Necessary my arse!" Crushma swore. "Curse this house. Curse all of it. We all know you mentored the girl in sword play. You can't be trusted."

"My loyalty has never been up to question," Jorgan replied. "Trust me when I say it belongs to this house, and this house alone. Kira has already declared that Keneira belongs not to this house anymore. I will kill her and bring back Jera."

"But you cannot bring back my son," Crushma wept. "Go. Someone hang Kira!"

"And then the house will die!" Jorgan said. "He is the Count!"

"I don't think that's necessary," Mala spoke, Crushma watched her whispering something with one of her messengers. "I think we can hold off on any executions for the treasonous bitch. But, Nezkama are coming. They appeared to have broken off the rest of the flank and are making their way here. Seems they really wanted a red wedding," she laughed. "Well, they got one!"

"Fine," Crushma agreed.

There was a ruckus in the crowd of people, still too shocked to move to permit them to process anything other than the two bodies on the floor, murdered in cold blood, but there was one person who was moving outside his own agency. A man trying to escape, and the King's hand raised up. "Seize that man immediately!" Men and women clad in armor immediately seized him, and he was not one for struggling, and was escorted to the king. He recognized the stableboy; this was the man with whom Keneira shared the cup.

"Where will your wife go?" Crushma asked. He turned to the messenger. "See to it word gets out, a king's gold reward will go to the man who brings me her head."

"My Lord," Mala snapped. "You clearly are out of touch with the Count's subjects. They don't want money, it's useless. All that will do is provide reason for others to come and steal from them. Offer them a seat at your table for food; indefinitely."

"No," he said. "Another mouth to feed—"

"Well, you've a Prince no more, so I think you can well afford it," Mala suggested.

Crushma gritted his teeth, this Count wasn't exactly replaceable, and she knew it. A bastard of a combination to have amongst the ranks, someone worth more than their weight in gold and untold riches, and likely, knew their precise worth. Shit circumstances all there was, but he could deal with it later, he always did. But now, to this man. "Answer me!"

Grieved as everyone was, soldiers from among the ranks started to depart by way of orders from their captains, to prepare the way for despair, and the violence which would ensue shortly. Why, why can't he get a minute to grieve? Damn Nezkama bastards!

"No!" Baudet said, that was his name, he remembered. "No."

"A man has his price," Mala said, tilting Keneira's husbands face to her, a gleam in her eye. "What's yours?"

Keneira fled with her sister towards the armory that was much further down. She had not the time to get her own sword, but a practice blade would do, it would fit for her purposes. Running, panting, sweating, her little sister too, hands on her thighs as she bent over, breathing heavily. Thanks to the Four Gods they don't dress up so fabulously as the dastardly women in the South do. Dreadful, she found a sword, tied it to her waist, and just in case, scouring over the weaponry with the smith and foundries unattended, she found a crossbow and some bolts, heavy, still. A good solid one-hundred-fifty pounds.

She took her sister's clammy hands in her own. "We're getting you out of here." *South? Yes, we'll be safe there.* "Look," she said to her. "I know it's hard, but we have to keep running. We'll go down to places they cannot or will not follow."

"Mummy," she whined. Of course, she'd be sad about it, the one such course of her actions, the consequences which would no doubt arise with the risk of futility. What other consequences await her tonight? After all, she did not once think this through. "Mummy!"

"Jera," Keneira put her hand on her sister's shoulders. "You were going to be separated regardless, I wish things could be different. I'm saving you." was she? Or was this something she was trying to convince herself? "I have a friend down in the slums. We can stay with him for a time. Let us go now, we can take a moment, think before they come looking for us."

Exactly how much time had passed? It certainly hadn't been a full day, and yet, a spirit of sleep was coming upon her. She knew she had to be aroused, for she knew not she was going to do what she ultimately did, and let alone, for how much longer she'd have to force herself awake.

"Very well," her sister wiped her tears. "Thank you."

"Thank me not yet," she said. *What else am I going to lose tonight?* By the Four Gods, she did not think this through.

Dreadfully aware was she of the uproar throughout the fief, people scampering about, wheels carting as if there was nothing to see there. Horses roamed, pulling the carts along. Some people rested, stayed inside their own little homes of iron walls, and some candles lit here, some torches there. She needed one, where to find one? No telling really, when she might need to traverse the Abyss, which was almost an inevitable fate, for there was not enough light in the night to go around to traverse the roads. Was she mad?

Coming to the door of Mirkur, her sister tugged on her hand firmly. Keneira sighed, squatting with her free hand touching the door. "Jera, it's alright. I know you don't know him, but he's a good person. We can trust him, if, no one else." Her sister nodded, grunting with the pain in her thigh, no less. She noticed it on the sprint to the armory she forced her to undertake. They had no choice really. Keneira nodded, showing her sister she understood her pain, standing up, she knocked on the iron door.

Footsteps echoed from behind it, a light illumined from the crack underneath the door. At last, it pulled open, a man with a slender face, a weak smile, and above all, rags that smelled with flies buzzing around him. Father, another companion of whom he simply would not approve. His smile was brighter, seeing who it was, and with nervousness besides, his eye seemed to be looking at something past her. "Keneira," he said. "Lovely to see you again, it's been an age, since you've been married I think."

"Aye, Mirkur, I agree, it's been too long," she said. "May we come in; this is my sister."

"Of course," he spoke sharply. "Hurry."

She walked in with her sister, permitted Mirkur to shut the door quietly as to not arouse suspicion from any suspecting pursuers. She led her sister to the table, chairs, and hoisted her up to the stool so she could sit relatively comfortably. She took an intense inhalation and permitted herself a moment to think as Mirkur walked over, sitting across. "What's your name?" he asked.

"It's—it's—" she began to say.

"It's alright," Keneira leaned in close to her sister, their cheeks kissing. "It's alright, you can tell him."

"Juh—Jera," she stammered.

"Lovely name," he smiled. "Trust, based on the attire, you look like you came from a wedding. Yours?"

"A—aye—" she replied.

"Look," Keneira spoke. "I need help. We need your help."

"Well, by the looks of it, you murdered the groom," he pointed at the blood on her sister's face. "Now, I may not be a smart man, but I recognize blood when I see it. Please tell me who it was?"

"You didn't know?"

"Four Gods," he said with gaping eyes. "The Prince. You didn't kill the Prince. Tell me, Keneira! Did you, or did you not kill the Prince?"

She heard scattering footsteps from above the ceiling. "Yes," she admitted. "A foul man, if ever there was one."

"We're all foul," he said with a fading smile. "You need to leave. I thought you'd be in trouble, but I didn't think this. Your being here puts my family at risk. I'd do many things for you, Keneira, but not this. Leave, immediately! I'll speak of your presence to no one. Get out. The back door you can use, now leave before—"

"Keneira!" a voice called from the other side. *Shit.* "We've come for Keneira, come out now. We know she's in there!"

Mirkur stood from the table, walked briskly to the counter, palms slapping the surface. Drawer was pulled out, and a kitchen knife he grabbed. Turning to her, the knife behind his back, he opened his mouth. "Out the back! Now. You brought them here!" Terror seized his face. "You must leave!" He turned to go to the door as she helped her sister from the stool. Fear gripping her, biting a lip until red blood dripped out from her mouth.

"Come," she said, quietly walking towards the back of the house.

"She's not here," Mirkur said. "Get yer own food. I've not enough to spare. You know that."

"I don't want yer food, open the damned door peasant bastard!"

"That's just ru—"

The door swung open, knocking him in the face. Mirkur dropped to the ground, the knife behind his back flew out, spinning on the floor. Keneira looked away as she hurried to the window, footsteps echoing faster behind here. "Keneira! Get over here. Get back here!" She hoisted her sister out the window of the house, and her little body scurried like a rat, looking for cover.

"Hide!" She felt a hand on her shoulders. Before she could vault herself out the window, she was pulled, tripped by her feet onto the ground, slapping it with her back. "Gah!" she grunted; the man jumped atop her. Before she could grab her sword, his hands were clear around her throat, squeezing tightly. Gritting her teeth, unable to breathe, she pushed her fingers into the man's throat, but he was too stubborn.

Mirkur pulled the man up, the knife in his hand, thrust it into the chest. The man grunted as he twisted the blade, pulled it out as blood poured from the ground. Another wound, another pierce, and he pulled out again, until the crimson liquid painted the floor, and he fell to the ground. Mirkur took a bloody hand, helped Keneira up from the ground, and another cry, a peasant, one she didn't know pointed at her. "It's her. She's here."

"Get out!" Mirkur cried. "Now!"

He pushed her; the ledge tripped her out the window, landed on a bed of hay, flies buzzing. The smell of shit in the air, her heart pounded with screams coming from inside the house. She stood, looked briefly, Mirkur was a bloody mess, barely recognizable, and the several men inside were looking for her, shrieking like one bloody K'hara. The bird of the air of the Abyss, a foul thing. She turned, saw her sister whimpering behind an iron box, and she took her hand, and pulled her up immediately.

"Run, Jera, run!" she squealed.

Keneira, her heart felt like it was going to burst through her chest and suffer a heart attack before any blade might pierce her, or weapon of bludgeoning her skull open. Her feet took her to the main pathway, and she heard the cries of those calling for her head coming out from behind. She turned her head again, the blood and markings of Mirkur flashed through her, and sweat beaded through her palms, so she squeezed her sister's hand tighter. Her legs lifted up with strides as several people came running at her with violent dogs, and pitch forks.

She turned her gaze forward, and people poured out onto the streets as if someone relayed information to her treasonous efforts. Word could get out quickly here, for reasons she knew not, but she kept running. A loud cackle, whistling wind there was, pushing through the cracks between the houses, brushing past her hair, she nearly fell over, and several pieces of scattering debris, fecal matter, hay, bits and pieces of stone from the ground.

"Give us the girl! Give her to us," someone called, hurling a pitchfork at her. She pivoted her feet, the fork thrust right past her head, scratching her face. Hissing, she gritted her teeth, gripping her sister firmly, ignoring her screams of terror. Her heart pumped, beating to her ears.

"You won't take her," she swiveled as the crowd of people advanced nearer to her. Bolting away as fast she could, they ran in a straight line forward, getting closer to the road, which of course, she'd have to brave the

Abyss, the one place she wouldn't be followed, least not of which, without a torch. "Stay away from my sister!"

A loud crash there was behind her. Head turning, the buildings were struck, creaking with stones as they struck against the flesh of her pursuers. Knew she did, this was not a blessing as buildings came down, the people inside screamed in agony as their own flesh, bones, and blood littered the earth behind her. Only one thing made in this land could collapse buildings. Catapults. Were they that desperate to come after her? Wait. No. This was far worse as smoldering flames scoured over the land, of all things that could be burned. A loud horn, three blasts it made. Three for war. She didn't have time to remember if it was the Nezka, or the Nezkama that the king managed to piss off recently, but the timing couldn't possibly be any worse!

Horses galloped, clopping their hooves against the stone coming from the right side of her. Hissing, swearing, she was certain had she not gone to the privy before rescuing her sister, she'd have shat her pants ages ago. Her ears rang as she neared the stones leading out of this village, heading further, and further away, towards the Abyss. The soldiers on the horses were clad with armor and lances as they came forward. Snarls and glares to her left side, she saw giant wolves and goats ripping up the terrain with their strides, and the Nezkama, that's who he pissed off, rode upon them, flails, and scythes they wielded.

"Keep running!" she cried. As if to assure herself her little sister would run.

Strides came forth with the shaking of the ground. Cries pierced her ears of battle as the hoards came, encroaching upon them. Wolves howling, horses neighing, iron creaking, metal clashing, and shrieks of pains, whines of wolves followed, and the dying screeches of horses followed. Chest pounding, exhaling, sweat dripping from her, she refused to be separated from Jera, who screeched in terror, a high-pitched scream. She couldn't tell what it was, the sound of battle around her was too fierce, and far too loud.

"Keneira!" A loud cry, and a horseback. A warrior, on a horse with his lance, she didn't recognize. Rearing his horse, he charged at her. She breathed, looking to the ground as the rider hunted her, and a loose cobblestone was what she found. Reaching out, the moving of horses distracted her for but a moment. Lifting up the stone, she hurled it at the horse. The leg of the horse buckled, neighing as the armored rider was flipped off the steed at her feet. Neck cracked, but he was very much alive. She pulled out her sword, stabbed him in the neck, and sheathed it, before she could let the guilt weigh in upon her soul.

Continuing to run, the soldiers were too distracted with one another, and with what she thought amounted to several turns of the hour glass, she finally made it out of the fray, blood soaking her clothes. Turning behind it, a Nezkama came at her, a large creature with a war hammer. Grimacing, she pushed her sister to the side, the beast struck at her. Jumping to the opposite flank, the strike hit the ground. Drawing her sword, she struck at the hands, slicing off his fingers, blood painting the handle crimson. With a deft flick of her wrist, she impaled him in the chest, twisting the blade before ripping it out. All before the purple bastard could scream.

Behind the fallen corpse of the nezkama, she beheld the level of gloom already behind her. Men, women, nezkama, lay on the ground with numerous wounds to their body, many trampled underneath the strides and struggles of the beasts. And both horses and wolves alive littered the ground, and a few pockets of foot soldiers survived, fighting against one another with no hesitancy, and neither side was willing to give an inch.

"Come!"

"I'm scared!" her sister wailed. "And you're, you're hurting me!"

Keneira shook her head and released her grip. "I'm sorry, but we have to go."

"But Keneira!" her sister cried, tears streaming down her face. "My legs."

"Then I'll carry you!" Keneira without hesitation put her hands between her sisters armpits, hoisted her up and started walking away from the scene of battle. "But remember, when we get to the abyss, I must light this lantern."

"Very well," her sister embraced her with the hug.

Keneira and Jera arrived at the road, the flames still lit around from the chaos of missed shot catapults. Oil burned; the scent rancid. Crinkling her nose, she looked around her. Surprisingly, there was no sound, save for the now very distant clanking of metal, clashing battle. A siege like this only ended one way, and that of those who lived here who knew where the food was. The humans of the north would slay the Nezkama and enslave them, they always did, and then, they'd regroup their efforts shortly to find her. If the King was persuasive enough, they'd even dare traverse the Abyss to find them.

"Alright," she said, letting her sister down. She opened the lantern from its top, pulled out some tinder and lit it aflame. "You're on foot now, remember, stay close to me. And if we're ever separated, don't go into the darkness."

"What if there's nowhere else to go?" she asked, one hand tightly enclosed to a fist. She bit it gently.

That was a reality far too likely for her liking. There was little that could be assured in a time like this, with opportunities running amuck for anyone else looking for whatever it was the King promised them for her head. Clicking her tongue as she looked her sister in the eyes, attempting to give her an assuring smile as her soul searched for the right words to speak. There was nothing significant that came to mind, and while the truth was far from reassuring, she chose to tell her. "Then do whatever seems best to you. But don't wander too far into the dark that you can't find the light again. Always look up, whenever you do, and look for the green orbs in the sky."

"They're gone," her sister pointed.

"For now, yes," she said. "But there are lanterns scattered across the road. And when the morning comes, the green lights will guide you back to safety. Do you trust me?"

"Yuh—Yes," her sister hesitated. "More than, anyone else."

Keneira hoped her sister didn't misplace her trust.

They walked through the road. The pathway still lit by the preliminary torch set apart to provide the first sanctuary from the Abyss, the cold black fog of unknown origin. The light from her lantern pushed the darkness away as she approached. The large streams tried to penetrate the light, but to no avail, thank the Four Gods! She hurried with hastened steps, and it was not too long before she and her sister were completely surrounded by the Abyss, the preliminary torch no longer in sight, neither was the next torch in the road, not yet.

Her heart raced, and settled. Just silence, minus the creaking of her lantern which swayed on one side of her, their steps, silently making their way across the road, and the occasional screech. A familiar one she'd heard before, but thankfully, didn't see what made it. The K'hara, great birds flew above the Abyss, while at all hours of all days, they were more active when the green lights faded, like they do. With tremendous fear and trembling, that was one horror that would stay away from the light at all costs. She and her sister arrived at another milestone, where a stone held an iron rod impaled, and upon it, a lantern. An orb of light, one in which would give them a sense of ease as the arms of the Abyss tried to penetrate this barrier, and again, to no success. For now, they were safe.

Or so she thought.

Armor clanked in the distance from the direction from which they came. Clopping hooves, and a flame. Jorgan came at her, riding on a horse with a lance. A light on the horse's side. A scowl wrote itself upon his face. The horse neighed violently as he pushed the beast towards the light, and the darkness tried to claim him, but the light was too strong, even from that measly lantern. Blood was caked against his face, and a limp arm had he. The horse reared into the light; the lance aimed at her.

Her mentor, her protector. That's the role he was to play, his tradition. She gritted her teeth as if felt like someone stabbed her heart, trying to rip it from her chest. He trained her for years in swordplay, taught her the value of tradition, despite how religiously she tried to escape it, but now, here he was abandoning his tradition. No. That wasn't it. His tradition was, and always would be tied to the House, and through Keneira's actions tonight, the House all but fell. Killing her wasn't betrayal, by killing her, he would be fulfilling his tradition.

"Stay in the light!" she cried, pulling her sister away, releasing her grip. *Don't stray too far.*

Jorgan got closer, so too, the spearhead meant to impale her. Drawing her sword, she swept it up, striking the spearhead. The horse ran past her as the tip of the spear flew up, the metal clanking at the strike. The horse ran in the abyss, and the light protected him. Rearing the horse around, the spear soared at her. She leaned backwards, the spear nearly taking off her head. He drew his sword; charged at her. The horses hooves came, clopping, drowning out her sister's screams. Her sword, she clutched with two hands, aiming for the horse. Nearing her, his blade slashed. She ducked. The blade barely missed her. She cried out, twisting her body as she struck the horse's hind legs with all her strength.

The horse neighed, tumbling down. Jorgan was thrust off the back of the horse, rolling off to the side. The blood on his face was certainly his, as he stared at her, getting up before she could attempt to strike back at him. His gaze, stern as it was, looked at her with rage before turning solemn to his steed. His blade in hand, he walked over to the beast, on its side now, and he impaled its head till it knew no more.

"Give Jera over to me, Keneira, and I might let you live," he said, barring his teeth at her, a dark mood must have plagued his spirit. "Stop running."

"No," she nodded curtly. "You can't have her!"

"Then I'll kill you!" he lunged forward, but stopped with the first step, for it limped.

"You'd have not offered me the chance had you think you can take me," she said. "Least of all," she pointed her sword towards him in the dueling position. "Not in your current condition."

"Had you still the stance ye had yesterday, it matters little," he frowned at her, his sword raised in response. "We're here because of your actions, Keneira, you are the best student I've ever had. This makes it all the more harder."

"You can, not, do it," Keneira said, brows furrowed. "You can live. Just abandon your tradition, and then it's over, and we can leave."

The night was short, and the road long. She wanted it to be over, but the more she tarried here, the more time people would have to organize and hunt her, should the battles be over. She hoped earnestly, that there was something inside her teacher that would permit him to throw caution in the wind like she had, but actions had consequences. In an ideal world, she never would have asked this of herself, nor asked him to abandon the values he held above everything else. But this world was far from ideal, and no amount of cruelty with the grim pits of despair and ceaseless violence and starvation could or would change that.

"You don't get to decide when it's over," he said. "You don't get to uproot tradition. You don't get to change the will of the King!" sharp was his words before releasing a sigh from his lips. "I gave you an out, just walk through the Abyss, leave your sister to me, and then it will be over. Just leave!"

"You know I can't do that," now she felt herself frowning.

"Then this will be the last fight one of us will know,"

"So be it,"

Keneira clashed with him. Sword against sword, her shoes and his boots in the mud and blood of the horse, spraying, slipping. His strong strikes were significantly weaker than she was used to, caught in the fray of battle, clearly he was wounded by a nasty Nezkama. However, all this to suggest that he was still admirable, pivoting against strikes he normally would have taken. A slash struck towards her, unarmored, she parried it with the pommel, twisting her body, pushing him aside. His free hand twisted into a fist, punching her square in the face. Grunting, she was pushed back on her feet. The dirty trick!

He swung his blade. She bent backwards, the steel nearly nicking her nose, stepping further from him. Dancing, she returned to her feet again, her stance, firm as she could manage. He thrust one at her again, and she twisted herself to permit the thrust to past her. She struck his wrist with his pommel, hard. The blade came free. She swiveled the blade to his throat, but he pivoted before she could kill him, a braced moved upwards, parrying the strike. His blade clamored into the Abyss, and he charged at her, tackling her to the ground.

"Keneira!" her sister cried. "Jorgan, stop this, please."

"No!" was his response. "These are the damned consequences!"

Keneira felt a strike to her face, the back of her head hitting the ground. Grunting, her hand stretched to his waist, pulled out the dagger he kept tucked away in his sheath. Impaling him in his under armor, twisting the blade. He grunted, grimacing, she pushed him off, rolled atop him. Ripped the blade out as blood poured out the wound. The mentor, she looked him in the eye, a man well respected for his prowess in battle; terror wrote itself upon his face as he was bested, and the knife impaled his neck, his screams silent in the light.

Panting, her mentor was dead, and she leaned back, the blade struck the ground. Blood pooled, ad already, she started to feel it wet her buttocks as she sat in the mess. Her hands shaking, she stared down, and felt a presence behind her. "Keneira," her sister's high-pitched voice brought her to. Her right hand immediately grabbed hold of her sister's arm. *All for you. I do this all for you.* Her teeth gritted once more, and she took the knife, hurled it into the Abyss, screaming. Just a little peace, that's all she wanted now. But there was now only but one choice, standing, ignoring her sister's plea for her to address her, she stood.

"Ha," she grunted, a sharp pain hit through her abdomen. Limping, she reached for her sword, and put it to her waist, and that of Jorgan's, strapped to her other side. "Come, Jera, we must get going. She moved and turned, grabbing hold of the lantern, and looked towards the direction leading South, away from the Kingdom she knew, and she walked towards it. A free hand with her touched her sister's hand, and she was pulled close to her side. Someone was bound to hear the screams of their battle, there was no time to waste contemplating the consequences of her actions. Oh, Lords, why did she not think this through?

"Very well," Jera spoke, her hair tucked behind her ears. Respectable, she would make someone happy, but not that bastard prince.

"We keep walking, until we're far away from this place, and we can rest," she said. "Then, we'll show you the whole world!"

What kind of promise was that? This world was dark, plant life existed rarely, and that tree, that fruit from yesterday was the most lively thing she'd ever come across in ages. The flowers died, the vegetables died, and those that were deemed unfit for human consumption were tossed to the animals. Breathing heavily, another pain shot up, her gaze looked downward. Some dust upon a cobblestone, shaking. Her eyes gaped open in terror, looking upwards, and the Abyss still remained disturbed, save for a few lights, moving along the dark, traversing it with lanterns. Scores of footsteps, marching towards her, from the one direction she intended going. Her way had been cut off. She could traverse the Abyss, but in the pain she was in, she doubted she could very well outrun a beast, outrun the corruption inside it, and the K'hara especially, still screeching. Seeing the world was the only silver lining in this Hell.

What if she was to kill King Crushma? Tradition would come crumbling down with him. There would be no power, and the counts would struggle, fighting one another for the next several years for the King's crown. A fight from the Nezkama soldiers that plagued them now, perhaps it might not be considered the best course of action, and then the humans of the north would end up enslaved to the Nezkama. But she was also uncertain, if it was nezkama troops that were in front of her or the king's men. She let out a sigh, there was no good option here. Just the best worst option. But she must still keep her sister close. Or else all her efforts would be rendered meaningless.

"Hey," she said, kneeling down. "We're going to go back."

"Why?" her sister whined. "I don't want to go back to awful men."

"Our way is blocked," she said, pointing to the Abyss with the faint orange hue of moving flames. "See there? We cannot survive the Abyss for long, so we must go back. I will not let him have you. You hear me, Jera? I will not let anyone take you."

"I understand," she said.

Keneira took her hand and turned. As they passed Jorgan's body, her sister said, "I really liked him."

"I—I know," she stammered. "I did too. There's not much we can do now, just head forward."

The fief was overturned. Flames still scoured, and volunteers were pulling the dead off the streets, dragging them into larger pits, before setting them aflame. Corpses of animals were cut up to pieces for manageable chunks, discarded into wheel barrels, horses and wolves, arms, legs, heads, ribs, thighs, all cut up to pieces, and the blood coated the land. There would be no time to recover, and the fighting all but ceased, and the sound of the marching band behind them seemed all but insignificant now, but it was still on its way, and in Keneira and Jera's way from escaping. And without resorting to drastic measures.

Her sister whimpered, again, of course, why wouldn't she? Animals, things of the like she loved, and things, of which she herself took for granted. Life was short and worthless in this world, bleak, despairing. What was the point of any of it? No. She mustn't think like that, not for her sister. She turned to her, knelt down, clasped her hands over hers. "I need you to be quiet," she whispered. "We're going further in, and we can put an end to them hunting after us. I will kill that bastard King!" her teeth gritted. "And maybe we can save our house, and not have to leave. Unless we do just that, they will never stop hunting us. I need to get closer but—"

"You'll die," her sister said. "Everyone will."

"Not today," she assured her sister, she knelt down, held her sister's shoulders within her palms tightly "If I can kill Jorgan, I can kill him. I need you to be close, I can't have you getting too far from me. Stop whimpering, stop grieving, there will be a time for it, just not now. You hear me, Jera?"

"Very well," she said, and put her free hand over her mouth.

"Good girl," she whispered to her.

She led her sister through the fief, well, what was left of it. Disappearing behind shattered remains of buildings, stands, people, carcasses, boxes, and various debris. Weapons and shields broken, wrenched into pieces of steel and iron more hazardous to use, than to their intended target. Even the arrows were bent out of shape. Moving further, she heard the distant scream, another battle horn, and the soldiers of the North went back to war, the Nezkama prepared another offensive, another wave, but fortunately, most had completely forgotten there was a prize for her head. Amazing what one forgets when violence is at the front door.

They crept through the fief, and there was a steady line of steel bars, and rope. Looking upwards, creaking, swaying in the wind were several bodies. Blood covered their face, but she recognized them. Her hand turned, holding her sister close so she wouldn't see her father hang there, dead. He was swaying back and forth, creaking, likely croaked, hopefully with the snap, and he didn't have to struggle till the air he breathed was finally snuffed out. And here she was, she and her sister, the last line of their house. There was no two ways about it, this was her doing, and her fault, just to save her sister. Was it worth it? Gritting her teeth, in one fell swoop, her sister had been exposed to the gritty pits that is violence that could only be produced by people.

"Cover your eyes," she said. "I don't want you to see this."

"See what?" she said.

"Trust me," she assured her again. "You do. Not. Want to see this."

She watched as her sister closed her eyes, shutting those lids. Leaning forward, she pulled her sister close to her, and her chest puffed with tears. Swelling, she came to the realization that unless she replaced the King, her house had indeed fallen to decay. No Lord there was, over her fief, and the King now lay claim to it, for however long he chose to keep it. Her heart was breaking inside, but she mustn't concern Jera with it. This would be her problem, yet, there was no running from the fact that this was a problem of her own making, and entirely her fault.

She hoisted her sister and walked her up the path leading towards the temple, but off the beaten path so they wouldn't be seen, the guards and soldiers rushing about to get to the front lines to kill the Nezkama invaders, once and for all. Refreshed as the Nezkama might be, the Northern humans were built of tough iron. They knew pain, and knew how to suffer, a virtue which the dirty little devils simply knew not. She found a small barn, some hay, and she put her sister atop it, hidden within these creaking walls.

"Stay here," she said. Her sister need not follow her. It would be needlessly distracting.

"Don't leave!" her sister pleaded, clutching tightly to her forearm. "I don't want to be alone."

"You won't be alone," she pointed at the chickens. *Stay safe!* "I'll be back. Like I said, Jera, I will not let them have you." She lost too much already. For her. She won't lose her too. "Remember, be quiet, don't let anyone see you until I come get you."

"But what if you don't come back?" her sister pleaded. She'd now seen death enough to know.

"I will come back, I won't die, you'll see. Just stay here," she replied, turning before she could see her sister's eyes glaze over.

The temple of the Four Gods was close. Reigning supreme with their superfluous ideals imposed upon people who would never know them personally, people who had no business following traditions. The temple, outside it, a bonfire. Mournful music played, still, instruments, her father's musicians, see, they spared them, but not that of the house. Of *her* house. This was the price. She crept up and beheld the king in the center of the circle by the bonfire, mourning, a bed of hay and iron rods, and on it lay his son, on fire, cremating and the ashes of his corpse rising to the Abyss above them.

Gritting her teeth, Keneira's hand rested on the pommel of her sword, and she'd kill the king, right here in front of all these instruments. If her house was to truly die tonight, so too will the kingdom come crumbling down with the man who cursed her existence and forced her father to agree to a child marriage, just to satisfy his sick bastard of a son's debauchery! What else was she supposed to do now? There were simply no good options for her to choose from. There never was, perhaps, in the thick of it, it was all meaningless. Was it too late? No. She'd never turn her back on Jera. Well, best do this now and get it over with.

"Crushma!" She darted out from the shadows, charging at the king.

He turned, a grievous line written upon his face, and a lone hand rested on his pommel. Armed to the teeth, and armored heavily with chain mail, and leather patches, he twisted his stance to face her. Eyes red with tears and swollen. The sad face turned ire, grimacing as he pulled his sword up, and he parried it with ease, kicking her a few steps away, and slashed at her. She parried the strike, pushing her further away; she realized the strike he made was merely to put her far away from him, and nothing else.

"Keneira," he spoke solemnly, gritting his teeth as she swung back at him. Pivoting his feet, a swift tilt to his back ensured he'd not get wounded. "You kill a man's son, and as he's grieving, and you seek to take his life. Why would you do this?"

"You know very well why," she gritted her teeth. "And I walked past my husband and father hanging! That only proves my resolve was correct," who was she trying to convince, exactly? "You tried to marry my sister into your family."

"It was your father's choice!" he snapped, wincing eyes and tears escaped, dripping down his cheek. She gasped. Could it be true? "I sent out the word to all the counts, those with eligible daughters for my son, and so too, did he make his choice. Yes, yes, my son has unique disgusting tastes, I know that, but I'd never force a count to decide. They had options."

"I don't believe you," she said.

"Then trust me when I say, your father was the only one willing to submit his daughter to this, to submit your sister!" he pointed. "Who's the real devil here? My son? The filthy swine? I can't help that. Me, for providing him options? You who killed my son? Or your father who offered Jera so willingly? It seems that our fates are more intwined than you might think."

"We're not," she snapped. "We're not. I'll kill you for what you did to my House!"

"What I did?" he scoffed. "You're a literal child! If you had not killed my son, they would still be alive. You'd still be heir to the count's seat. Your treasonous attempt to subvert your father's decision led to that, not me. Your house and mine were tied. Success and failure depended on the other. If the marriage went off, the union would make things more stable, and the line of kings would continue. Now, there is no line to continue, and when I die, we'll be thrust into chaos! Is that what you want?"

"No," she replied. "I just want to kill you."

"Stupid girl!"

Keneira grimaced and charged at him. Their swords clashed, the metal clang. Pivoting forward, her stance remained steady, after all, Jorgan, trained her, but he was not the best teacher in the land, the best was always reserved for the King. She pivoted, tired, as her legs proved to be true, and the King, older in years, was still nimble, dancing back and forth, pulling his blade to try to feint her. They nicked each other's sides multiples times but drew no substantial blood. Grimacing, Keneira knew what might await her should she lose, fail and Jera's life too, was forfeit. Lost her house, lost her husband, her father, and now, her life, and perhaps her sister too. She couldn't lose *everything!*

He kicked her. She twisted her blade at him when she was pushed back, pivoting, her ankle tripped, and sprained. "Gah!" she cried on the way down. Her hand swept up as the King walked over to her, kicking the sword from her hand, clattering against the ground, it slid, and the King's blade touched her cheek. Crushma, panting, sweat profusely dripping from his forehead. She wanted to push herself up, but his iron boot pushed against her chest, pinning her to the ground.

"Enough of this," he panted. "There is but one way out of this now, where is your sister."

"No," she grunted. "I'll not—" His foot lifted and pushed against her abdomen. The weight forced her to spit as her body responded to the pain inside her. "Gah! I'll not tell."

"Where is your damn sister!" he said. "I'll not ask again. This is the only way."

"No!" she said.

"Don't you understand, I am trying to save both our houses!" he hissed. "If I adopt her as my own, I can marry her off to someone that will gladly take her. Now, where is your sister!"

"Keneira!" Jera's voice cried.

She turned to where the voice came from. Her sister was there, right in front of Count Mala, whose hands firmly grabbed hold of her sister's shoulders. A sneer was upon her face. How did she find her? Raspy breaths escaped Keneira's lips, still in pain, and her heart thumped hard through her chest. She wanted to vomit. The king looked up, the blade still scratching her cheek with the point, warm blood dripped down.

"Well, I don't really need you now," he said, raising the sword up for an executioner's blow.

"Crushma," Mala opened her mouth. Keneira turned her head from the blade to her sister. Frightened was she, and deservingly so. There was no telling what Mala would do, not with a hostage as now valuable to the King than anything else. Was she trying to help? She was so kind to her last night, if, a little unsettling. "I," she took something out from her side; Keneira couldn't rightly tell what it was. "Had other plans."

Mala took the item, deftly brought it upon her sister's throat, red blood poured down. Coughing, her sister did, and as the blood rolled down the neck into her dress, Keneira cried, "No!" her sister collapsed to the ground. The king swore, as Mala laughed. Her sister, the blood was on her hand. The foot of the King released from her grip, and she sprinted to her sister, crying, tears rolled down her face as she tried to stop the bleeding but alas, the eyes already faded, and the life seeped from her body. Her soul had departed this disgusting world. Jera's life, and her happiness and joy, the innocence behind those eyes was the reason Keneira did anything tonight. Now she was dead.

"You don't get to decide—"

"Keneira killed the Prince, an act of treason, and yet you failed to enact your own justice!" Mala replied. "You're not fit to wear the crown."

"It was for the good of the kingdom," he sprinted at her with a drawn blade.

Mala deftly disarmed the King with her dagger, thrusting it in his throat, twisting, his sword clattered to the ground, lifeless, as soon he was. The Count turned to her, and she had nothing to defend herself with. What did it matter. In a single night, her attempt to save her sister from a rotten marriage only got her killed, and so too, the line of the King, and their house was destroyed. Pitted against her mentor, she killed him; her husband, her father, executed, and so too now, her sister slayed right before her eyes.

"Keneira, dear," Mala said, sly was that smile on her face. "Why, oh why did you have to go and kill the King?"

Keneira felt a rock strike her in the face.

Keneira groaned. Waking up, she found herself tied, ropes and all, to the bottom of an iron slab. Holes within it, being tied to four horses. A pain seared through her face; a tongue moved around her mouth. The cheek was swollen from the rock, and the air, and light as she moved, seemed thinner. How long was she out? Where was she? No one around her at all, simply put, she was just where she was. Where was—a vision flashed before her, her sister.

"Jera!" she cried. Seeing her death, a second time wasn't any easier. She lost everything. *I don't want to be alone.* Alone was exactly what she would become.

"You're awake," Mala's voice rang clear through the air. Her dress was beautiful, but for such a person it was ill suited. "Nice to see you again. You ready for another grand adventure? One of which you—"

"Damn you, you bitch!" she screeched. "Damn you. I'll kill you!"

"By the Four Gods," Mala gasped. "Here I am doing you a favor."

"After killing my sister, your favor can go throw itself over the wall!" she kicked against the slab to no avail.

"You killed the king," she said. "And plunged the north to chaos."

"You did that you treasonous bitch!"

"Well, you killed the Prince," Keneira gasped with the accusation. "Since you've been gone, the North quelled the invasion of the Nezkama. We're whole yet again. We will have a summit as to who will replace him, and likely get into more petty squabbles. Not that I mind of course," Mala sneered. "Your house, the King's house, are now combined into one, and whoever is crowned king or queen, I hope yours truly quite personally, will inherit that. Why, we're practically sisters, now aren't we? Well, you being alive complicates things, for if you were found alive, you'd be crowned, but so many people would ask for your head, you'd barely last a week," she clicked her tongue. "So that you're not surprised, I'm going to tell you what I'm going to do with you. I'm taking you to the south, selling ye to a brothel. Got a nice fancy reward down there for those who used to own land, which, you very much qualify," she cackled. "You're out of my way, and you get to live. This is a wonderful exchange, if you ask me."

Keneira gritted her teeth, eyes narrowed so she could stare her hatred into Mala's eyes. She hated this count, and soon, perhaps, this queen. She was involved with one royalty assassination, which got botched up so bad it cost her everything. Literally everything, and now, she was to be downgraded to the common whore, used for some miller's breeding sow, no, there would be no breeding into her womb. Not one bit. She would bite their cocks off before they touched her!

"I will buy my freedom, Mala," she gritted her teeth. "And when I do, I'm going to raise your land to the ground."

"Well, suit yourself, and good luck!" Mala walked past her, all the while cackling at her misfortune.

Letters from the Front

By Ali Jon Smith

Ali Jon Smith is an archaeologist from the misty fens of eastern England. Academically, he specialised in the Bronze Age because "there's less you have to know about people before they invented writing." Somewhat ironically, he now likes to relax by reading ancient works of literature, especially classical Greek texts and about the voyages of early explorers. When not digging up skeletons or contemplating the wine dark sea, Ali Jon runs games of D&D and sculpts miniatures.

###Target: For Xersus – ◇1 Senior Propaganda Officer ###
  ###Access verified, proceeding###
  ###Author: Hashnus Foe – ◇◇◇Propaganda Officer###
  ###Subject: Gellmar assignment###
  ###Message:

Dear Xerxus,

I must thank you dearly for recommending me for this assignment. I never hoped I would see my home world of Gellmar again, and certainly not at the forefront of its liberation! Already I have had a stroke of luck. Upon the command carrier where a large number of the invasion troops were stationed, I happened to pass his lordship Varloth Chlorinus and snapped a few stills! He is such an intense man; why he fixed me with a glare that made me think he was about to order my execution. I positively quailed! Fortunately, he was merely concentrating on what must have been higher matters before boarding one of the dropships.

I have attached the stills in case you have use of them, though I fear they convey more of the psychopath than benevolent general. It is such a blessing to have this legend who has crushed worlds and made alien empires cow, take personal charge of my home world's rescue. I suppose, sometimes it takes a psychopath to win a war.

I know this assignment will only be a ten minute piece to show off the Durgan troops to my fellow Gellmar natives, but I have high hopes that after the end of the war it can form part of a more complete historic record. This counter-invasion will be the biggest event in Gellmar's history since the initial founding. Therefore, allow me to include material with these messages that may not make the final cut of my current assignment.

My initial encounter with the Durgan troops was awaiting the drop ships on the command carrier. They were neatly arrayed in ranks and being ordered about by naval personnel. They did not strike me as being as quite as disciplined my native Gellmar troops; they did not stand to attention well and their brown and grey uniforms had been adulterated with little charms and trophies, so there was a whole sense of disunity to the scene.

I have a strong suspicion that is the last time I will see them in well-ordered mass ranks. But in truth I do not know what to expect once Electron Disruption Pulses start firing. I have never seen men fight in EDP, when something as basic as a bullet's cordite propellent is rendered useless. What does a war fought with spears and flamethrowers look like? I just hope I can find enough gaps in the pulses to get some good shots with my vid-corder.

Please find my first images attached. I will update you as often as possible, but I do not know how reliable communications will be during the war. Hopefully they will at least reach you in the right order!

[*Images Attached*]

Yours respectfully,

Hashnus Foe###

****

###Target: For Xersus – ◇1 Senior Propaganda Officer ###
　　###Access verified, proceeding###
　　###Author: Hashnus Foe – ◇◇◇Propaganda Officer###
　　###Subject: Gellmar assignment###
　　###Message:

Gah! Bitter disappointment! I had to wait two days to join the landing troops. It meant I missed Varloth Chlorinus's welcoming ceremony and will be behind the frontline for some time until I can catch up with his vanguard.

Once we hit the ground in the dropships, the Durgan men spilled out and started to do everything conceivable to get away from the navy's rigour. They hollered and whooped and bounded around the muster yard, like school children in camo-fatigues. Some men even started to piss against the vessel's sides. At least one fight broke out when two men with a grudge found each other in the chaos. The officers seemed to let it reach its conclusion before stepping in. I did not film these scenes. One can hardly blame the Durgans for the respite they took. I spoke with one of them and discovered they had been cooped up in orbit for months. It was not until now that Varloth had felt confident of launching a mass drop without Scythrial counter-batteries ripping through the landers.

They seem a crude, but likeable people. The ones I spoke to had few pretentions. They know they are here to kill aliens, and whilst that is at hand, nothing else really matters to them. Apparently, apart from some high-level officers, they are all conscripts, so they are not keen about fighting for another people's world. But that is understandable. I weigh that the greater measure is the pride they have that troops from their world were personally requested by Lord Varloth, and if they resent fighting away from home, they are doubly keen to prove their worth to the rest of the empire.

There is another propaganda officer here. His name is Karl Riftus, a Mossian. You taught him as well, but he assures me you will not remember him. He was quite the 'grey blur' at the college. He was never due to come here, but his ship was commandeered for transport of the Durgan troops. He writes poetry in Syndicate Standard, so he should not infringe on my work – you know how much I despise that rigid and inexpressive art form. I never did understand what niche of people find Syndicate Standard more stimulating than their own language. Insipid bureaucrats, probably.

Together we met the welcome delegation. It was all very formal, though a little small. The usual chorus that greets off-worlders was reduced from forty sopranos to four amateur warblers. I think, given the situation of total war, we were lucky to be shown even that courtesy. The head of the welcome committee was a young Militia lieutenant called Cama Beese.

Mercy! I have never known the Militia to be good at finding the right person for the right job, but someone was doing it perfectly when they threw her in front of two Propaganda Officers! She is the only woman I've met who can make the one-size-fits-no-one fatigues look good. I melted just a little as she kissed me on each cheek then planted those bee-stung lips on mine. I shall make sure she is in a few shots – every woman will want to sign-up to be her and every man sign-up to prove themselves to her.

After me, she moved on to Karl and – well you know what prudes Mossian's are? – he went bolt stiff as she touched him.

"Officer Riftus, if you stand to attention any harder you shall break a bone!" she said, almost managing to conceal a smile.

He overcame his chronic rigour just enough to whisper, "Umm...are you a courtesan?"

Cama and I creased with laughter.

"No, Officer Riftus! I am the Militia's adjunct! I will be chaperoning you two to the frontline."

"Karl, this is a Gellmar tradition! The 'kiss of peace,' a happy welcome to all outsiders who come to this world bearing aid."

"Humph, on Mossia we only kiss our spouses."

"It must be a very boring world," said Cama with a shrug. "I hope you're not quite so boring, Karl because I intend to find you something interesting for your vid-corders."

"I am a literary Propaganda Officer, I write," said Karl.

"Oh, how terribly sad, you have my condolences."

She span and started leading us away before he could respond.

"Uh, Lieutenant Beese! Have we missed Lord Varloth's greeting?" I asked, chasing after her.

"Unfortunately, that was yesterday – you're late. *Fortunately*, I was on the welcoming committee for him too, so I had one of the choristers snap some stills while I gave him the kiss of peace." She smiled to herself at the memory, "What a perk that was! Not often one gets to press flesh with one of the Empire's heroes!"

She handed me a poorly rendered picture of her straining on tiptoes to touch Lord Varloth's lips while he remained impassive. What a waste! Nothing speaks so much of the authorities being on top of the situation like a well-framed pompous ceremony. I would have had her looking up at him adoringly, as he gazed off with paternal pride at the horizon and the Empire's future.

All I got from today was some good footage of the dropships landing and disgorging thousands of Durgan troops. I suppose they will be landing like that for weeks yet.

[*Images Attached*]

Yours respectfully,

Hashnus Foe###

****

###Target: For Xersus – ◇1 Senior Propaganda Officer ###

   ###Access verified, proceeding###

   ###Author: Janus – ◇◇Scribe /// on behalf of Hashnus Foe – ◇◇◇Propaganda Officer###

   ###Subject: Gellmar assignment###

   ###Message:

Dear Xersus,

I am forced to write this report by hand. We are now well within the EDP zone and the data slates are all but useless. I have employed a courier to transport this back to the rear area and transcribe it for transmission. Therefore, I apologise for any creeping errors.

Lieutenant Beese is both wonderfully charming and utterly frustrating. I barraged her with questions as we were driven towards the battlefield.

"Will Lord Varloth be commanding from the frontline, like he did at Blanus Prime?" I asked.

"I can't comment on that," she said with a smile.

"How long is the counter-invasion likely to take?"

"I can't comment on that," she said, her smile not fracturing.

"Which city will be the first to be liberated?"

"Ah! I do have a formal answer about that from Militia HQ!" She took a piece of paper from her pocket, unfolded it and read aloud "I – Can't – Comment – On – what's that word, oh yes! – That!"

Karl tittered with laughter as I frowned.

"But you *know* that last one, don't you? You're directing the driver where to go well enough."

She raised an eyebrow and whistled, "my secrets are undone! You really are smarter than your face lets on. A promotion to the Provosts is no doubt coming your way, Hashnus Foe."

"Is there anything you can tell me? You are *supposed* to be our adjunct to Militia intelligence."

"I can't comment on tha...no I'm larking now! I can tell you this – the powers that be would like you to know there are eight-million Durgans joining the fight. You can put that in your vid-cast."

"Eight-million!" I exclaimed.

"Is that a lot?" asked Karl. "I lose myself when so many zeroes are involved."

"It is, Karl. This is a young colony world, we don't have more than twenty-million people in arms on the whole planet."

Our progression is painfully slow. Our old EDP-compatible truck is akin to a rusty cart and we keep having to clear off the roads for the Durgans in their faster trucks. There is nothing like enough transport for everyone. Long columns of Durgans are also making the journey on foot.

Nevertheless, the Durgans have not been slow in getting to work. Only a day's travel from the drop site and we started to find dead Scythrial. I have never seen a Scythrial before. At least not in person. The variety in shape is remarkable: Some of them have four limbs, some six. Some are a bit smaller than a human, some twice the size. Their beaks are sometimes avian and sometimes like serrated bolt cutters. They all have a sandy-orange skin complexion, but in some it is soft and smooth like that of a mushroom cap and others, particularly the larger ones, knobbly and rough like tree bark. Forgive my expressions, I realise you may never have experienced these objects, but they will be familiar to everyone on Gellmar. Karl Riftus struggles to find appropriate metaphors within the realm of his experience. I think the strangest thing is that I assumed they would be somehow humanoid, like a perverted version of ourselves. It is true they have a head with a mouth and two eyes, and limbs that end in digits, but they seem closer to invertebrates. The limbs are a good two metres long even in the smallest examples, and the 'digits' are three opposing claws, not our delicate fingers. In the absence of any stills, here is a sketch I made whilst we stopped for our evening meal (I praise you for insisting I learn the skills of an artist):

[Transcriber's note: Most respectful apologies sir, the manuscript became blotted with a small quantity of motor oil during transit and the pictured was obscured beyond recovery.]

Karl is full of poetry at the moment. He sees a strange kind of beauty in the bodies of the dead aliens. He asked me to listen to some of his verses with a critic's ear, but I declined. Declined, and banned him from reciting them out aloud for his own amusement. Lieutenant Beese took sympathy and asked to hear some. After a painful number of 'you-must-understand-it-isn't-quite-finished-yet-s' and 'this-is-only-the-first-draft-s,' among other equivocations, he finally began. Cama could not do anything but nod her head and smile. She knows just enough Syndicate Standard to do her job chaperoning foreigners around, but never had the education in literature that would equip to appreciate the style. She barely understood two lines of it. She was a little politer than me about it, but blunt enough to say she would not be volunteering for the experience again. Karl was a definitely upset, but I like to think we are doing him a favour. Whoever heard of a happy poet?

As much as I complain about Cama's obfuscations, her witty company has been a blessing for me. The problem is, that among the dead Scythrial, there are also dead humans, and I think more of the latter. I am not used to seeing the dead of my own kind – certainly not men razored in two by genetically engineered claws. Cama notices when I am disquieted and hits me with a wry joke as if this were all just a college field trip. When she tells me the stories of her brothers' and father's hijinks in the Militia, I cannot help but laugh through the dreadfulness of war. Her eldest brother is [Transcriber's note: The next eight lines are also obscured by motor oil]

in   as   much   pipeline

grotesque   walking

with   burst forth

complete glutton   timely   but

vacuous

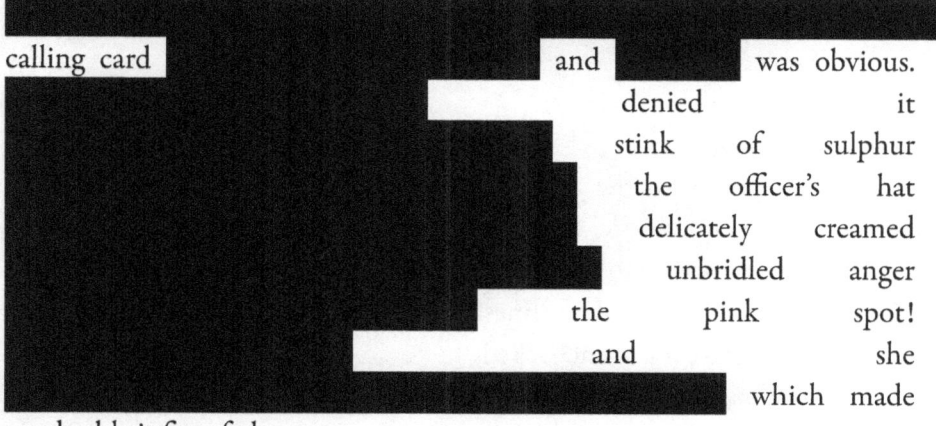

calling card   and   was obvious.
                              denied   it
                              stink   of   sulphur
                              the   officer's   hat
                              delicately   creamed
                              unbridled   anger
                    the   pink   spot!
                    and   she
                              which   made
me double it fits of glee.

Alas, as much as Cama keeps me from dwelling, my job forces me back to the scenes all around me. Most of the dead are Durgan soldiers, but there are a few Gellmar civilians as well. Even worse, the injured lie or hobble beside the sides of the road, begging for transport, food and water. I can only assume that the battle is pushing forwards with such speed that provision cannot be made for those invilided out. We cannot stop for them, there are simply too many to help. Some of the Gellmar civilians do not beg, but instead try to avoid our sight and scramble from the road before us. I can only imagine what terrors they had to endure under Scythrial occupation. Surely it must have taken the greatest courage just to leave their hiding places? Settlements are sparse here, but all of them have been looted and vandalized. The Scythrial may be scorching the earth as they retreat.

Soon enough we should be nearing the battle lines. No army can maintain the pace the Durgans have achieved for long. When we get there, the real reporting begins.

Yours respectfully,

Hashnus Foe###

****

###Target: For Xersus – ◇1 Senior Propaganda Officer ###

###Access verified, proceeding###
###Author: Hashnus Foe – ◇◇◇Propaganda Officer###
###Subject: Gellmar assignment###
###Message:

Dear Xersus,

We have been on the road for a few days now and just reached the aftermath of a large battle. In a grand stroke of luck, the EDP was lowered shortly after our arrival so the Durgan troops could use scanners to check for Scythrial stragglers behind our lines. The Scythrial seem to excel at this kind of guerrilla warfare if left unchecked.

We now have an escort. Not far from the front, we were waylaid by a unit of Durgan soldiers with black armbands. They were armed with sword breakers (these look a little like crowbars) rather than the crossbows and spears most troops have. The lieutenant in charge of them was a stocky man with thick scars on his face and deeper wind-blasted wrinkles. He introduced himself as Cluff Grimmus and asked our business.

"Lieutenant, these smooth-looking chaps are Propaganda Officers, I am escorting them forwards," Cama explained.

"Propaganda? A bit redundant when we are half way through a genocide, no? Why not just make it up, show a few old scenes of dead Scythrial? No one cares really."

"I can't make it up I'm afraid. We have a rule – it has to be ninety-eight percent truth. My mentor, Xersus hammered that into me. So, we are here to help teach Gellmar about the Durgans, get you the credit you deserve for turning up in our hour of need."

"Hmph! Don't so much az give a piss what milksop Gelmarz think. Though it'd be nice to get some respect when this is done. What protection do you have?"

Cama pointed to the pistol on her hip.

"Ha! That'll not help you in EDP!" he said.

Cama turned and whispered to me, *"we also have a poet who is a deadly soporific ward."*

Cluff barked at his unit, received some nods, then turned back to us. "Theez parts are in chaos. Me and two of my men will come with you."

I was grateful for the protection their strong arms and clubs offered. Cluff explained he was a *Kossan*, which I think translates most readily into 'blocker.' It was his job to guard roads from the battlefield against deserters or the occasional Scythrial.

"How many have you caught?" I asked, meaning Scythrial. He showed me the haft of his sword breaker. There were two notches cut into it.

"One notch for each dezerter's skull I have cracked," he said with pride. One of the other blockers displayed his haft notches with a similar pride. That had not been the response I had anticipated.

When we reached the site of the last battle, the Durgans were already in wild celebration at their victory. Somehow they had managed to obtain a large quantity of alcohol and they sang around fires, danced, and gambled. They were gambling anything and everything, including captured Scythrial weapons, shroot (a medicinal plant with a strong sedative effect), alcoholic spirits and items of military equipment. Some of the Durgans passed out and were relieved of their possessions by other soldiers. The officers did not seem to act so long as the one doing the taking was of an equal or higher rank.

The Durgans seemed to like the attention my vid-corder offered them and they started to perform tricks for me. One inebriated man had perfected the art of balancing an upright spear on the tip of his nose. When he dropped it, he rubbed his head and seemed to become angry.

"What am I doing turning trickz for Gellmar scum? Because you can't take care of the Scythrial by yourself, I had to leave my wife and son to get the harvest in by themselvez. How are they going to survive? It's your fault our families will starve!"

Karl stepped in. "Hey, I'm no Gellmar, I'm Mossian. I didn't want to be here. I got dragged here for the same reason you did!"

The Durgan man looked a bit confused for a second, then he hugged Karl.

"Oh, I'm sorry my friend! The Gellmarz screwed your family as well," he said, before hugging me as well. He obviously thought the whole team was from the same place and I did not want to correct him. He went to hug Cama as well, but stopped just short and starred at her blue uniform.

"Hey, *you* are a Gellmar!" The man got a violent look across his face and I thought he was going to strike her. But Cluff stood behind Cama like an ominous ogre and tapped his club in his hand. It was enough to make the drunkard think twice and he threw his arms around Karl and myself again. He looked Karl up and down then asked "Hey, where is your vid-corder my friend?"

Karl shrugged his shoulders. "I don't use a vid-corder, I write *poesis*." The man looked confused. I was not sure if it was because he did not understand Karl's Syndicate Standard or he did not realise anyone could actually make a job out of writing poetry, so I used a looser term.

"He writes *cantus*," I said.

"Ah, songs! You come now, teach uz a song!" The man pushed and prodded Karl towards a big fire. Karl shot me an evil glance. I am sure he would never describe his works as anything so lowbrow as songs. But he acquiesced and was taken off into the night.

It was not long afterwards that the first patrol came back with a captured Scythrial. It was bound up and trussed to the shafts of spears. The men carrying it were cheered on like heroes. Indeed, perhaps they were. I do not know. I thought all Scythrial prisoners were to be taken for interrogation, but the Durgan officers did not seem to care. Some Scythrial I'd seen lying by the side of the road were three metre tall monsters, with genetically engineered scythes for limbs; this was something small and mewling, not even the size of a human woman. If I had to guess, I'd say it was one of their civilian caste, bred for clerical duties.

Cluff grinned at the sight of it and leaned in to my ear. His gruff voice could never be called a whisper, but he made it apparent his words were only for me.

"Hey, propaganda man, if I show you something good for your vid-corder, will you make sure I get some alone time with Cama?"

"That's her call Lieutenant Grimmus."

"You're not the boss?"

"I don't have a militia rank, Lieutenant Beese is the one in charge."

"Ah, so it'z like that." He turned to find her in the crowd gorping at the imprisoned Scythrial. "LIEUTENANT BEESE! Want me to show you something everyone will want to watch?"

"Sure, I mean anything that helps the Propaganda Officers helps me."

Cluff grinned and pushed his way through the throng gathering around the captive. He lifted his sword breaker into the air so everyone could see it. The crowd cleared from around him like a shoal of minnows from a pike. Ack, sorry. I know I keep using similes that off-worlders like you will not understand, but nothing describes the scene better.

Cluff turned to the Scythrial. I cannot read Scythrial expressions, but it made a keening sound and threw it's beak back in what must have been something like terror.

"Ok, you got that vid-corder on me, propaganda man? I'm going to show you how to kill a Scythrial." Cluff produced a machete and held it up for the camera to see. There was a chorus of appreciative grunts from the crowd. He grabbed one of the Scythrial's arms and held it out to its full length. "Now, the thing you have to remember about Scythrial iz that they used to live in trees. Their arms look spindly, but they are strong. They are also as flexible as a teenage whore." Cluff forcibly rotated the Scythrial's multi-segmented arm through every conceivable angle and met little resistance. Then he raised the machete high in the air and hacked though one of the joints in a single blow. The Scythrial's eyes rolled back and its tongue clicked rapidly in what must pass for screaming to them.

Cama and me gasped at the sudden bloodletting while the rest of the soldiers jeered.

"Hacking off their arms doezn't work. They can stand, *or fight*, on two, three or four claws. Loosing an arm just doezn't matter to them."

He tossed the hacked arm into the crowd and there was a momentary scuffle as two men caught it like eager brides to be.

"Now another thing you have to remember about Scythrial iz that most of them are infertile. They've messed with their own DNA so much that they have to make babyz in vatz. To be blunt, they don't fuck. And that gives us a big advantage, because after all, what have they got to fight for without that?" Cluff smiled mischievously at my vid-corder, then winked at Cama. A wave of sniggers passed through the crowd. "Now if you want to test if your Scythrial has some gonadz, you can't go looking here." He groped between the Scythrial's legs. "They keep theirz up here." He raised the tip of the blade up to the Scythrial's neck. The clicking it had been making stopped almost straight away. "If they've got a working set, they're even more precious about it than we are." Cluff pressed the edge into the Scythrial's throat and began to cut just deep enough to raise a bead of blood. The clicking resumed with even greater intensity. Cluff grabbed the creature's throat and squeezed, so the clicking tongue lolled out.

"See any Scythrial gonadz in there?" he asked the crowd. All I could see was blood. "Ha ha! To be honest, I wouldn't know what to look for!"

The crowd laughed.

Cluff slipped behind the Svythrial and traced the machete along where its sternum would have been, if scythrial had sternums.

"Enough foreplay! The real way to kill a Scythrial iz to go for their chest. They only have one lung and a weak heart. Hurt either either and they freeze up and die without a fight." Cluff hacked at the Scythrial's chest with the machete. He was right; the wound was shallow, perhaps only enough to cause a human some pain, but within thirty seconds the Scythrial was dead. The crowd did not wait a beat, they descended on the corpse to tear off trophies.

I have to say, this streak of bloodlust in our guardian disturbed me. I looked to Cama and we shared a hollow look of revulsion.

"These people are gross. You'd think it was them who had been at war with the Scythrial for ninety-four years, but I've never seen a Gellmar soldier so cheery about slaughter," said Cama.

"It certainly was not pleasant to watch."

Cluff stood proud in front of us.

"Well?" he solicited.

"It was certainly something," I said diplomatically.

"I'm suddenly glad I'm in the admin corps," Cama confided.

Cluff wiped the alien blood from his machete. "Soft jobz for soft people," he asserted.

What a strange cultural chasm between us. Untimely deaths, even in combat, are a tragedy to Gellmar natives. The *humanitas* of caring for each other is a key foundation of the Gellmar spirit. What other world would have greeted Lord Varloth Chlorinus with a kiss of peace?

But I reserve my judgement. I have never fought. I have never faced an enemy at half an arm's length and felt my blade enter them. I have never spent night after night without sleep for fear of them. I have never seen my friends shredded before my eyes and been so terrified that I defecated upon myself.

These men have, and I cannot imagine what kind of hatred that can engender. Of course I hate the Scythrial, but as a fellow sentient race that the confines of the universe happened to foist us next to. Not on that deep visceral level I saw as men hollered at its death.

I do not think the scenes of Cluff butchering the Scythrial will make my documentary, but they make interesting viewing for troops on other worlds like Durgan. Therefore, I attach the file under the name 'How To Kill a Scythrial.'

That one was just the first of the Scythrial captives. Through the night more and more came into the camp in sporadic drips and drabs and each time the scene was repeated in some form or other. I did not stay for any of the others. Instead, I retired to our accommodation with Cama. The nearby slaughter put me in mind of casualty figures, so I asked her if there was any chance of getting them through her Militia contacts.

"That might take a while to get approved, but I will ask." She paused for a second, twiddled a loose hair then asked, "Want me to see if I can find out what Lord Varloth is up to at all?"

"It sounds like *you* want to know what Lord Varloth is up to."

She looked guilty, but shook her head. "No, no, no. I'm not allowed to ask questions like that, they might take for a spy or something. But if I passed on your, *very professional*, question, then that's ok."

"Fine, then please ask as to Lord Varloth's activities. It may make good material for the documentary."

She gave me a full-on grin, "Thank you. I might have developed ever such a small crush since I met him in person."

"You, and the rest of the Empire."

We could hear Karl singing nearby. Despite what I am sure he would have us believe about him being a serious and astute poet, he had quite a talent for making up songs the soldiers enjoyed. *Bellicose and bawdy.* The Durgans belted them out alongside him, even though they were in an unfamiliar language. When he eventually tired and joined us, he was quite drunk.

"Hey, you two. Look what the Durgans gave me for singing." Karl held out a small wrap of shroot.

Cama looked concerned.

"Have you tried that stuff yet?" She asked.

"Yeah, it's great! Like smothering yourself in a warm blanket of molasses."

"Watch yourself, too much of that and you'll not want to move, Officer."

"Ha ha, I'll bare that in mind. You want some?"

Cama dismissed it with a shake of her head, "Not when I'm in uniform."

I declined as well. I needed my head to be clear to order my thoughts and write this letter. I think I have only succeeded in one of those. Until next time.

[*Images Attached*]

Yours respectfully,

Hashnus Foe###

****

###Target: For Xersus – ◇1 Senior Propaganda Officer ###

   ###Access verified, proceeding###

   ###Author: Hashnus Foe – ◇◇◇Propaganda Officer###

   ###Subject: Gellmar assignment###

   ###Message:

Dear Xersus,

Happy days! Today we passed a series of purple and grey cliffs that I recalled from my childhood. It places us near the city of Hulam. It is the most remote of the cities on Gellmar. When the war started it was considered likely to be surrounded and was left to its own devices. I remember its giant defensive walls, no less than ten metres thick, and all the towers and siege machines that surrounded it. If any city could survive a siege, it is Hulam. This will make a great piece of propaganda indeed.

Yours respectfully,

Hashnus Foe###

****

###Target: For Xersus – ◇1 Senior Propaganda Officer ###
  ###Access verified, proceeding###
  ###Author: Hashnus Foe – ◇◇◇Propaganda Officer###
  ###Subject: Gellmar assignment###
  ###Message:

Dear Xersus,

I am certain this will be my last letter you. I am afraid I must resign my commission. Even if this leaves me open to prosecution, it is a necessary act. I simply cannot continue.

We heard the Durgans had liberated Hulam when we were just hours from the city. It put us in great anticipation. I had high hopes of catching the victory celebrations that were sure to breakout. It would have been the perfect finishing touch for my documentary. We were even elevated enough to ignore the miasma of carbonized bodies. The Scythrial had been using flamethrowers as they retreated.

When we arrived, the city was in ruins. There was smoke billowing up from a dozen different parts and the cacophony of fighting came from every direction. I thought we were too late. I thought the Scythrial must have broken the siege just as the reinforcements arrived.

It was not so.

The Durgans are beasts! It was *them* destroying the city. After months of holding out against the Scythrial, the people of Hulam threw their gates open to the Durgans and were rewarded with carnage. I cannot recount all the individual acts I saw. It was no systematic killing or destruction; it was just uncontrolled men running rampant. Which meant rape. No woman they found was safe from the Durgan gangs. The officers did not stop it, in fact, mostly they went first.

And they did not seem to care that I was vid-cording them.

I was hoping that might put them off, but no one cared at all. We were all scared, standing in that city, but I cannot imagine how terrified Cama must have been. I am sure that the only thing that saved us was Cluff Grimmus standing by our side. If anyone came too close he gave them a deathly look that seemed to say: "*my* woman." One swish of his sword breaker and the Durgan soldiers kept well clear. We got off the streets as soon as possible. Even so, I cannot count how many women we saw left bleeding, faces swollen purple, clutching scraps of torn clothing and searching for a place out of sight.

Of course people fought back against the looting and molestation. The entire population was in arms to resist the Scythrial! But the Durgans killed anyone with the temerity to stand tall. So no, the killing was not systematic, but I would not be surprised if thousands of Gellmar citizens were already dead. And I doubt the killing will stop until the Durgans leave the city. What they shouted as they fought - the Durgans have a genuine hatred of the Gellmar. It has been fermenting ever since they got here, though I dismissed it as bluster and typical soldier discontent. They blame us for having to fight the Scythrial. They think we are cowardly for co-existing with them for ninety years. They think they are due everything they take! It makes me wonder about those strays we saw on the road here. Was it really the Scythrial who brutalized them?

We were distraught; we just did not know what was going on or what we should do. Cluff found us a large house to stay in that had been gutted, but still had some decent beds and its own well. Later some other Durgans came and asked Cluff if they could use it to house injured comrades. He agreed and we huddled into one corner and ringed our hands with worry while they filled most of the floor space. It was Cama who was first to whisper what must be done.

"Tomorrow we leave the city at first light. We have to get to the nearest Gellmar regiment and let them know what has happened."

"Agreed," I said.

"Bastards. Fucking *animals*," Karl repeated more than once. "Don't they know who the enemy is? Humans shouldn't do this to each other. Brute force is the only thing they respect. Someone's got to stand up to them."

He began frantically scribbling notes on his ledger. His normal, precise hand was a mad scrawl. And I realised then that my incomprehension was nothing to do with Gellmar *humanitas*; Karl Riftus was right, the Durgans were animals. Karl gripped his stylus so tight that it snapped in two. There were tears of frustration in his eyes. He took out the small package of shroot he had earned a few nights back.

"Anyone, want to join me?"

"Yes," Cama and myself said before he had even finished the sentence.

Three Durgans came in carrying a wounded soldier on a stretcher. Cluff followed in behind them. They put the soldier down in the centre room, then one of the Durgans noticed the shroot in Karl's hand.

"Hey, you wanna give that to some heroez of the Empire?" one of them asked.

Karl looked him dead in the eye,

"Let me know when you meet one."

The Durgans did not like that at all. The one who had asked for the shroot grabbed Karl's hand and tried to prise the lump out. Karl did not let go. There was no time for escalation; no threats, no posturing, no punches. One of the Durgans simply took out a machete and cut off Karl's hand. The poet screamed and reeled back. But they did not stop; all three of them piled in and started kicking him. Cama tried to grab one of them and pull him off, but I held her back. They did not need much of an excuse to turn on the Gellmar woman in their midst. Instead I looked to Cluff, but he was not moving at all.

"Cluff, help him!" I implored.

"Why?" he asked.

"You are a military police officer, enforce discipline!"

"It is my job to make sure men don't run away. Do you see anyone trying to run away?"

When the Durgans got off Karl, he was not moving. One of the soldiers puffed the shroot and patted Cluff on the back as he left. I could not believe Cluff's attitude; I could no longer look him in the face.

"You could at least get a medic!" demanded Cama.

Cluff shrugged and went looking in one of the other rooms. Karl was bloody all over and the stump of his arm had liquid pumping out of it. I wrapped the arm in some clothing to try and stem the flow. When he roused, he gasped in pain. I tried to ease him with some soft talking, but there was not much I could do. He sputtered some words.

"Hashnus, I can't see."

When the medic eventually came, he said Karl had detached retinas and it was already too late. Karl was blind.

I cannot say how sorry for him I feel. His job was his life and there is not much call for a blind Propaganda Officer who cannot hold a ledger and a stylus at the same time.

You see, I must resign my commission. You always taught me that the golden rule of propaganda is that ninety-eight percent of it must be true. How can I finish my assignment having seen what I have seen? How can I lie to my own people? Does the Syndicate know what the Durgans were like? Normally I would say no, but Lord Varloth has a reputation for the most intimate micromanagement. He must have known what would happen? Or at least guessed? It does not matter. Please present the video images attached to the relevant authorities so proceedings can be brought against those it incriminates. I doubt you will hear from me again.

[*Images Attached*]

Yours respectfully,

Hashnus Foe###

****

###Target: For Xersus – ◇1 Senior Propaganda Officer ###
   ###Access verified, proceeding###
   ###Author: Hashnus Foe – ◇◇◇Propaganda Officer###
   ###Subject: Gellmar assignment###
   ###Message:

Dear Xersus,

You may be surprised to have received this letter. I must ask that you ignore my previous communication and, if it is not too late, reinstate me. Things have changed down here, or at least how I understand the events has changed. Let me continue where I left off.

The next day we planned to leave at first light, but word reached us that the roads were closed to all vehicles except troop transports heading to the new frontline, and that did not include us. We would have to sit still.

"I feel terrible doing nothing. I'm a Militia officer and I'm hiding," said Cama.

"There's nothing to be done. At least not by you. The only thing either of us can do is gather more evidence to present when we get out of here, but I daren't leave you here alone."

"No, you should go, Hashnus – please. I don't want to think criminals walked free because of me. I'll ask Cluff to stand guard."

"After he stood back and did nothing for Karl?"

"I'll make him swear! LIEUTENANT GRIMMUS!"

"You don't have to shout, it'z a hollow building."

"Hashnus wants to go out and get some more shots of the town. Karl and me need to be kept safe. Will you swear to protect us from looters."

"Fine, for the pretty one, I swear not to let anyone new in here. *Unless I get a direct order*. Propaganda man, you can have my two subordinates out on the street."

I did not like it, but it was the as much of a plan as could be hoped for.

"You sure, Cama?" I asked.

She nodded and we left her with Cluff.

The scene on the street was a lot more subdued than the day before; most of the fires were out and there was not that urgent lust in the men's eyes, although the cruel liberties were still being indulged in. Sporadic sobs and screams piecing the air attested to that. Where previously many of the Durgans had sewn on Scythrial trophies to their uniforms, now many had pieces of Gellmar uniform and, I am disgusted to say, some had women's gussets, as if it were something to be proud of.

I got some good close ups of peoples' faces as they committed their crimes. All the better to identify them with later. I got some pictures of the victims as well, so they could give evidence if it came to a hearing. It seemed to amuse my bodyguards; they openly joked that I was making a private snuff film.

"Kinda makes you want to join in," said one of my bodyguards. We were watching a group of soldiers who had managed to find a crate of alcohol, rather than anything more sinister. However, his statement was not necessarily limited to the scene in front of us.

"I have too much work to get distracted," I said.

"Cluff gave us permission to enjoy ourselves if we wanted," he insisted. "He's a good man, he doesn't want us going without whilst he finds his own entertainment."

"Finds his own entertainment? He's supposed to be guarding Lieutenant Beese."

The guard laughed,

"Don't worry, he'll be *looking after her* well enough!"

Gads, that snide tone, that casual mockery. They must have seen my face go dead as I contemplated what they knew about Cluff's intentions towards Cama that I did not.

The guard gawfed again, "Why surprized? Of course! Why do you think he has uz out here helping you? He doezn't care about some Gellmar vid-corder project. He'z been itching for a chance to spend some time alone with a fine woman like Cama."

"...And what if she blows him off?"

He scoffed, "Bah! Why would she turn him down? Boss iz a catch. A brave man, well respected!"

"Why? She's fucking angry at him for letting her friend get mutilated!"

"She won't say 'no' for long. Trust me on that, Propaganda Man."

I churned the situation over in my head. It seemed obvious to me that Cama would sooner shoot Cluff than hook up with him. I stopped dead.

"Hey, I left some equipment back at the house, I need to go back."

The guards looked at me sceptically.

"Forget them! We shouldn't disturb Cluff."

"No, I mean, I do actually need some equipment. Batteries. There's no need to disturb anyone. Besides, how long do you think you could last with a girl like Cama? He's probably done by now!"

"Ha ha, good point! She's a two-and-a-half second wonder alright! Fine, letz -*quietly*- get your stuff."

I got back to the house as fast as my escort would allow. Once there I shed my guards with a sudden sprint and dashed to Cama's room, barging in. Cama was cowing in the corner, a great red welt on her face where she had been struck. Cluff loomed over her, his belt discarded on the floor. I had arrived *just* in time.

"Let her go!" I demanded.

The two guards came running in behind me. Cluff smiled. There was no way I could intimidate all three of them. I doubt I could even have handled Cluff by myself.

"Why should I do that?" he asked with cruel amusement. He slowly reached down and closed his hand around Cama's neck.

What could I do? The honourable thing and go out fighting like Karl? The sensible part of me was screaming to just turn around and leave Cluff to it. It might not be so bad if Cama did not struggle. But no. This was Lieutenant Cama Beese and Lieutenant Cluff Grimmus; they were the same rank, and if Cama reported it, Cluff would face a court martial for sure. That meant, if Cluff raped Cama, he would have to kill her. Probably me as well. There was only one thing I could think to do. Lie.

"Because Cama is Lord Varloth's sweetheart."

All three of the Durgan's laughed out loud. I switched my viewer on and flicked to the picture of Cama greeting Varloth on the first day of the landings. The kiss of peace. But what did the Durgan's know of Gellmar culture?

"Look."

Cluff took my viewer and the colour drained from his face. All he saw was Cama lip-locked with a man so much more powerful than himself that he feared for every bone in his body. Karl had been wrong. The Durgan's did not respond to brute force, they met it head on. They had not respected the Scythrial and they were stronger than any human. What they respected was rank. We saw that every time Cluff's black armband made men fall back, or when they refused to steal from a superior even when blind drunk, or the way they let the officers take the women first. And Varloth Chlorinus was at the very top of the tree.

"And I've already sent a report back mentioning you volunteered to look after us," I added in case he had any ideas of making us 'disappear.'

Cluff let go of Cama's neck.

"No hard feelingz, eh?" he suggested.

Cama's face turned into a snarl.

"Out! Now!" she screamed at him.

All three Durgans shuffled out of the room and I shut the door behind them.

"Thank you," said Cama, readjusting her uniform.

"You...ok?" words failed me. Me, the professional wordsmith.

"No. Not at all."

We spent that day and night sat in her room, not daring to sleep. Cama had her little pistol in hand, trained on the door.

We had been hit with sporadic EDPs the whole time we were in the city, which kept cutting communications with the outside world. Towards the next morning, the EDP cleared and a flurry of messages got through to Cama. She glanced at them.

"Oh, they have given me an official response about Varloth's activities."

"And?"

"I can't comment on that."

I think I even managed a little sardonic snort at that.

You may be wondering at this point what changed to make me reconsider my assignment. The truth is nothing I have mentioned yet. All of this merely served to reinforce my convictions. What changed was what Cama showed me next.

"It's the stats you asked for," she said, handing me the data slate.

I perused the data, then became stuck on one small table. It was the casualties since the start of the war.

Gellmar dead: 2.2 million

Durgan dead: 4.3 million

Scythrial dead: 5 million

Since the start of the war. In the months the battles had been raging only a few million Gellmar out of a population of a hundred million had died, but in a couple of weeks, almost twice the number of Durgans had been killed, and out of just eight million. The Durgans had achieved their spectacular pace in taking land not through any remarkable tactical innovation, but by their willingness to die in doing so. In just a few short weeks more, it was likely nearly all the Durgans I had met would be dead.

The breakdown of the Scythrial casualties was even more revealing.

Scythrial dead on Gellmar front: 1.5 million

Scythrial dead on Durgan front: 3.5 million

They were killing the enemy far faster than we could hope to. Suddenly the huge sacrifice and contribution they were making became apparent. I think I said in my first letter, *sometimes it takes a psychopath to win a war.*

I think I may have been right. I think in order to save civilization, we have to embrace the barbarian. We have to embrace the Durgans.

In my opinion, one of the Syndicate's greatest moves was to call us 'Propaganda Officers.' Not war reporters or communication executives, but *propaganda* officers. It makes our job transparent and reminds us who we serve. And why do people still listen to us? Because of that golden rule. Ninty-eight percent truth. Very well, here is my documentary for the people of Gellmar, and to boot it is one-hundred percent truthful...just not one-hundred percent *of* the truth.

[Images Attached]

Yours in melancholia,

Hashnus Foe###

****

###Target: For Diona – ◇2◇ Propaganda Distributor ###
   ###Access verified, proceeding###
   ###Author: Xersus – ◇1 Senior Propaganda Officer ###
   ###Subject: Hashnus's Gellmar assignment###
   ###Message:

Dear Diona,

I recently received a request from ◇◇◇Hashnus Foe for dismissal from his post. Fortunately, his communications were delayed and his letter containing a recantation arrived at the same time. Let the record show no action is to be taken. Hashnus has provided us with several pieces of unsolicited work that I think merit publication. I have checked the anatomical facts of his 'How to Kill a Scythrial' and they are basically correct. Send this to the Militia for first refusal on distribution. The main documentary is satisfactory and has the format as follows:

1. Opens on a scene of the Durgan troops in ranks aboard their transport.

"The Syndicate is sending help!"

"Over eight million Durgans are on their way!"

2. The drop ships are shown thundering towards the ground.

"The Durgans have landed right in the thick of the fighting."

3. Shot of dead Scythrial.

"Already the Durgans have killed three and half million Scythrial. Soon there won't be any left for us!"

"But who are the Durgans?"

4. Shots of Durgans drinking and gambling and performing tricks. A few short interviews with them.

"The Durgans love to have fun, just like you and me."

"But mostly they love to fight!"

5. Shots of a Durgan lieutenant cutting off a Scythrial arm.

"In fact, they can't understand why we left it so long to have a war!"

6. Shots of Hulam city burning on the horizon.

"People of Hulam will not forget the Durgans. The Durgans put flight to the Scythrial within hours of the city falling.

"If we work together, perhaps next time we can stop the flames altogether."

"And never forget who we have to thank for giving us the Durgans."

7. Archival footage of Lord Varloth Chlorinus and the Syndicate insignia.

The only change I am making is to remove the last reference to the Syndicate. Given the tension likely between the Gellmar and Durgans, these parting words could be seen as subversive.

As for Hashnus's other footage labelled 'Evidence,' put it in permanent storage at level ◈1. It is unlikely to be accessed again.

Yours respectfully,

Xersus###

Puellsua

By Sierra Trabosci

Author of The Curse of the Cypress

The cold seemed to creep in that night, the thick fog blocking everything out but the sounds of screams from the Abyss. Puellsua had grown used to the sounds of suffering, hearing it nightly for as long as she could remember. She could hear it in the day, too, if you could call it that. Even with the orbs shining above, there was still barely enough light to see more than sixty feet. Puellsua sighed as she looked out the window, hunger gnawing at her and too many worries to count. Inside, her parents spoke in harsh whispers around the candlelight. While they had saved and only gotten the candle a few days before, it was already halfway down the wick. It would be months before they had the chance to buy another, so other means would have to be used. Of course, that wouldn't be for a week or so yet. Puellsua turned her gaze to the candle, tuning out the angry tones of her parents.

Luelle, Puellsua's younger sister, sat absentmindedly at the table. So young, so naive, so happy. She knocked a small piece of metal to her own beat, not bothering to see if it annoyed anyone. And of course, it didn't. Puellsua pursed her lips, the irritation on her face slowly turning into a smirk of appreciation. At least, through her hunger, she had her sister for entertainment. Luelle caught her eye and gave her a full smiler, wrinkles crinkling at her young eyes. Puellsua smiled back, offering a wave from the window. Soon it would be too dangerous to remain there, but for now, she was going to enjoy every moment of it.

"Puellsua, get away from the window," Mother snapped her voice firm but not unkind. Puellsua did as she was told. "Good, now come get prepared for supper."

Puellsua trotted over to the table, taking one last glance at the window. She let out a small gasp as the shadow of a tentacle seemed to pass by her vision. She pointed and looked toward her family, but nobody noticed. In fact, as Luelle sat at the table and Mother scraped up the last bits of meat from two nights before, Father could only seem to keep his eyes on Mother. He didn't blink, but his eyes grew wider and his fists gripped around a flintstone. Mother glanced up at him and shivered, but didn't look as if she was worried. Puellsua sat gently next to Luelle, who now tapped the piece of metal faster and louder on the table. Still a steady beat, but it rattled Puellsua to the core.

"I don't know if this is enough for all of us," Mother sighed, keeping her eyes on the meat; a small cat with its hair ripped off and singed in the flame, and avoided Father's gaze. "I know we already discussed this, but I'm not sure if the children will make it at this rate. We need to do something, and fast. Maybe we can—"

Father struck before Mother could let out another word. She gasped and felt her head, blood seeping out of the back of her skull where the flintstone had done its damage, blood caked at the back of her head, the wirey thin strands of hair dripping with red crimson fluids. She looked up at him with wide eyes, but not ones unknowing. Puellsua let out a silent gasp, the beat still drumming on the table by Luelle. It was faster now, harder as Luelle did her best not to focus on the scene unfolding. Puellsua was not so lucky. Father raised the flintstone again, yet he didn't immediately strike.

"You're right, my darling. The children do come first, after all," his voice was low and gruff, the huskiness of a life lived mixing with the struggles of hiding among the darkness. "Do you remember what we spoke of, all those years ago?"

Mother opened her mouth to speak, her brows furrowed and her lips contorting. Father raised the flintstone again, and her mouth slammed shut. She raised her arm and flinched away, but nothing came. Father's arm remained poised in the air, stiff as a board and ready to fall at any moment. Mother stared up in fear, the flinch still etched on her face. Puellsua grinned, unable to decide if the fate to come was for the best or otherwise.

She had always loved Mother. When the monsters raged on outside and one barely had a moment's notice to survive, Mother had always been a source of love and peace. She cooked, cleaned, and kept the outside away as the two girls had grown to survive. She endured Father's rage when something went wrong, and she was always sure to include the mostly silent Puellsua in her moments of affection. Father had never done such a thing, but that's what made him the ultimate goal. If Puellsua kept as silent as a mouse and approved of such an action, then perhaps he would show her some affection as well. After all, Luelle never disobeyed Father.

"What did I say we would do if we ran out of food? If I couldn't get enough to support us all?" Now the flintstone came down again, creating a bigger crater in Mother's head, bones brittle, and a crack send shivers up Puellsua's spine. She let out a small scream and closed her eyes. "You laughed at the time. Did you think it was a joke?" Lift, and down again. "One less mouth to feed is grand, especially when it can feed the rest of us."

The beat from Luelle's banging was deafening now, blending each mushy thud into a beautiful music of its own. Red splatted the floor, the consistency changing after each hit. First, it was liquid, pouring out in waves and pools across the sleek floor already covered in rust. Then, it was slime, oozing out in large chunks and falling in heaps to the ground. Father chuckled by the fifth hit, so Puellsua joined in. She started with a small chuckle, then a laugh, then into full-out hysteria. Laughs rang out throughout the metal hut, echoing into the Abyss. The thudding stopped, and the tapping from Luelle quieted, yet Puellsua laughed on.

Father dropped the bloody flintstone on the ground and clapped his hands to remove all the dust. He stepped over her Mother's corpse and around to the table to Luelle, ignoring Puellsua altogether. He knelt by the small girl and wiped the flowing tears from her cheeks, smiling at her gently to reassure her. Luelle dropped the metal she was tapping and rushed into his arms, weeping into his chest as he wrapped her into a hug. Puellsua laughed through her own pain at this rejection, the anger coursing through her and piercing her own skull.

"Puellsua, stop that this instant!" Father growled, his cold grey eyes shooting into her. "Do you want to attract beasts here? Get the rest of us killed?"

Puellsua slammed her mouth shut, stopping at once and grinding her teeth. She had done everything correctly, had she not? She didn't fight or complain, and she even laughed when Father did as well. It was Luelle causing trouble! She was the one crying and making noise with that ridiculous piece of metal. Puellsua crossed her arms and pouted as Father gave Luelle one last squeeze before pulling away.

"Don't fret, little one. Now she's actually of some use, see? Mother can feed us for days now while I go and find more food," Father spoke softly, setting her back at the table and handing her the piece of metal. "Go on, now, and keep playing."

Luelle went back to her previous activity, keeping the volume low and humming a small tune of her own. Puellsua grabbed onto her stomach, the next growl painful enough to knock her off her chair. Father stepped over her and around the table, hardly glancing at the starving girl. He stared down at the corpse lying in front of the fire instead, scratching the back of his head and sighed. He took the last of the old meat and served it on a plate, passing it along to Luelle with a pat on her head. Luelle dropped the metal at once and hooked her fingers into the meat, digging in without a second thought.

Puellsua pulled herself back up, grunting at the sight of Luelle eating. Why did she get two pieces? Had Father not seen Puellsua just a moment ago? She looked to Father with sad eyes, careful not to make a noise or complain in case he were to yell again. Father didn't notice as he began to sort through the cooking utensils. He glanced over at the corpse every once in a while, moving his hand along the tools. Puellsua stood next to Father, careful to avoid the soulless eyes stuck open in Mother's skull.

Father jumped at Puellsua's touch. "Oh, it's you. Don't scare me like that." Puellsua opened her mouth to speak. "Don't! Why don't you be of some use and help me prepare the rest of supper?"

Father handed Puellsua one of the utensils and gestured towards Mother. Puellsua forced down a swallow and turned to face it, resisting every urge to run or scream or even plead with Father not to make her cut up the only one who seemed to love her. Instead, she began the grueling process of chopping the meat off the bones so Father wouldn't have to chop the bones themselves. As she did so, her mind began to wander.

Was it wrong to eat Mother? It was clear she didn't want to die, but she did want to do everything for Puellsua and Luelle. In that way, it was right. Besides, Puellsua didn't mind so much as her stomach felt like it was shrinking by the second. What if Mother had survived? Luelle would go hungry, Puellsua would have starved to death, and Father would be alone when Mother eventually did the same. Would Mother taste different than any other creatures Father brought home? Puellsua didn't think so. After all, meat was meat. Puellsua began to salivate at the thought of food, and the meat she had just cut off was beginning to look more appetizing with every glance. She brought it closer to her mouth, her eyes widening and lips parting. Just a small bite...

"Puellsua!" Father scolded, taking the piece from her and threw it into the pot. He pointed back to the table. "Go."

Puellsua skulked back to the table and sat down next to Luelle, who was licking her fingers after inhaling the meat given to her. Luelle hadn't thought to save a piece for her sister, or to even save a nibble for later. It was disgusting. Father finished cooking the chunk of Mother and split it evenly among the three of them. By the looks of it, Luelle would be full for the first time since before she ate solids. Puellsua wasted no time in eating, scared that it might be taken away at a moment's notice. She ate her entire serving before Father sat down, using it as an excuse to steal a scrap of seconds. Father didn't seem to notice.

As the candle flickered away, Father stood and hovered over the rest of Mother. There was much to prepare for before the night was through, and although he would never know it, Puellsua would be right there, looking on.

***

The days seemed to pass in one never ending cycle, the third glow orb hovering in the sky since they lost Mother. The light never seemed to be too bright, but at least it was enough to keep the monsters back in the Abyss. Puellsua and Luelle sat behind the house, awaiting their father's instructions. They had very rarely gone on foraging trips in the past, but now there was little option in the matter. Luelle grinned at Puellsua, excited for the day to begin. Puellsua smiled back, but it didn't reach her eyes. Luelle would be nothing but dead weight, and Puellsua knew she'd be responsible for keeping everything in check.

Father emerged from the hut, a bag and heavy rock in hand. He huffed as he checked everything one last time before turning to his girls, a mix between a grimace and a smile etching across his face like an illusion. He turned away and scanned the perimeter, deeming it safe to continue. Not a soul was in sight...nothing but the barren wasteland for miles. Father began walking as if his children weren't there, marching without a second thought or a slight change of pace. Luelle happily skipped along behind him, struggling to catch up already and hardly looking away from her feet. Puellsua rolled her eyes, skipping forward a few steps and nudging her along. Had she fallen behind, it would have been all Puellsua's fault, and she couldn't have Father believing that.

"Fa-Father..." Puellsua cried weakly as he began to pick up his pace. It was as if they weren't there. He continued on, only bothering to look once she tugged on him.

"What? You can't be slow in a world like this," He snapped out the words, cold and harsh. Father sighed and ran his fingers through his thin and wiry hair, glancing around one more time. "This isn't going to work! I can't catch what we need and focus on you."

Puellsua bowed her head and took a few steps back, shame filling her. Here she was, complaining about keeping up and watching little Luelle when Father had so much more to be concerned about. He had to keep food on the table and risk his life! Luelle whimpered, and Father's irritation seemed to dissipate.

"It's alright, we just need to think of something," Father grunted under his breath. He looked around, eventually gesturing to a small field. "Here, just go over there and stay put. I won't be too long."

Puellsua held her sister's wrists and looked around. Sure, there was nobody around now, but that wasn't a guarantee of safety. With a nod to Father, Puellsua took off in a sprint. Luelle shouted out, her wrist wiggling under Puellsua's grasp, but it made no difference. Puellsua kept her eyes focused on the field, running across the barren road with eyes shifting from left to right. The moment both of their feet hit the brittle ground below them, Puellsua released Luelle's wrist.

"Puellsua! You hurt me!" Luelle whined, rubbing her now red and sore wrist. "Where are we? Where's Father?"

Puellsua brought a finger to her lips and let out a large huff. "Stay put!"

Although Puellsua repeated Father's instructions exactly, Luelle wasn't quick to listen. Luelle's eyes welled with tears as she clenched her fists and looked out into the road. She then shouted into the Abyss, crying out without a second thought. Puellsua clamped a hand over her mouth and pulled her further into the field. She looked up and scanned the road, which was luckily still empty. They waited in silence, the stillness suffocating in the darkness that surrounded. Puellsua squinted into the Abyss beyond, looking for any sort of trouble that came their way. Once the silence was thick enough to cut through, Puellsua let go of Luelle's face.

"Puellsua!" Luelle dropped her voice to a whisper. "What are we supposed to do now?"

Puellsua looked around. She had to find a way to quiet down her sister for hours, a task that was near impossible on its own, let alone for so long. There was nothing to entertain the irritant with, leaving them completely at the mercy of the world around them. Fear began to set in as Puellsua thought, the silence beginning to grow into uncertainty and doom. The weight of it was heavy...too heavy to bear.

Thud.

The sound rang out through the silence, rippling like a wave and destroying the tension in one blow. Puellsua jumped, every muscle tensed to run when the moment called.

Thud.

Puellsua winced, daring to follow the sound with her eyes. The thud was not from some unforeseen threat, in fact, but from Luelle and her new toy. She tossed the rock in the air, hand out expectantly for it to land in the same spot. The rock flew before gravity took its toll, moving the rock directly back to the ground below. Luelle pouted and picked up the rock once more. She tossed it into the air, only for Puellsua to catch it above her. She raised it up to hit the girl, then thought better of it. What good would it do for Luelle to cry again?

"Can I have it back?" Luelle asked, completely unaware of Puellsua's threat.

Puellsua glanced around one last time, then nodded and pointed to a select spot on the field. "There."

Luelle smiled wide, racing to get to the spot with her arms wide open. Puellsua couldn't help but smile back, tossing the rock while little Luelle turned. Luelle caught the rock with ease, sloppily throwing it back. Puellsua ran and caught it an inch from the ground, waiting until the silence returned to throw it again.

For the first time in years, they were both having fun. Puellsua couldn't remove the smile from her face as the catches grew more creative and the time seemed to pass by in an instant instead of in hours. They were having so much fun, however, that neither thought to look around for a threat. On the road behind them, a child made its way alone. He looked from side to side, careful for any threats. Little did he know, however, that a threat could be just as silent as a monster.

Puellsua tossed the rock to Luelle, but this time, Luelle's skills didn't match up. She missed the rock by less than an inch, the rock hitting the ground louder than ever before. A roar cried out from the road, then a shrill scream. Puellsua immediately ran to Luelle, grabbing her hand and preparing to run. Before she did, however, she froze at the sight of it all.

Three older boys were on top of a poor child, no older than Puellsua herself. His screams quickly turned to gasps as the boys ate him alive, tearing off the flesh of his throat first to silence him, then ripping the rest in fast movements. They let out cries of their own, angry animals perfectly fitting in the world that built them. Blood splattered the road and stained their clothes as they wiped their faces. Chunks of flesh flew through the air, only ignored for a moment and stolen off the road by a weaker boy. The oldest of the boys wiped his cheek, smearing blood on his cheek and leaving a crumb of the child. It was enough to make one vomit, had they any meals to bring back up to the surface. Within a minute, the heap of the young boy lay still and devoid of flesh, although his scream still echoed into the silence. He was nothing more than a hunk of bone, stained crimson and shattered from the blunt force. The older boys licked their fingers, but she could see in their eyes that they were still hungry for more. One of them scanned the area, finally locking eyes with Puellsua.

Puellsua took off once again, this time much faster than before. Luelle tripped over her own feet but had no time to fall, Puellsua moving much too fast for any accidents. The boys were almost just as fast and would've easily caught up if not for the distance between the field and the road. They let out shouts of aggravation as Puellsua shoved Luelle into a crevice and followed suit. There was no escape from it, leaving Puellsua to only hope that the boys couldn't reach.

An arm shot into the crevice, merely an inch from Puellsua's face. It flailed up and down, its owner grunting angrily. Puellsua took the opportunity and bit down on one finger as hard as she could. Blood spurted out of his hand and across Puellsua's face, the metallic taste flooding her mouth and almost begging her to come back again. She didn't have the chance, however, as the hand and arm shot right out of the crevice. Three sets of footsteps took off, much too desperate for food to risk getting hurt. Puellsua wiggled her way out of the crevice, offering a hand to Luelle as she did the same.

"Puellsua, Father said to stay put!" Luelle was whining again, but it was shortened by a glare from Puellsua. "Oh! Puellsua, look!"

Luelle bent close to the ground, careful to step quietly. Puellsua saw the rat, too, but didn't feel the need to chase it. She was never great at catching things, anyhow, and neither was Luelle. She still tried, however, and Puellsua was not ready to protest. Luelle pounced a few steps in, managing to just catch the rat's tail and drag it in.

The rat withered in her grasp and turned to bite her, earning a bite or two before meeting Luelle's hands on its throat. Luelle pushed with all her force, shaking the rat around to disorient it. It didn't take long for the rat to die, and the pride Luelle felt was nothing but irritating to Puellsua. With a snap of her fingers, they began their journey home. Luelle dragged the rat along the ground by the tail, eventually finding a lone bucket on her path. She stuffed the rat inside the bucket, careful to balance it the rest of the walk home.

They returned home before dark, the metal hut cold and lonely in the silence. Luelle slid the bucket onto the table and laughed victoriously, looking to Puellsua for encouragement. Puellsua didn't grant it, however, but returned to her place by the window. She stared out of it for hours, not focusing on one thought but allowing her emotions to bounce around inside her head. As the hours passed by and the orb sank further down in the sky, Father's bulky figure emerged from the shadows.

He came inside, struggling to hold his rock, and now a slightly larger bag filled with his foraging for the week. It wasn't enough, but it would keep them full for at least a little while. Father dropped the bag on the table and sighed, looking around the hut with faded eyes. He then noticed the bucket and looked up at the two girls, confusion on his face.

"Luelle, did you do this?" He asked.

"I did, Father! You won't believe what we did today!" Luelle was beaming from the inside out. "Puellsua and I-"

"Wonderful job, Luelle!" Father lifted up Luelle and spun her. "Just like your father, huh? You're so talented!"

Puellsua's face grew red with rage. She coughed, attempting to get Father's attention and failing. Another day, and Luelle was always the chosen one. Puellsua turned back to the window, hiding her tears as she looked back out into the night.

**

"Damn!" Father cussed into the room, addressing no one in particular as he looked at the rotting flesh before him. "Now what the hell am I supposed to do?"

Puellsua was unsure if Father had even seen her enter the room, but she frowned with him nonetheless. It seems Mother had not been that useful, after all. She glanced around the room for Luelle, glad to see her asleep, and ignored for once. Father took the meat and set it on its own while Puellsua watched, silently counting each piece. Realistically, the meat should've fed them for at least another week or two, but Puellsua knew they could never be so lucky.

"Puellsua, wake your sister," Father ordered. "It looks like we have another long day ahead."

Puellsua grunted and walked over to Luelle, pushing her onto the floor. Luelle hit it with a heavy thud and a groan, her eyes heavy from the middle of whatever dream she was caught up in. Puellsua snickered at her sister's minor misfortune, yet stopped instantly at Father's frustrated grunt. Puellsua helped Luelle to her feet and cleared her throat, waiting for the instructions of the day.

"Are you awake and listening?" Father asked Luelle with a voice like honey. She nodded. "Good, because I have something for you both to do today. You're both old enough to help out around here, so we're going to go find some food."

Puellsua couldn't keep the smile off her face. Finally, a chance to prove herself! She would find the biggest animal she could, something that could feed them for at least a week! Father could finally be proud, and maybe he'd even be as sweet to her as he was with Luelle. It was a stretch, but it was possible.

"Now, it will be just like last time. I'm going to set out some bait and work on what I can find here. You both will explore and catch what you can then bring it back here by nightfall," Father instructed. "Understand? Good, then go grab something to catch with."

He smiled as Luelle skipped away to find something. Puellsua took a few steps to go look for something of her own when her father called her, one word that froze her feet in an instant. She looked at him with a hopeful glance, a small smile etching her face. Was this the moment she had been waiting for?

"Puellsua, I have a special job for you."

Puellsua hurried over and stood in a ready position. She put her hands behind her back and looked up at him, eyes wide and brighter than they had been in a long time. She wanted to speak, to thank him before he had graced her with responsibility, but she couldn't bring herself to do so. After all, what if those few words were to somehow ruin it all? Each millisecond passed as if in slow motion, an endless waiting.

"Are you ready for it? This is very important," Father pressed, and Puellsua nodded. "Good. I need you to look after Luelle for me. She's a lot smaller than you, not to mention a lot weaker."

He had hardly started, yet Puellsua's face had already turned as red as her rage. Once again, even in her best moments, Father had still managed to put Luelle first. She pursed her lips and took a small deep breath. Any way she could make Father proud was a good thing, even if she disproved of it.

"You can't take your eyes off of her, not even for a second. You can't let anything happen to her," Father continued, his face expressionless despite Puellsua's reaction. "She can't defend herself if someone- or something- gets ahold of her. I'm trusting you with this. Should I trust you?"

Puellsua paused before speaking, her brow furrowing in her hesitation. Finally, she nodded and forced out a smile. "Yes, Father."

Father smiled a rare genuine grin. "I'm glad. You better go catch up with her now, before she decides to go without you."

Puellsua hurried off to find Luelle, leaving Father to his own devices. Puellsua found Luelle outside, waiting patiently and looking out into the void around them. Puellsua could see the fear in her sister's eyes, and although she didn't show it, it gave her some relief. At least Puellsua knew she had some control over the favorite of the house. Luelle hugged her bucket closer to her chest and looked up at Puellsua, a slight smile etching across her face.

"Are you ready?" Luelle asked, glancing inside to see Father. "Did he say to go?"

Puellsua nodded and gestured out towards the field. It was a dangerous spot, especially if the older boys were back again, but it also offered an opportunity to prove herself. One more daring save, and Father just might see her as more than a shadow. Luelle went in the direction that Puellsua pointed, humming a tune as she did so. Puellsua followed, glancing in every direction in order to spot danger a mile away. The Abyss was no less terrifying, but Puellsua felt some comfort in it. As long as she was aware, she felt she could take it on with ease. As they approached the field, however, Luelle froze.

"They're back," She whispered, pointing to the road. Puellsua looked up to see the boys once again, prowling like wild animals. "Let's go the other way."

Puellsua nudged Luelle forward another step, but Luelle refused to budge further. "Fine!"

Puellsua turned around and marched off in another direction, her awareness gone in a flash of emotion. Luelle struggled to keep up, tripping over her own feet as she practically ran. Puellsua didn't slow down until the road was nothing more than a blip on the horizon. An animal scurried in their path, waking her up from her trance and stopping her in her tracks. Luelle, still intent on just keeping up, ran directly into her back. Luelle tumbled to the ground, grunting as she hit the dirt.

"Puellsua..." Luelle groaned, pulling herself off the ground and rubbing her back. "What was that?"

Puellsua put her hand to her mouth and shushed her, eyes glued to the ground where the animal had scurried. It hadn't been a predator, or else they'd have been goners. But what was it running from? Puellsua looked to where it came from, but there wasn't even a noise to warn them. They stood frozen for a few moments, eyes locked on the darkness. After a few more minutes, Puellsua relaxed and the silence thinned. Another critter scurried by, a cat trying to get out of the open.

Puellsua reacted without a second thought. She lunged at the cat, wrestling it to the ground and wrapping her hands around its neck. It tried its best to fend her off, scratching and hissing and spitting. Puellsua tightened her grip flexed her arms away from her face, the pain only spurring her on more. Blood flowed down her arms from the cuts like a river, staining the cat's fur and her skin. Puellsua let out an enraged cry, one that silenced the cat instantly. She put her weight into the strangle, letting out a shaky breath as the cat finally let out its last breath. She kept her hands around its throat as the stinging kicked in, her arms in bloody agony with no option for relief.

"Puellsua, are you okay?" Luelle whimpered, her hand stretched out to her but not quite daring to touch. Puellsua took one more deep breath as she unclenched her hands, letting the cats corpse fall to the ground in a dull thud. "Puellsua?"

"Yes," Puellsua answered, standing up and wincing as her arms move. She pointed to the cat. "Dinner."

Luelle grinned and grabbed the cat. "I'll carry it with mine!"

Puellsua raised an eyebrow and turned to look at her. During the fight, apparently, Luelle had managed to catch a rat of her own. Luelle scooped them both up and dropped them in her bucket, picking it up with excited hands. Puellsua took fast and shallow breaths, pointing weakly towards the direction of the house. She wanted to keep going, to catch more, but she had no more energy left to give. Luelle slowed down to her speed, and together they stumbled home.

As the house came into view, Luelle picked up the pace and began to run. Puellsua couldn't keep up, but continued to hobble on. She was so excited to see Father again, to get his praise and her kill. The cat had been a large one, and she took it on single-handedly. It would be a feast, and she was finally going to get the attention she deserved. On top of that, but she had completed her special job. Luelle was safe.

She walked inside to Luelle scooting the bucket onto the table and Father cursing outside. It seemed the bait had yet to work. Puellsua slid next to Luelle, trying to hide her pride until Father saw. The surprise in his eyes would be more than worth it. Father came in with an angry growl, slamming his fist into the wall as he did so.

"Father, we caught something!" Luelle exclaimed, unaware of his anger.

Not that it mattered. Father's anger seemed to melt in an instant. "You did, did you? Let's see what you caught."

Father glanced at Puellsua, but didn't address her. He pulled out the rat and cat and set them out on the table, lining them up next to each other. He judged them both silently before turning to the girls, eyeing them in the same light. Luelle was a star in his eye, and he smiled at her approvingly. Puellsua, on the other hand, earned nothing but a sneer. He didn't know which one was which, but already Puellsua knew the outcome. She lowered her gaze, the pride wiped from her in an instant.

"Judging by your arms, I'd guess that you caught the cat," Father's voice was cold as he turned to Puellsua. "You shouldn't have picked something so dangerous. Maybe that will teach you."

He tossed the cat back into the bucket and admired the rat. "Now, this, on the other hand, is perfect. A little small, but it'll make a great meal. Good job, Luelle!"

Father gently put the rat into the bucket before going to cook them. Puellsua sat there in silence, fighting the tears that were threatening to spill over. She had done so much, and so well, and yet he didn't care. Why wouldn't he pay attention to her? Why did he ask things of her and ignore her after? It couldn't have been her fault. It had to be something else, something that she could overcome. She would figure it out, even if it killed her. They waited in silence, and when the food was done, they ate in silence.

And, once they all went to sleep, Puellsua thought.

In silence.

***

Puellsua's brain felt like it was being torn in two as she contemplated the evening. Father's words were a blade to her chest, and somehow it stung more than any of the scratches along her arms. She looked down at Luelle in disdain as she slept peacefully, completely unbothered by the world around her. Why did she get all the better treatment? She didn't work, watch out for anyone, or even pay attention to the danger outside. She didn't deserve it, which was worse than any other sin. No matter how hard Puellsua tried, she never could get past the perfection of Luelle's innocence.

She turned over the thought of dinner, and how much better the cat tasted compared to the rat. It must have eaten better than its smaller counterpart, something Puellsua could only dream of for herself. Just the same, Father made no note or even an ounce of praise towards it. He didn't even lecture her on how foolish her choice was during dinner, or acknowledge her. He didn't try to help her wounds, but she refused to blame him. He had to be ignoring her for a reason. Maybe it was to make her stronger, to prepare her for the harsh world outside. After all, the world was a dark and cruel place. He never taught Luelle that, and perhaps that was for a reason as well. Maybe he didn't expect her to survive, even if he somewhat trusted Puellsua to handle it.

Thinking back, she couldn't remember a time when Father had mentioned Luelle surviving on her own. Even at her birth, Father was concerned that she wouldn't make it, just like Mother, who at least died for a purpose. Puellsua paused, glancing once again at Luelle. She certainly looked a lot like Mother, not that she knew it. No mirrors meant one could only catch a glimpse of their reflection in their family, and no one cared to tell Puellsua who she resembled.

Did Mother know she would perish for her family? Puellsua assumed she did like Father said. Even if it was a surprise at the moment, she had to have known deep down. Was Luelle the same way? Did her sweet younger sister know deep down that there was a chance she wouldn't make it? Puellsua thought she did. That was the only thing that would make sense, otherwise Father wouldn't have been as kind to her. He was being merciful, as he always was.

Puellsua stood up and paced, careful not to cause even a squeak and wake up either of her family. Father needed all the rest he could get, especially as he had to watch the two of them all on his own. If only he had less on his plate, then he could really take the time to train Puellsua as he most likely meant to. He'd be able to teach her how to avoid the cat's claws when it leaped, or how to get rid of any obstacles in her path. She could eliminate anything that she had to, but every waking wish was to do so at his side. They could be close, and as he grew old, she would take care of him like he took care of her. They would be the strongest family in the world, with no one to stand in their way. That was, assuming they didn't have any extra weight.

Puellsua resisted the urge to let out a gleeful shout, slamming her fist to her mouth. It was all possible, especially with her will! She could eliminate any obstacle, and why shouldn't that be in her home as well? She could bring them to glory, but she had to earn Father's approval. She had to show him that she was worth his time and attention, that he could make good use of her. There had to be some grand gesture, some way to blow his mind and get his acceptance without a second thought...

This time, when her eyes fell on Luelle, they were dark with the thoughts that clouded her mind. She smiled, but it formed in an uncanny twist as she began to plan. Perhaps Luelle's true purpose was approaching faster than she could possibly imagine...

***

Puellsua tightened the ropes around her sister's wrists with a grunt, falling backward and wiping her brow with a sigh. As much as she appreciated that Luelle slept so heavily, it was difficult to move all of the limp weight. The sound of Father's footsteps caught her attention, inciting a minor form of panic. Puellsua rolled Luelle onto her stomach in a rush, silently hoping Father wouldn't find it strange her hands were hidden. Puellsua had to be in her best shape if this plan was going to work, so she had to be careful not to get a thrashing. A moment later, Father appeared from around the corner.

He looked from Puellsua, standing at attention, to Luelle. "Is she still resting?"

Puellsua nodded.

"Good. I've got work to do, and I'll be gone most of the day, so I need you to watch her," Father instructed, his voice like stone. "Don't disappoint me."

Father left before she could respond, but it wouldn't have made much difference. In fact, Puellsua was glad Father left early, not to mention in a rush. It gave her time to not only watch Luelle, but to show her own worth once and for all. She stood in that same stance for a minute more, until she was sure Father was long gone. Once certain, she turned and nudged Luelle awake.

"Puellsua? Is it time to get up?" Luelle mumbled through a yawn before reaching to rub her eyes. "Huh? What happened to my arms?"

Puellsua put her fingers to her lips in a hush, then gestured for Luelle to follow, whom struggled to stand, her eyes still stuck together from sleep. Puellsua rolled her eyes and helped her up, leading her by the wrists to the cooking pot. Sitting her down gently on the bench, she moved the cooking pot off the fire and looked around the kitchen. It would be difficult to get her to fit, but it wasn't impossible with the right tools. She walked slowly as she grabbed what she needed, careful not to seem too eager. Luelle wasn't going to enjoy this, so she had to be careful not to frighten her. After all, it was a lot harder to catch prey when it was tense.

"Where's Father?" Luelle asked. "Are we going out today?"

Puellsua sighed. So many questions, more irritating as they went. "No. We cook today."

"Cook?"

"Yes," Puellsua kneeled down and wiped the sleepiness from Luelle's eyes, waiting a few moments for her to blink and gather her surroundings.

It may be easier to catch peaceful prey, but the look of fear was intoxicating. Luelle hid it well as she processed the line of utensils, the pot off the fire, and the flames roared, but Puellsua could see it deep in her sister's eyes. Puellsua tried to give a reassuring grin, but Luelle's shudder told her she had failed. Oh well. In the end, none of those feelings mattered when it came to the hunt.

"Into the pot," Puellsua instructed, dropping all expression. Luelle shook her head, but Puellsua continued to point. "Now."

Luelle stood, her knees shaking as she took a few steps. She turned back, eyes wide. "What did I do wrong?"

"Into the pot," Puellsua repeated.

"No!" Luelle turned to run, but it was too late.

Puellsua tackled her to the ground before she could get three steps. They tumbled to the ground with a hard thud, blood seeping out of Luelle's head out onto the floor. Her sister whimpered from the pain but still clawed at Puellsua. She ignored the reopening of her wounds from the cat the day before, the blood dripping into Luelle's face as she forcefully pushed the girl's shoulders down into an iron pin. Luelle struggled under her grasp, but it was no use. Puellsua moved her knees to Luelle's shoulders and sat up, making her completely immobile and waited for her to stop struggling, pulling her hair back and smearing blood on her cheeks as she did so.

Once Luelle finally gave up, her eyes slightly glazed over from the head wound, Puellsua risked standing only long enough to grab some more string to tie her with. If it had to be done the hard way, then so be it. She tied Luelle's ankles tight enough to make her cry out, making sure it was extra knotted. Luelle whimpered as she moved her ankles together, her skin turning instantly red and threatening to seep red at any moment. She then lifted Luelle and attempted to slide her into the pot. Luelle was just too wide, however, her hips keeping her from fully fitting. Puellsua grabbed one of the utensils, holding it in the air to determine if it was truly the best one for the job.

"Puellsua, please!" Luelle begged. "Why are you doing this to me? What did I do? I can make it better, I promise! I'll be quiet when you tell me to, or I can go away! Is that what you want? I can run away, then I won't bug you anymore!"

Puellsua snarled at her sister, disgusted that the two could even be related. At least Father never had to hear this yammering. It was pathetic. She twirled the utensil in her hand, suppressing a giggle at the light clogged in her sister's eyes. The girl moved her arms around in a helpless flail, but there wasn't enough energy to succeed. The put squeezed her where she didn't fit, leaving deep pits that made her skin swell. All the more fun to fix up, in Puellsua's eyes.

"Please let me go!" Luelle pleaded. "Or...or I'm gonna tell Father!"

Puellsua laughed, cutting off a piece of Luelle's flesh at the hip and ignoring her screams. "This is for Father! With you gone, he won't have to work anymore. You'll feed us for days, and you won't be able to take him from me! He's going to be so proud! I'm helping the family, just like he did with Mother!"

As Puellsua ranted on, she sliced more and more of Luelle's body. Luelle screamed and withered around, but Puellsua hardly noticed. She took each piece of flesh and shoved it down into the pot, pushing around Luelle as if she were already dead. Luelle fought as hard as she ever had before, twisting and turning to avoid the attack despite the pot slowly sucking her in. Soon she wasn't just cutting at her waist, but up by her stomach and shoulders. Luelle tried to block with her arms, but her armor of flesh sliced through like paper.

"He'll be so proud that he'll finally love me! He won't just be Father to 'daddy's little girl'," Puellsua made an effort to cut deeper as she said it. The cut was enough, and Luelle slid into the pot. "That will finally be me!"

Luelle, eyes glassed over, finally went silent. She slumped forward, panting heavily as the life left her with each breath. Puellsua paid no attention, struggling to lift the pot and returned it to its place over the fire. Luelle would make a delicious dinner, and she could almost see the face of pride already. It would be perfect, and they would be a perfect family at last. She laughed at the thought, the energy turning the laughs hysteric in a matter of moments. She threw mounds of salt in the pot recklessly despite how much they had to ration in the past. She was not in the present but lost somewhere deep into the future of her own mind.

"Sorry...Puellsua..." Luelle let out her last gasp, finally falling lifeless in a crimson heap.

From there, Luelle turned into what Puellsua always saw her as...a useless piece of meat. Puellsua remained in her own world for the entire preparation of the meal, which took hours. She was careful to cook it to perfection, adding more salt for more preservation. With just the two of them, there was no way they'd finish it all in one night. She removed all the hair, strand by strand until the meat in front of her looked nothing like the sister that haunted her most of her life. Once the meal was complete, she set enough for the night on the table carefully before putting the rest in buckets for later.

She toiled at the table for another hour before finally sitting down herself, frozen in her excitement for Father to sit down.

Father didn't return home until well after green orbs in the sky faded, but the enthusiasm Puellsua felt didn't fade. He didn't address her at first, setting down a variety of tools and a bucket of his own. The meat inside it didn't look human, but where else he could've gotten it, she couldn't be sure. He also carried with him a bag of salt, much needed after her own endeavors from the day. She crossed her fingers as he finished putting everything away, and then he glanced at the table.

"Where did this come from?" Father asked. He tried to be snide, but the smell forced him to sit in front of it.

"I made it," Puellsua gleamed. "Is it good?"

Father took a cautious bite, then a few more. "It is. Where's Luelle? Did she help you?"

"You're looking at her."

"What?"

"I did what you did, Father!" Puellsua clapped. "She was useless! She couldn't find food, posed a constant danger, and ate all the food. Just like Mother! She had to be useful in...other ways."

Father looked at her with mouth agape, completely speechless at her confession. She beamed at him with pride, awaiting the onslaught of praise that she had come to expect all day long. A few moments went by, and the fierce enthusiasm turned to nerves. He gagged twice but was unable to spit out the remains of his youngest daughter.

"And isn't she delicious! I have more for the next few days, too, so you won't have to go out and find some," Puellsua spoke to break the silence, but it was much quieter than when she began. "Father?"

Father stood up, a looming figure as he stretched out his arms to full length. Puellsua stood up in a rush, a wide grin forming almost immediately. For a moment there she feared he was upset with her, but she was wrong! She was going to get what she could already tell was going to be the beginning of a great bond. This hug would be the connection between them for all time! She ran towards him, hands outstretched to embrace him. Without a second thought, she grasped his mid-section and absorbed his warmth.

One moment passed, then two, before his hands finally came down upon her head.

Then, all she saw was black.

***

When Puellsua awoke, every inch of her body was screaming in ache. She fought the tears falling from her face, although she couldn't be sure why. The last she remembered she was locked in a warm embrace with Father. Was there an attack she missed? Something that was just too strong for the two of them? Impossible. She winced at a bump on the road, waking her up to her senses.

Her hands were clasped behind her back and tied tightly together, as well as her ankles. When she struggled in them, the rope attached was painful and blood oozed around the binds. Her head was killing her, pulsing in pain to her own heartbeat. She could hear a multitude of voices around her, a busy square in a world where isolation was key. Where was she? She caught a glimpse of armor out of the corner of her eye. Knights? What place could be so grand that it had protection? Perhaps she had been stolen away, and Father would also find this place in an attempt to rescue her.

She turned her head to the front of the horse, sucking in a gasp from the sharp pain in her temple. She was wrong again. Father led the horse, walking slowly and not uttering a word as he passed through a crowd of people. They were approaching a building like nothing she had seen before, the letters *INN* hastily marking it as a meeting place for those in the area.

"Father?" She called meekly, but he must not have heard her. "Father, where are we?"

This time he glanced back at her but offered her no response. Fear gripped her like iron, and her heart began to race. She struggled in her binds some more, tearing into her skin as panic hit hard and fast. She didn't understand. She had done what he wanted! Even if he didn't want Luelle gone, she had at least given him enough food to be of use. Why did he refuse her at every turn? Tears stung her face as she scoured for a trace of good intention. Maybe he was just confused. Yeah, that was it! He couldn't see how life would be better with all she had done, but in time he would learn.

Then, perhaps, he could approve of her! The thoughts rambled in her mind a mile a minute, her hopes clashing with the sense of the impending doom approaching at any moment. If she could manage to just get herself off the edge of the horse, she might just have a chance to get away and get home. That would give Father time to come to his senses...

The horse stopped in front of the inn, where a robust man leaned against the wall. He wore a smug smile and was coated in sweat and dry blood, a sack of coins hanging from his waist. Father picked Puellsua up off the horse and slung her over his shoulder as the man pushed himself off the wall and into the street to meet them. Puellsua wiggled in his grasp, but a single squeeze told her to stop resisting in an instant.

"I was worried you wouldn't make it," The man laughed, but Father didn't smile. "So, what have you got for me this time?"

Father threw Puellsua off his shoulder and into the dirt below. "She's wild and violent, but she could be of some use to you."

"Hmm..." The man licked his lips and spun around her, tapping the bruises on her and laughing and her winces. "What's with the damage?"

"She decided to get rid of her sister."

"I see..."

"Father, please don't do this!" Puellsua begged. "I'm sorry for hurting Luelle, I am! I'll do better, I promise! You don't have to speak to me. I'll cook, I'll clean, I'll do whatever you want!"

Father didn't respond, keeping his eyes on the man. "How much for her?"

"Well, she seems sturdy enough, and I bet she can do good work..." The man unhooked the sack from his waist. "Half our usual?"

Father scoffed. "She's worth more than that! She'll last you a lifetime. I want full price."

"Three-quarters?"

"Deal."

"Father!" Puellsua bawled. "I'll do anything! Please don't let him take me! Please!"

The man swept her up as if she weighed nothing, tossing him the entire sack of coins. "For some of your troubles. Pleasure doing business!"

Puellsua screamed and struggled, but it was no use. The hand had been dealt, and her father showed no signs of remorse. As the man carried her away down the road, talking to himself, Father walked inside the building. His ears fell deaf upon her cries and her pleading, but she never stopped. As she disappeared into the crowd, her final sounds rang out into the night.

Just like all the times before, she was ignored. Just like all the times before, she was invisible. And just like all the times before, that's how she would remain.

Armanis Ar-feinial, in the gritty pits of despair, he comes from: Bridgeton, Maine, a terribly dreadful place. Currently residing in the Greater Boston Area with his family, he studied Criminal Justice, English, and currently dabbles in a little bit of Finance. His unfaltering passion for writing came from his first exposure from the Lord of the Rings, which he drew inspiration from in his first stories, but alas, as all good things come downward into the grimdark pits, adopting tones from Joe Abercrombie. He loves reading, playing games of all kinds, and he is what you call a practicing writaholic. He is personally known for his witty sarcastic unasked for remarks.

Kieran Ferrara is a creature of many interests and loves. Of particular note are his interests in the fantastical genres of horror, fantasy and science fiction as well as his love of Heavy Metal, tattoos, and his family. He graduated in 2019 from Southern Hampshire University with a Bachelor of Arts degree in Creative Writing and English. When not writing, editing, or working at his day job, Kieran enjoys spending time with his wife (the enteral soulmate and frenemy), two children (the female spawn, and the boy child) in his home in the Pocono Mountains of Pennsylvania.

www.ingramcontent.com/pod-product-compliance
Lightning Source LLC
Chambersburg PA
CBHW020955180626
46814CB00003B/1109